Controlled Burn

A Blackbridge Security Novel
Marie James

Other Books in the Blackbridge Security Series

Copyright

Synopsis

As the mechanic for Blackbridge Security, when I make a mistake things don't work properly.
Correcting that mistake is the only way to get things operational.
I meet issues in my personal life with the same mindset.
How was I to know the woman I've been flirting with at the gym is the same woman I called a noise complaint on?
I got her kicked out of her condo.
My first response: *Move in with me.*
When she confessed to having three kids, it was too late to back down.
I thought keeping my hands off of her was going to be a problem, but the tiny terrors she brought along with her are extremely effective at solving that problem for me.

Chapter 1

Kendall

"Stop staring at me. I already answered your question." Ezra sighs again, his agitation growing with each roughly exhaled breath.

I cross my arms over my chest and dig my feet in.

My brother has acted like this for as long as I can remember, and since he's ten years older, that has been my entire life.

"You're annoyed," I say.

"I'm not," he argues, but then he clamps the bridge of his nose between two fingers and sighs again.

"If you just tell me what's wrong, I'll fix it and you can relax."

"It can't be fixed," he mutters.

"So, you admit that something is wrong." I feel victorious for getting him to admit at least that something is bothering him.

My brother is the laid-back sort. It's very seldom that something bothers him, but when it does and that irritation comes to a head, stand back and take cover. This is why I've been needling him for the truth for the last five minutes. I don't want him to get so annoyed that he explodes. He's as prone to off-the-wall reactions as I am.

"Do you see this place?" he asks, sweeping his arm out to indicate the living room.

"You want me to vacuum?"

He shakes his head, sighing again in a way that makes me believe he thinks I'm a little slow on the uptake today.

"Dust?" I continue. "I promise I'll get it done today."

His eyes find mine, and with the tiniest shake of his head, I know that the dusting and vacuuming are the least of his concerns.

"What about the rest of the clutter?"

I look around the room, trying to see it all through his eyes, but it only looks like a normal, lived-in room to me.

"Where else am I supposed to put it?" I ask, my own irritation growing.

"Your own house?"

My eyes turn to slits as I glare at him. "I had a house, remember?"

"Those were the days," he mutters.

"And somehow it's my fault for the owner selling it right out from under me?" I shake my head, trying to ward off the familiar burn at the backs of my eyes.

Although crying solves nothing, I do it much too often lately. I can normally wait until I'm in the shower, so no one is the wiser about the disappointment I feel in myself. Suffocating under the weight of failure is bad enough. I don't want eyes on me, witnessing the way I break down nearly daily.

"If you didn't want me here, you shouldn't have offered."

I stand from the sofa, needing to get away.

"Kendall," he mutters. "It's not that I don't want you here."

He doesn't add a but. There's usually a but when he states things in this way.

"I think my trip will help level me out."

I turn back to face him. He hasn't mentioned a trip, or maybe he has, and it was when I wasn't focused completely on him. I have a lot going on in my life, and I always feel like I'm split in a hundred different directions. Nothing in my life ever gets all my attention. Even now as he speaks, my head is wondering about finding my own place, not forgetting the dusting and vacuuming, and a million other things.

"Trip?" I manage to ask before losing complete focus once again.

"I'm going to Vegas," he says with a groan. "We talked about this at least three times in the last week."

I nod with a small smile, but his frown tells me that I'm not fooling him. I've grown used to the disappointment in his eyes, but the recognizable look doesn't ease the sting of it any.

As if I couldn't be distracted any further, Evie swoops into the room.

"I can't think with all of this yelling," the parrot snaps, sounding so similar to my and Ezra's mother it makes me smile.

"And then there's that," my brother snaps, his irritation growing even more. "That damned bird shit on my suit jacket yesterday morning."

I frown at the bird. She's completely housebroken, knowing she's only allowed to use the bathroom in her cage. She only does what Ezra is describing when someone makes her mad.

"Sorry," I mutter. "She doesn't like men."

That's the only other reason for her shitting on his clothes.

I have no idea why Evie hates men, but she has since I got her. She loathed my ex and would fly around and crap on him every chance she got. It should've been a warning sign, but I have several reasons I can't hate the man. Despite being a total loser, he gave me three reasons to live.

"Men are pointless," the bird mutters as she walks around on the coffee table separating my brother and me, and before I can scoop her back up to carry her to her cage, she stomps her foot and hisses in my brother's direction.

He slides back further on the couch as if he's facing an angry lion rather than a bird weighing only a pound and a half.

"I'm going to work," Ezra grumbles as he stands up, skirting the long way around the table to avoid the bird.

She tracks him with her eyes as he gathers his things from the console table near the front door.

"Walk away," Evie snaps. "That's what you're good at."

My brother shoots me daggers before walking out of the condo. The door snaps closed, making me turn to gape at my bird.

I had a more off than on relationship with my ex, and Evie was a purchase from a pet store because I felt like I needed companionship during one of the times he disappeared. She was calm and mostly silent, only saying hello when the phone rang, or someone knocked on the door. For the longest time, I figured she just wasn't a talker, but when Ty Penman showed up the first time after I purchased her, she came out of her shell. She had to have been a man-hater before I bought her, but it was the first time having someone of the opposite sex in my space. If Ezra thinks he has it bad, then he has another think coming. At least Evie tolerates him. She hasn't defecated on his person yet, and that's progress as far as I'm concerned.

"Stop antagonizing him," I snap at her as I walk out of the room.

Unable to ever not get the last word, she's perched on my shoulder before I can even open the door to the guest bedroom Ezra is now obviously regretting offering me.

The living room looks perfect compared to this room. There are literally boxes and plastic totes stacked nearly to the ceiling. Looking at the contents of the room makes me feel like the biggest failure of all.

You see, it's not only me wedged in this room surrounded by as many things as I could manage to move out of the house I was renting. Those three reasons my ex gave me to live, the very reasons I get up and keep going each and every morning, stay in here with me. My seven-year-old twins, Kason and Kayleigh, and my five-year-old son, Knox, also live in this room. The boys share the double bed against the far wall, and Kayleigh and I sleep in the queen bed wedged into the corner.

This room is a silent reflection of my life. It's cluttered and confusing. It's full of things I have to have. Layers and layers stacked upon each other that makes so much of it unused and neglected.

I can't give the things in this room the attention it deserves, and I feel the same way about my kids. I have no friends to speak of, but it's not like I'd have time for them if I did. I can barely juggle the other four people that live in this condo.

"This place is a pigsty," Evie squawks as she flies across the room to the perch sticking out from the side of her cage.

"Tell me about it," I mutter.

I argued with the damn bird the first time she said it. Then, she was speaking about a couple of dirty dishes in the sink, and she's said it a million times since I brought her home. It bothered me the first time, and I rushed to clean those dishes, but this isn't a mess I can tackle today, so I quietly change into my gym clothes, keeping my back to the mess.

"Ignoring it won't make it go away," Evie calls after me as I leave the room.

She's like the grandmother I never had, giving sage advice, especially during those times when no one asked for it.

I take several calming breaths as I climb into the elevator, thankful for the in-building gym. Working out is the only calm I get during the day, and I tend to take full advantage of it. Before moving in with my brother, I had to either exercise outside or hold my breath at the gym that was closest to my house. Considering the importance of breathing while exercising, I usually opted to hit the great outdoors.

I take another deep breath as I walk inside the gym, loving that it smells of cleanliness and lemons, unlike onions and dirty socks, like my old gym.

Maybe when I move out, I'll be able to convince Ezra to let me keep the key. Access to this state-of-the-art gym is almost enough to stay piled into one bedroom. Knowing that thought isn't serious because my kids deserve better than a cramped life with no room to play, I frown as I walk toward the filtered water machine with my Hydro Flask.

My frown does a full one-eighty as I approach. My other reason for wanting to keep coming to the gym, and the motivation I've used to get out of bed several times in the last couple of weeks, is standing there.

"Hey there, stranger," the man says, that thick accent of his making the hairs on my arms stand on end.

"Good morning," I tell him.

"Finnegan," he says.

"I remember," I say, unscrewing the lid to my reusable water bottle.

He grins down at me, and when I say down, I mean the man has to tuck his chin into his chest because of our height difference.

Normally the size difference would make me worry, and that's on having a horrible ex who used my small size as a means to regularly intimidate me. The man never lifted a hand to hit me, but I knew it was only a matter of time when he started getting so angry that he'd break things around the house. Sooner rather than later, a broken vase or smashed picture frame wasn't going to be enough to satisfy his fury.

Finnegan never looks angry. His bright green eyes are always smiling in a way that proves the man is always in a good mood. He's happy, always. He's polite, offering to switch machines at the gym when he notices someone hovering around.

This is how we met. I wasn't the one hovering, but I was watching as another woman stuck close to him, so close he noticed and offered her the leg press he was working on. I smiled when he wiped the thing down for her, nearly laughing out loud when he bent in the middle to blow on the seat to dry it faster when she just stood there and smiled at him.

Eventually, he nodded at her and walked away, landing on the exercise bike directly to my right. It put me between him and the woman settling on the leg press, and I could feel the irritation in her eyes as I blocked most of her view of him.

His grin grew wider that day when he noticed me beside him.

"She wasn't interested in the leg press," I told him, thinking he was oblivious to the woman's blatant desire.

"I know."

Those two words lit a fire inside of me. St. Louis is a melting pot of many nationalities. Accents aren't something new to me, but the rumble of his voice just lit me up.

It took three more trips to the gym for us to finally introduce ourselves, and we've chatted nearly every day since.

He's cordial, asking about the weather more often than anything else, but his eyes sparkle when doing so, as if he's waiting for me to change the direction of our chats.

"The leaves are starting to turn," he says, and the tone is lower, as if he's whispering something different.

I swallow thickly, nodding as one does when chatting with a near stranger.

"They are," I tell him, but honestly, I haven't even noticed. I don't have much time to stand around and take in the world these days.

"Glad the gym is in the building," he says, drawing another smile from me.

I pull my now full water bottle away from the machine and recap it, wishing I had a two-gallon jug, so I had a reason to stand here a little longer.

"It's very convenient," I return.

"It means you won't have to put on more clothes once it gets cold."

If there was ever any doubt that he was flirting, that flies out the window when his eyes sweep down my body. I'm no stranger to men looking at me with heat in their eyes, and I want these looks from him. It's why I'm in skintight athletic leggings and a sports bra, rather than the baggy t-shirt and sweats I used to wear while working out.

"We wouldn't want that," I say with a shy grin, wondering what it's going to take for this man to actually ask me out.

I'd have to say no because I have way too much going on to get involved with anyone, but the request would be nice.

"What are you focusing on today?" he asks, the same way he does every day.

"Legs, more specifically, the very top of my legs."

"Your glutes?" His eyes sparkle mischievously.

"If my ass gets any bigger, I'll have to switch back to my sweats."

"That's a shame," he says, his eyes studiously locked on mine, whereas most men would probably try to look around me to see the ass in question.

"Sweats aren't that fun to work out in."

"It's a shame you're trying to shrink your ass. It's a great ass." He winks before walking away, and I swear I stand there with my jaw hanging open before someone else approaches to fill their own water bottle.

I keep my eyes on the mirror as I work out, appreciating my hourglass figure more now than ever before. Because of these little interactions, I feel like I'm in the best shape of my life. I work out harder and longer than before, and in an effort not to be like that creepy woman from the first day I met him, I keep my eyes to myself, all the while picturing him watching me. It's really helped me not give in as easily as I used to. I push myself more, up my weights, and exercise longer.

Finnegan has been the best thing to happen to me in a long time, and I don't even know his last name.

Chapter 2

Finnegan

"Have a good time last night?" Kit asks as I take a seat across from him.

My body sinks into the sofa, and I know I'm going to have a little trouble getting up. My workout this morning was extra intense, but they all have been lately. Ever since Kendall showed up in the gym, obviously a new resident in the building I live in, I've felt the strain in my muscles. Her smile makes literally every part of my body perk up and take notice.

"I was in bed by nine," I tell my friend, shaking my head when he chuckles.

He doesn't believe me, and that's fine. I have nothing to prove to him.

"I did have a great workout this morning."

"Yeah?"

"At the gym," I say, knowing exactly where his mind went. "The literal gym. The one in our building? If you worked out a little more, maybe you wouldn't be getting so soggy around the middle."

Kit smiles wide, lifting his shirt to reveal a mountain of ridges down his abdomen. "So soggy."

"Put those damn things away," Deacon, our boss, mutters when he walks into the room.

"I really don't mind," Anna, Deacon's wife, says with a wide smile.

The look Deacon gives Kit is murderous.

"What?" he asks with a scoff. "She's the one looking, and you're mad at me?"

Anna chuckles as she shifts her little boy from one hip to the other.

"Keep your clothes on when on the clock."

Kit's eyes dart from Deacon to the big clock on the wall. Noticing it's after nine, he simply nods in agreement, his face falling a little because he's missing out on the ability to tell him the workday hasn't technically started.

"You got it, boss," Kit says, blatantly winking at Anna just to rile the man up even more.

Anna leans in and whispers something in her husband's ear, and although he points at Kit like he's got a shitstorm coming, he follows his wife toward his office.

"He's going to end up murdering you," I mutter, pulling the box of mechanical parts from the floor and putting it on the table in front of me.

"He'll kill Brooks first. I lifted my shirt. He dropped his pants in front of her."

"What are you two assholes gossiping about?" the man in question asks as he appears from the hallway that leads to our offices.

"You," we respond at the same time.

"I was telling him that Deacon will kill you first because you flashed Anna your ass," Kit explains.

"I was seeking medical treatment from a wound. She walked into the room. I didn't flash her."

"She still saw your ass," Kit reminds him.

"How is that tiny bite on your ass?" I ask with a wide smile. He'd made such an ordeal about getting bit, but Jude, our in-house medic, said it was not much more than a scratch.

"Healed," Brooks mutters as he pours himself a cup of coffee before sitting down beside Kit. "Why are you in such a good mood?"

Kit chuckles. "He had a good workout this morning."

"Oh yeah?" Brooks asks with a smile, quick to get in someone else's business, but less than forthcoming when it comes to his own life these days.

"At the gym," I say. "Literally the gym."

"Like in the steam room?" Brooks asks. "That far corner is really dark, and you have like a five-second warning before anyone can spot you."

"The steam rooms are gendered," I remind him.

"Yeah," he says. "Yeah, I know that. Did you guys watch the game last night?"

My eyes narrow, and they've done that so many times in recent months with Brooks, people are going to start wondering if I need glasses.

Kit goes on about how the umpires were the worst, and I lose my train of thought. My mind takes me back to the gym and imagining being able to sneak Kendall into that dark corner Brooks mentioned.

The day goes by slow as molasses, but that's not unusual. The days always drag by. The mornings at the gym are the only quick times in my life these days, and it's as if I'm living my life one workout at a time. I look forward to the gym and can never wait to get back in there. I would've asked Kendall out, but dating someone that lives in the same building means things get awkward after the appeal fizzles out. I've had it happen once before, and it was months before that woman finally moved away, and I didn't have to spend extra time looking around corners and avoiding certain areas of the building. I don't want to go through any of it again. It's why I haven't pulled the trigger on asking her. Dating within the building is messy, and after what happened last time, I'll avoid it at all costs.

I groan as I plop down into the recliner in my living room. I'm normally not home very often, but as the guys have started pairing off, the appeal of staying at work nearly twenty-four seven has dwindled. Since Kit had something else to do, and Brooks disappeared midday and didn't return, there was no point in me sitting at the office all alone.

I'm lifting a forkful of whole wheat pasta to my lips when the chaos begins.

My condo used to be damn near silent, but lately the man next door has been making enough noise to wake the dead. Lazy evenings at home have turned into more than a little irritating.

I take a deep breath before shoveling the food into my mouth, hoping on the off chance this evening would be different.

That hope flies out the window two bites later when a god-awful shrieking echoes around me.

"What the hell," I mutter.

Standing from the recliner, I place the plate of food on the coffee table before making my way to the door. Like a weirdo, I press my eye to the peephole to look at the condo across the hall. I don't even share a wall with the guy that lives over there, but it sounds like whatever is going on is happening right in the middle of my own damn living room.

The door doesn't open, and after a few minutes, silence fills the room. I'd swear the man is breeding monkeys with the noise they make every evening.

Kendall isn't the only reason I head to the gym so early and workout for such a long time. The mornings are just as rambunctious and noisy.

I settle back in to finish my dinner, but it doesn't take long for the noise to start back up.

I'm an easy-going guy. Normally, I wouldn't pick up my phone and call Deacon, but this place is my sanctuary, and I can't take much more.

"I can't do anything about it," Deacon says after I explain what's going on.

"But you own the damn building."

He chuckles. "I don't own the building, Finn. I own ten condos in the building."

I frown. I was certain my boss owned this entire building. "But it's called Blackwood Estates. Your last name is Black."

"Mere coincidence." I hear his son start to cry in the background. "I have to go. I'll text you the information to the guy who owns that unit."

He hangs up, and it's another thirty minutes before that information pings on my damn phone. I can't really get mad at the man for meeting his son's needs before catering to mine, but in the meantime, I had to listen to screaming and the sound of things bouncing off the walls.

I cringe as I dial the number, wondering if I'm going to reach the man who lives there. If Deacon doesn't own all the condos, then there's a good chance other people own individual units.

I won't get anywhere if that's the case.

Suddenly, having this condo doesn't seem like such a benefit for working for Blackbridge Security.

"Hello?" the man answers. I've never had an interaction with the man across the hall other than a quick head nod when passing each other, but he doesn't seem the type to have a voice like a three-pack-a-day smoker.

"Mr. Crosby, this is Finnegan Jenkins."

"You're one of Deacon's guys," he says.

"I am. Listen, I'm calling about the guy across the hall."

"Ezra? Has something happened?"

"You could say that," I mutter. "He's got something off the wall going on over there. It sounds like he's living with a pack of wolves."

"I can assure you, the man lives alone. He has for years."

"Pets then?" I ask because there's clearly more than just him in that condo.

"He's not approved for pets," Mr. Crosby assures me.

"Can I ask you to check things out? It's pure chaos over there."

"I'll handle it," the man says, irritation lacing his tone. "Good day, Mr. Jennings."

"It's Jenkins," I say, but the man has already disconnected.

I don't know how long it's going to take him to get control of the situation, but things over there don't calm down for another hour and a half, but just like every night, it's like a switch is flipped and silence ensues.

Chapter 3

Kendall

Despite it being Friday night, or should I say very early into the morning of Saturday, I like the silence when I get off work. The drive home is quick because most people are in bed asleep at this time. I don't have to wait for the elevator like I would if I worked a regular nine-to-five job. Despite my feet killing me from being in heels all night, I quietly enter the condo with a smile on my face.

I take my time slipping my shoes off and putting my purse and keys on the console table, but then I stop dead in my tracks.

Ezra is sitting in the armchair in the living room, looking more upset than he had been this morning. He had calmed down by the time he got home from work and didn't seem to have an issue when I had to get ready to leave. He's an amazing uncle and doesn't mind watching the kids while I'm gone. Last night was no different from any other night.

"What's happened?" I ask, my mind immediately racing to consider something terrible happened to one of the kids while I was gone, but that can't be it. I keep my phone close at all times in case he or the kids need me. I haven't missed a call or a text tonight.

As I approach, Ezra holds out a single sheet of paper.

"What's that?" I ask, rather than taking it from him.

"An eviction notice."

I freeze, my mind racing. First it goes to wondering where we'll live. I only moved in with him because we had nowhere else to go. Then my mind settles on guilt.

"Why?" I ask, already knowing the answer.

"Because I'm the only one on the damn lease, Kendall. Someone found out you and the kids were living here."

"I'm so sorry," I tell him. I have no idea what else to say.

"I've lived here seven years. I've never been late on my rent. I've never had any problems until—" His jaw snaps closed.

"Until we came in and ruined your life," I mutter, feeling the weight of just one more thing on my shoulders.

Maybe it's life that's strengthening my muscles, not the extra gym workouts. Carrying all of this around threatens to break my back.

"I didn't say that," he says with another one of those sighs I've grown so used to in recent weeks.

"You didn't have to. What are we going to do? Can we get added to the lease?"

He shakes his head. "It would triple the rent. Besides, the condo isn't rated for five people. It's only a two-bedroom."

That doesn't make sense. What if we were a married couple with three kids? Surely, they wouldn't require a bigger apartment. I have no leg to stand on right now, so I don't even open my mouth to argue that point.

"Do they have a bigger condo here?" I ask, grasping at straws.

I'm living here to save money for a house. I'm already getting behind on that task because, despite Ezra's generosity, I still insist on paying half the rent and other bills. I refuse to live with anyone for free.

I don't want my kids to live in a condo forever. There's not enough room, and they have nowhere to play outside.

"You'd have to ask at the concierge desk in the lobby," he says, making it clear he has no desire to move with us into a bigger condo, which means I'd be moving alone with the kids, and that's not possible. The rent here is already outrageous and possibly more than mortgage payments on a new house with a yard.

"I'm not canceling my Vegas trip because of this," he says, tossing the eviction notice on to the coffee table separating us. "We have thirty days to leave."

That calms me a little. If I pick up as many extra shifts at work as possible, I may be able to swing buying a house by the end of the month, but what about the time it takes for that process?

I slump onto the couch, tears stinging my eyes. I don't even have the ability to hold them back until I'm alone this time.

"What am I going to do?" I mutter.

"You're resourceful. You always have been. You'll figure it out."

You, not us. The distinction is very clear. I'm on my own in this. I don't have any right to feel bitter right now, but that doesn't stop the emotion from hitting me in the chest.

Being the older brother, he was the one left with the responsibility of taking care of me after Dad took off and Mom died three years later. He could've let me end up a ward of the state, but he stepped in and fought for me. Times were tough while he worked himself up the ladder as an analyst in the firm he works at, but we made it.

My life wouldn't look the same as it does now had I not met Ty. I would've finished college. I'd have a steady job with benefits.

But I wouldn't have my kids, and those three miracles are things I'd never regret.

I accepted that my life would never be perfect a long time ago, but I'm ready for the hits to stop coming. I don't even have time to get on my own two feet fully before getting knocked down by another curveball.

I bury my face in my hands as I cry.

Crying doesn't solve a damn thing, my mother's voice says in my head. *You have to take action if you want things to change.*

I scoff at the imaginary reminder. She was a woman of action. When Dad took off, she went to work. She went from being a stay-at-home mom to a mother with two jobs. When she realized she wasn't getting anywhere, she took action. That action, swallowing the bottle of pills left over from Ezra's dental surgery several years before, left her dead and the two of us parentless.

Ezra predicted Dad would come back, but he never did.

I've heard more than once that men go after women like their mothers and women look for men like their fathers. Ezra has avoided that fate by not getting into relationships at all, but true to that prediction, I clung to Ty Penman like he was my salvation. I welcomed him back into open arms on more than one occasion. That was, until the anger issues got out of control. One day, I told him I couldn't live like that anymore and asked him to leave. I never imagined he'd stay gone forever. It wasn't unusual for him to leave for a few weeks at a time, but he'd been gone for years. Knox was barely six months old at the time. He's five now. We haven't seen or heard from him since. See? Just like my dad.

I cry harder when I feel a warm hand on my back. Ezra may be distant more than usual these days, but he's always there for me when I'm feeling lost and desperate.

"What's wrong, little man?"

I jerk up at the sound of my brother's voice still across the room.

With a sad look in his eyes, Knox is standing beside me.

"Hi, honey," I tell him, quickly swiping at the tears streaming down my cheeks.

His own little eyes start to swell with tears, and I pull him to my chest.

"It's fine, sweet boy," I promise him. "Everything is fine."

Lying to my kids comes easier than it ever should, but my adult worries aren't their concern.

"You're crying, Momma," he says, his words getting lost in my t-shirt.

"It's fine," I tell him again. "I promise. Everything is fine."

When he pulls back, I have to look away from the despair in his eyes. In this moment, I'm grateful he never had to see exactly who his father was. Ty would tell me to stop crying and fucking get over it. He could be the cause of all of our problems and wouldn't bother to lift a hand to correct any of it.

All I see right now is worry and compassion in my son's eyes.

"Let's go to bed," I tell him as I stand from the sofa.

I pick him up, balancing him on my hip as I leave the room.

Ezra doesn't say anything to try to stop me, and I'm grateful for that.

He's given me so much already, but his apathy tonight leaves me feeling less than loved.

I hold on to my little boy, cradling him to my chest as I climb into the bed. I don't bother with changing my clothes until after he falls asleep.

The tomorrows are getting harder and harder to face, but I'm lucky to have three amazing kids. They keep me fighting. They keep me grounded.

Unlike my own mother, they keep me alive.

Chapter 4

Finnegan

"You're not just saying that to be nice?" I ask, running my fingers through my thick hair.

"What?" she asks. She seems extremely distracted this morning, and I know it has more to do with her than my proximity.

"My hair color. You really like it?"

"Almost as much as I like your accent."

I give her an easy smile. She seemed out of sorts when I walked in this morning, and I've made it my mission to change the trajectory of her day before she leaves the gym. A woman as gorgeous as her not smiling is a travesty.

"Yeah?" I ask, my own grin widening.

"Are you the type of man that needs compliments to function?"

I love the playfulness in her tone, and I would probably fall head over heels in love with this woman if she didn't seem so damned distracted today.

"As much as the next person," I say with a lazy shrug of my shoulders. "How do you feel about them?"

"Men who like compliments?" She shakes her head. "That's a lot of work."

"Compliments, Kendall. How do you like compliments?"

She pauses for a long moment, her eyes searching mine before she responds. "I like genuine people, Finnegan."

"Finn," I say. "My friends call me Finn."

"Is that what we are? Friends?"

I give her a wider smile. "Of course we're friends."

"I've never been friends with a Scottish man before."

My smile immediately fades away, but then she bites the corner of her mouth. My eyes narrow to slits.

"I'm not Scottish."

A sweet chuckle escapes her lips.

"But you knew that, didn't you?"

"What do you mean? Are you British?"

A rumbled growl escapes my lips, and she looks immensely giddy at my reaction, her eyes locked on my lips.

A tingle of awareness runs the length of me.

"If I knew you a little better, I'd take you over my knee."

She doesn't back away like some women would with the threat, and although I'm not really an ass smacker, I like that she isn't growing scared of me.

"I didn't really take you for the type of guy who is into that sort of thing."

"What sort of thing?" I ask, because although it's not really my thing, I still want to hear her say it.

"A guy who likes to smack asses."

"I'm an ass man," I tell her, giving her backside a quick glance in the mirror behind her. The woman has an ass for days, and despite her being insanely gorgeous, it's the first thing I noticed about her.

Kendall may think that the first time I had lain eyes on her was when I chose that exercise bike beside her, but I clocked this beauty the second she walked into the gym that day. I haven't really been able to take my eyes off of her since.

"But you're right. I'd never abuse one the way you're thinking. I'm more likely to worship it, than hurt it."

She bites her lip again, her eyes darting away from me.

"Where do you work?" I ask, steering the conversation away from anything that will make me have to explain the issue beginning in my sweats.

"Excuse me?"

"Sorry. Abrupt subject change."

"I work in the service industry."

God, words like service aren't doing anything to help me right now.

"Yeah? And what exactly does that mean?"

"Just what I said."

I grin wider. "The service industry? I bet you make a lot of tips."

"Because I have a great ass?"

Laughter bubbles out of my throat before I can stop it. "And you're sweet."

"I do okay. There are others that do better. Where do you work?"

"I work for Blackbridge Security."

She gives me a little head nod in acknowledgment, but she doesn't seem to recognize the name.

"I'm a mechanic," I clarify.

"For a security firm, or is it a play on words that's not translating?"

What a breath of fresh air. This woman isn't one of the ones that got wind of the organization and is salivating for what has been termed the #BlackbridgeSpecial.

"I'm also a safe cracker," I tell her, smiling when she does the same.

"Like Mystery Man Medano?"

"Who?"

"The viral safecracker guy. My s—I have a friend that's a little obsessed with him."

"I've never heard of him."

"He's not actually a safe cracker. His latest thing is trying to get into an old safe he found in the basement of a house he just bought. Several of the videos have gone viral."

"I'm not one to spend a lot of time on social media," I say, but I'm sure Wren, our IT specialist at Blackbridge Security, would have heard of the guy.

"Me either, but my... friend is a little obsessed."

Instead of worrying about whatever friend she can't seem to stop mentioning, I focus on other things.

"Where do you work?"

"You already asked me that."

"And you answered with what you do, not where."

"Why do you want to know?"

I bite my lower lip in an effort not to smile, but I fail miserably.

"I work weekends in the service industry."

"I'm a big guy who likes to eat. Maybe you can be my waitress someday."

"Why do you automatically think I'm a waitress?"

"Do you work in a hotel? Which one? I might need to stay there sometime."

"I don't work in a hotel."

"Which bank? You can help me switch my account over."

"Not a bank," she says, taking a step back. Until she moves, I don't realize just how close we've been gravitating to each other.

"A retail store?"

"You going to tell me you need lingerie next?"

I lean in close, swallowing hard before I can speak. "Do you really work in a lingerie store?"

Her cheeks turn pink. "And if I said I do, are you going to tell me you need something for a friend?"

I shake my head. "I don't have any friends that I'd buy lingerie for."

"Is that so?" Her eyes drop to my mouth once again.

"It is," I tell her, my accent somehow deepening. "Do you try the items on?"

"I don't work in a lingerie store."

"You're a dream crusher," I tease, drawing a small laugh out of her.

"I work at a truck stop diner out on the highway." She begins to frown as if she's disappointed in herself.

"The Lucky Diamond? They have the best chicken fried steak."

She shakes her head, her eyes darting away. "I don't work at that one."

She suddenly seems uneasy with our banter, and since I'm not a creep, I take a step back.

"Were you still wanting me to spot you?"

"What?"

"The bar." I point to the rack behind her, making her turn back around to face the bar.

"Oh right. We got a little off track. Just pull them off me if I go down," she says.

"You got it," I say, stepping back as she situates herself under the squat bar.

I get lost in the movement of her body, the small yet strong lines of her physique. She's the perfect hourglass, and I don't imagine a man alive being able to ignore the fullness of her breasts or that perfectly round ass of hers. I'm fixated on it as she squats and stands over and over.

"You okay back there?" she asks, and I can't even feel guilty about where she found my eyes focusing.

"You have great form," I say, my gaze going right back to her ass.

She chuckles, and that's how the rest of her time in there goes. I keep my eyes on her ass, and she laughs periodically. She doesn't tell me to stop, but when she's done for the day, I tell her goodbye rather than follow her out of the gym.

For one, I didn't get any of my own workout completed with her there, and two, she started to get weirded out with my line of questioning. I figure she wouldn't appreciate me following her onto the elevator. I've really grown to like our time in the gym, and I don't want her to start avoiding it because I've come across as a super creep.

After she leaves, I work out three times harder than I normally would, returning to my condo to complete silence.

I can't get Kendall out of my head, and although I know how things tend to end with women in this building, I'm beginning to lean toward asking her out. Maybe she won't be a psycho stalker who shows up at all times of the day and night knocking on my door.

I barely make it to work on time because I got distracted with thoughts of that gorgeous woman more times than I can count, and I settle behind my desk to go through emails and work orders Pam sent.

Just like the many days before, by ten o'clock, I'm wishing the day away just so I can see her again tomorrow morning at the gym.

Chapter 5

Kendall

The kids are in full meltdown this evening, and although locking myself in the bathroom and ignoring all of it would be easier, that really isn't an option.

I refuse to ignore the problems going on around me. I had too much of an example of that growing up, and I refuse to let my kids see me the same way I saw my own mother.

"Tell me what the problem is," I insist, holding the collar of each boy in separate hands.

Knox relaxes, knowing he's been caught, but it's Kason that continues to struggle.

"Stop," I urge. "Tell me what's wrong so I can fix it."

"He's being a jerk," my oldest snaps, growling at his younger brother like a rabid animal.

"We don't call names," I remind him, my voice calm but tinged with frustration.

Kason has struggled the most with living here, and I know it has more to do with having to change schools in the middle of the year than actually living with his uncle Ezra. He idolizes the man, seeing as he's the only older male role model the poor kid has in his life. Change is hard, and in addition to losing the only house he's ever known, he's also had to give up the friends that he made at his previous elementary school. It's translated into bad behaviors both at home and at his new school.

"Then he shouldn't be a jerk," Kason insists.

Knox's lower lip begins to tremble. Where Kason looks up to Ezra, Knox has always looked up to his older brother. This mean streak Kason's taken to lately has affected him the most.

"Knox, why don't you go find Kayleigh and play with her?"

Knox bolts away the second I release the collar of his shirt.

"Let's have a chat," I tell my seven-year-old son.

He's tall like his father, and since I'm just a hair over five feet three inches, he's getting very close to being as tall as I am already. I forget sometimes that he's not as grown as he looks.

"Chatting is stupid," he mutters, but he allows me to lead him to the living room and out of earshot of the other kids.

"I can say the same for the way you've been acting," I say.

Every evening, there's a fight of some kind, and the mornings aren't any better. I'm already exhausted from staying up so late on weekends to work, and never have the ability to catch up on that sleep lost. The bickering and screaming have only made it worse.

"What happened?"

"Why does it matter? You're only going to side with Knox. He always gets his way." Kason crosses his arms over his chest, an indignant look on his face.

"I can't fix it if you don't tell me what's wrong."

"He colored in my math book. I turned my back for two seconds and the next thing I know, he's scribbled all over the pages. The teacher already hates me. This just gives her more reason. I'll miss recess for an entire week because of this!"

I'm sure the teacher is a reasonable woman, and I want to remind him that picking fights with his peers has probably more to do with the fact that the teacher isn't always excited to see him, but that reasoning would be lost on him.

"Did you leave it out of your backpack after you were done with your homework?"

His eyes snap to mine. I've seen that look so many times before, only I thought I got rid of the problem when Ty left. He's the only man, before now, that could look at me in a way that made me want to clench my teeth until my jaw hurt.

"Do not look at me like that. Did you?"

"I told you! You're siding with him!"

In a rage, Kason picks up the television remote and hurls it across the room. I watch the thing bounce off the drywall, denting it, before crashing to the floor.

Kason's eyes widen, and I see the instant remorse, but it's a little too late.

"I've told you more than once to put things up after you're done with them," I say calmly even though I feel anything but calm. "I was already going to have to replace your math book. Now I'm going to have to pay for the wall to be repaired, and possibly the remote now that you've acted this way."

"Sorry," he mutters, his head hanging lower as his shoulders slump.

"No *YouTube* for the next three days."

"What?" he snaps, his eyes widening as if this punishment is the end of the world. "I said I was sorry."

"Sorry doesn't fix the wall, Kason. You've got to think before you react like that. Now go put your school things away and send Knox in here."

Sulkily, Kason stands from the couch, and although I know he's livid about losing *YouTube*, he doesn't say a word. He's not a dumb kid. He knows giving me any more attitude will only lead to him losing what he loves most for longer. He learned that lesson two weeks ago when he threw a similar fit.

"Momma?" Knox says, his eyes already filling with tears as he approaches.

"You colored in Kason's math book?"

"I didn't have any paper, and you were busy cooking dinner."

And just like his father, I'm being gaslit by a five-year-old.

"You know better, and you also know that sometimes you have to wait to get what you want. Bring me your crayons."

He scurries away, already crying by the time he makes it to the bedroom. I don't have to wait long. Knox hates being in trouble.

When he's on his way back to me, I speak up. "If you bring me that box again with the blue crayon missing, you're going to be in more trouble."

He stops in his tracks, his chin wobbling even more as he turns back around, disappearing into the bedroom before returning.

I learned my lesson a long time ago about how sneaky kids can be.

"This is all of them?" I ask as he hands the box over.

"Even the blue ones," he whispers, his little heart broken over losing what he loves the most. "How long?"

"Three days," I tell him, knowing that's probably too long of a punishment for his age, but I'd never hear the end of it if he got his prized possession back before his brother's punishment was over. Sometimes the punishment doesn't meet the crime, but in the end, it's better for the greater good.

The bickering doesn't end as I carry the crayon box to the kitchen, depositing it on top of the fridge before going back to cooking dinner. At least the yelling and fighting is at a tolerable level.

I'm thinking back, trying to remember if Ezra and I fought like that, but I can't recall a single incident. Maybe it's because he's ten years older, and by the time I was old enough to be annoying, he was already hanging out at his friends' houses. He avoided home as much as I wanted to back then. I think that's why he seems less damaged than I feel most days. He wasn't around to witness Mom's manic behaviors, and he was happy she wasn't bitching when she was down and could hardly get out of bed.

"I don't know how you can eat that stuff," Ezra mutters as he walks in. It's clear his mood is no better than it was a few days ago.

"This?" I say, stirring cut up hotdogs into the mac and cheese I just finished. "This is an excellent meal."

Ezra makes a gagging noise, and it irritates me more than it should.

"The kids are still up," I tell him, knowing he's been purposely staying away most evenings until it's past their bedtime. He's trying to avoid the chaos that goes along with having three kids confined to a small space. I don't blame the man. He never wanted kids in the first place, and although he loves his niece and nephews, they're a lot to handle on a daily basis.

"We need to talk," he mutters, pressing his back to the edge of the counter.

I don't miss the fact that he's all the way on the other side of the room.

"Let me guess, we don't have thirty days to move out," I say, trying to lighten the serious mood he walked in here with.

He doesn't answer. I don't even hear a frustrated chuckle, and my gut sinks when I turn around to face him.

"Tell me we still have thirty days, Ezra."

I whispered the words *it could be worse*. I spoke those words out loud when I was looking in the bathroom mirror this morning after my shower. It was a way to try to lift my spirits, clear my mind of all the things that were out of my immediate control.

I never should've spoken them. I put that bad juju out into the world, and here it is coming to bite me on the ass.

"Ezra?"

"I think getting the noise complaint was a sign. It's like, forcing me out of the apartment forced me to make a decision I've been struggling with for a long time."

"Noise complaint?" I scrunch my face in confusion. "You said it was a lease issue, that there were too many people here."

"That was the main reason, but the noise complaint was secondary. You know I never wanted kids, and I love you guys, but I'm out of my element here. It's just too much for me."

"Noise complaint?" I snap, still stuck on that part because listening to my brother and what he's confessing will only break my heart further. I choose to stick to the anger instead.

There's only one other condo on this floor, and since I never hear anyone walking in the condos above us, I know that it didn't come from them.

How could he do this?

The man across the hall is none other than Finnegan, the man that will only be known as the Irish Asshole in my mind from now on.

How in the world can he flirt with me daily at the gym and then do this? Does he have any idea what he's done? He smiles in my face then calls the landlord on us? I've never met someone so damn two-faced in all my life, and I was a teenage girl that went to high school, so that's saying something.

"Yes, noise complaint from Finnegan Jenkins," Ezra says, confirming what I'd already figured out. "Are you even listening to a word I'm saying?"

"What?"

"Exactly! You never listen. That's why I took the job in Vegas."

"You took a job in Vegas?"

Ezra sighs again, and as much as he'd hate me saying it, he sounded exactly like our dad right before he— "You're deserting me?"

"I'm not deserting you. I made a life decision that benefits myself. It's not selfish to think about myself every once in a while, Kendall."

"Now you're calling me selfish?" The hits just keep coming.

"Do you ever listen?" he hisses.

That same familiar feeling I used to get that urged me to do something insanely crazy comes roaring back despite having shoved that part of me down long ago after the twins were born. I'm antsy with the urge for chaos, to do something off the wall just to feel alive again.

"I'm giving up the apartment early. The landlord said I could get my deposit back if I'm out before the first."

"The first is only a week away," I say, after picturing the calendar in my head.

"Yes."

"Yes? Yes!" I snap. "You're telling me I'm going to be out on my ass with three kids in a week."

"I need the money for my move. I hate to put you in this situation, but you knew living here was temporary. God, Kendall. Please don't look at me like that. It breaks my heart."

"I can't worry about your heart, right now, Ezra. I have to worry about being homeless with my kids."

"Now you're just being dramatic. I can't talk to you when you're acting like Mom. You have money saved up, put it to use."

He doesn't even give me time to form a rebuttal to his insistence that I'm acting like our mom before he walks out of the room.

"Knox!" I holler a few minutes later once I get my bearings again.

My youngest walks into the kitchen.

"Bring me your entire box of craft supplies."

"But, Momma! You already took my crayons!"

"I just need to use some of them. You can have it back when I'm done."

Satisfied with my promise, because I do my best never to break them, he scurries away to get what I asked for.

I move around the kitchen, gathering everything else I'll need. I'm scared to death of what my future holds, and if that man across the hall can so easily make me feel this way, then the only way to turn the tables is to make him feel the same.

Chapter 6

Finnegan

"There's that smile again," Kit says.

He just got back from doing who knows what, but as the weapons expert for Blackbridge Security, it probably has to do with guns and ammo.

"Can't I just be a happy guy?" I say, the smile even bigger today since I received a call from Mr. Crosby that not only were the people across the hall moving, but they'd be out in a week's time.

"You can, but you seem happier right now than Gaige, and that man just walked in with Leighton, and you know what the two of them have been up to lately," he argues.

"She seemed upset," I say, speaking of Leighton who just walked through here with Gaige and into Wren's office.

"It'll get sorted," Kit says. "It always does."

"Haven't you guys got anything better to do than sit around here?" Deacon asks as he walks into the room.

"Not all of us have a gorgeous wife and a cute little boy to get home to," Kit says.

Deacon narrows his eyes at Kit for the gorgeous wife comment. He knows his wife is gorgeous. It's just that Kit is an idiot for saying it out loud, especially so soon after the lifted-shirt, ab-reveal incident a few days ago.

"I'm getting out of the line of fire," I mutter as I stand and make my way to the coffee pot.

I don't really need caffeine this late in the day, but I also don't need to get blood spatter on my favorite t-shirt when Deacon decides to take Kit's head off either.

Wren's office door opens, but the crying Leighton that entered the office, isn't the same woman who exits.

"Daddy needs love, too!" Puff Daddy, Wren's obnoxious African grey parrot, squawks from inside the office.

Gaige ignores the bird. Like everyone else, he knows that giving the thing more attention only makes things worse. He's too busy whispering in Leighton's ear as they walk across the office.

I grin, feeling a little warmer to the idea of all my friends falling in love, but that has more to do with the hot blonde I've been chatting up at the gym than their own happiness. I cringe thinking just how selfish that sounds in my head as I turn back to the single use coffee pot that's sputtering out the last of my cup.

"Finnegan Jenkins!" a woman screams.

I'm lifting my cup to my lips as I turn around, and I can't help the smile that spreads across my lips when I see that it's none other than Kendall from the gym.

She doesn't seem very happy as she rips open her jacket, but I'm happy to see her. Despite the very clearly fake bomb she's strapped to herself, I smile.

What isn't funny is the pure terror in Leighton's eyes as she witnesses this crazy damn woman in the middle of the office.

To make matters worse, Puff Daddy flies out of Wren's office screaming, "Take cover, we're going to fucking die!"

Kit chuckles on the sofa, but I'm no longer seeing the humor in the situation.

"You crazy woman!" I yell. "Are you trying to get shot, coming in here like this?"

I highly doubt Kit would even point a gun at this woman, but everyone in the office, including Pam, the office manager who is standing directly behind Kendall, is armed.

"I'll blow this whole place up!"

"You'll do no such thing! Get your pretty ass over here!"

Kendall glares at me as if she truly wants me dead, but she doesn't move in my direction. Instead of listening, her thumb hovers over what she wants us to believe is the detonation switch on a bomb. Hating that she's turned out to be another crazy one, I smack my cup of coffee down on the counter and cross the room to her.

I don't hesitate to lift her off the ground and drape her over my shoulder. Smacking her ass is just a bonus as I carry her out of the room toward my office.

"Put me down, you asshole!"

I don't put her down until we're both in my office. I kick the door closed, turning around just in time to see her swiping some of her wild hair out of her eyes. It's a nice look on her, and the first time I've seen it not tied up for a workout.

"Do not look at me like that," she snaps when I let my eyes sweep the length of her. "Are you all crazy?"

"Really? You're asking me that?" I ask, trying to hide the humor in my voice because she seems so serious right now.

"That's right. Did you forget I have a bomb?"

I walk closer until I'm standing in front of her. She glares at me when I pull what she's trying to make look like a detonation switch from the spray-painted roll of Lifesavers and pop the thing in my mouth.

I cringe when sweetness instead of spice hits my tongue. "I thought it was a Hot Tamale."

"Mike and Ike's," she mutters. "My kids don't like spicy things."

I tilt my head, my eyes roaming down her body once again. "Come again?"

"Mike and Ike's. They're—"

"I know what Mike and Ike's are," I snap. "You have kids?"

"As if you don't fucking know," she hisses before peeling away the paper on the Lifesavers, pulling one off the top and popping it in her mouth.

She moans like she's in heaven or at least like a woman who hasn't eaten candy in a while. The sound bypasses my confusion and heads straight to my dick.

"First things first," I say, pointing to the boxes taped around her waist. "Can you take that mess off and put it in the trash? It's getting all over the floor."

"Don't," she says, smacking my hand away when I reach for the leaking box of baking soda. "I have to put that back in the fridge when I get home."

I shrug. I hadn't planned on vacuuming my office today, but it seems like an unavoidable task now.

"Now what is this about your kids, and why does it have you in my office, threatening to blow the thing up with baking soda and candy?"

"You ratted us out!" As if she can't help herself, she crunches into the candy in her mouth before pulling another one off the roll and popping it in her mouth.

"I assure you, I didn't—"

"Don't lie to me. You get all flirty at the gym and then you turn around and betray me!"

She plops down on the sofa, coughing when a baking soda cloud puffs up into her face.

"I like flirting with you, Kendall. It's seriously the highlight of my day, but you're going to have to explain the other half. I have no idea what you're talking about."

I haven't been this confused around a woman since Mrs. Tidwell came down into the basement naked when I was sixteen. Apparently, she wanted more than her dryer vent cleaned that day. That was the first time a woman mentioned liking my accent. Who knew the power an accent could wield?

"Don't play me for a fool, Finnegan Jenkins. You know what you fucking did."

I inch closer to her. "Such filthy language should only be reserved for my bedroom. A pretty thing such as yourself shouldn't—"

"Don't use that Scottish accent on me," she snaps.

"I'm not Scottish!" I hiss.

She smiles a little, making me realize she's only trying to rile me up, and I'm giving her exactly what she wants. Then her face falls, eyes dropping to her lap as her fingers toy with the edge of the duct tape securing the boxes around her waist.

Then the tears start to fall.

"You have no idea what you've done," she sobs.

Jesus, I can't handle a crying woman. I'd walk the length of the earth a hundred times over to silence their tears. Kendall is no exception.

"If you tell me, I can fix it. No matter what it is," I vow.

Her eyes are rimmed in red when she looks up at me. "Why cause a problem if you're just going to turn around and offer to fix it? How about not causing the issue to begin with? Why are men so stupid?"

I've spent more time than I'll ever admit wanting to get to know this woman better, but this side is making me want to both run for the hills and give her a hug at the same time. It's a massive change from just wanting to run for the hills the last time I had an encounter with crazy.

"What happened?" I ask again, because we're getting nowhere.

"You got us evicted," she says on another sob, and I'm grateful when she drops her head again.

I know exactly what happened. I don't need further explanation.

Guilt slams into me.

"You're the one living across the hall?"

She scoffs. "As if you didn't know."

"Swear to God, I didn't. I had no clue. Are you dating that guy? He seems a little old for you."

"He's thirty-six, and gross. No, I'm not dating him."

He looks much older than thirty-six, seeing as how I'm thirty-two.

"He's my brother, and he's abandoning me, but not before he kicks me while I'm down. I have to move by the end of the week. Where the hell am I supposed to go?"

"Stay with me," I say, the impulse to make her stop crying speaking for me.

She jerks her head up, a look of pure disgust on her pretty face.

"Are you nuts?"

I want to point to the "bomb" still strapped to her body, but now doesn't seem like the best time to point out the obvious.

"You want me to move my three kids in with a damn stranger?"

"You have three kids?"

"Do you think I was over there making all the damn noise you called and complained about?"

"I didn't know it was you. I've never run into you other than the gym. I thought that guy got into breeding wild animals or something."

That is the wrong thing to say. Kendall stands from the sofa, prowling toward me with a look that says if she did have a real bomb, she'd shove it down my throat right about now.

"Do not insult my kids," she says, her voice low and measured.

She's a little terrifying like this despite our height difference. She's way too pretty to be considered a troll, but she's got that very same menacing look in her eyes I remember watching on a television show as a kid. She's scaring me a little more than it did back then.

"I'm not," I say, holding my hands up in surrender. "I promise, but the offer still stands. You and your kids can stay with me until you find something else."

And the words just keep coming. She asked me if I was crazy, and I'm beginning to think that I just might be. I couldn't stand the chaos next door. How would I ever survive if it was right in the middle of my own condo?

"I'm sorry I ever met you," she mutters before walking out of my office.

I'm frozen in place for a long moment before running after her. The trail of baking soda she left behind ends before the end of the hall, and before I can get to the breakroom area, she's gone.

"You have to explain that," Kit says from the sofa.

"I'm sorry I missed the action," Brooks says. "Give me a play-by-play."

Deacon, Gaige, and Leighton are all gone, and since it's inching up on six in the evening, I'd wager that we're the only three left in the office.

"I don't want to talk about it," I mutter as I take a seat beside Kit.

More than that, I don't want to feel guilty.

She may have bolted out of here, and I may feel like I dodged a bullet with her not accepting my offer, but I get the feeling this will not be the last I hear of Kendall.

"You can't have a woman walk in here with a fake bomb and not explain," Brooks whines. "Tell me."

"She's a girl I met at the gym," I murmur.

"In our building?" Kit clarifies.

"Yep."

"Shit, man. What did I tell you about that?" Kit hisses.

"Didn't you learn last time?" Brooks adds.

"She's different," I mutter, understanding that more now than ever before.

I've dealt with crazy before, and never once did I find myself wanting to run after it when it left.

"Seems like it," Kit says with apparent disbelief in his voice.

Chapter 7

Kendall

The audacity of that man to offer me a place to stay after creating the entire problem himself has me floored. I'm so annoyed, I mumble hateful things about him under my breath the entire drive home. Agitation makes my muscles tight, and although I know a good workout would probably solve that problem, I can't take the risk that he'll be in the damn gym.

And that's another thing I'm mad about. Finnegan Jenkins, the too-sexy Irishman, has now ruined the damn gym for me. I guess it shouldn't really matter seeing as I'm fixing to lose that perk as well.

I only have a couple hours to stew in my hatred for the man across the hall before it's time to pick the kids up, and I plan to use the time wisely.

That plan is derailed when I get back to the condo and find four strangers inside.

"Can I help you?" I snap at the one standing around, observing as the other three proceed to remove furniture through the open doorway.

"We're the moving company hired by—" He glances down at the clipboard in his hands before looking back up at me with disinterest and boredom. "Ezra Stewart."

"My brother?"

"I don't know who the man is to you, lady. I'm just here to do a job."

I stand to the side, wondering where Evie is because she's usually all over things like this. Four strange men in the apartment would mean her losing her shit and screaming at the top of her little bird lungs.

"Did my bird fly out of here?" I ask as I pull out my phone to call my brother.

This makes the man smile. "That thing is deadly. It dive-bombed Jack and shit on Rocky's head. Clay had to catch it in a sheet."

"Evie is wrapped up in a sheet?" I squeal.

"Clay put it back in the cage and then covered it up with the sheet," the man informs. "I should charge extra for having to deal with that."

"Yes, you should," I agree, thinking of it as payback for Ezra not giving me a heads-up about them being here.

He scribbles something on his paperwork and winks at me before barking out an order to one of his guys.

After checking on Evie and assuring her the men would be leaving soon, I sit in the corner on the sofa that's not on the man's list and wait for them to finish. By the time they leave, the condo looks barren. Wishing I could spread out my own belongings, I close the door behind them. Doing so would be pointless. I have to be out in less than a week, and it would be only wasted energy.

Ezra doesn't answer for the fourth time when I attempt to get ahold of him, but he texts a couple minutes before I have to go grab the kids from school.

Ezra: Headed to Vegas early.

That's all I get in explanation about strangers being in the condo.

Ezra: You still have a couple days to figure things out.

I want to cry with his apathetic responses, but that too, would be wasted energy.

The kids are extra lively when they get home, but I manage to get them through homework and dinner with little incident.

When they start getting stir crazy and the volume of their playing grows to nearly an unbearable level, I encourage it. Ezra deserted us, and the man across the hall is the reason we have to move, so as far as I'm concerned, the louder the better.

If he thought my kids were annoying enough to call and report us, then we might as well prove him right.

Kason is still grumpy as he watches Kayleigh, Knox, and me have a little dance party in the middle of the living room. He's still mad about losing his *YouTube* privileges, but as the dancing continues, I can see him starting to give in to the excitement his siblings are displaying.

"Baby Shark" is on constant repeat, and as annoying as the song is to me, I imagine it being ten times as bad for Finnegan. I'm a mother. I can tolerate annoying. Finnegan doesn't seem like the type to tolerate it very long, so that's why I have a huge smile on my face when the doorbell rings.

I turn the volume up louder and encourage the kids to keep dancing, feeling accomplished when Kason climbs off the sofa and wiggles to the music as I walk toward the door.

My look is smug when I pull it open, but it isn't Finnegan.

"I love the song," the pimple-faced guy says with a smile. He wiggles a little to the music as he holds out a plastic bag with a local restaurant's logo on it. Maybe he thinks it'll bring him a bigger tip or something.

"I didn't order food," I tell him, watching his smile fade and his body stop moving.

He looks from his phone up to the number by my door before muttering a curse.

"Sorry to bother you," he mutters before turning around and heading right to Finnegan's door.

The delicious scent coming from the bag makes me even angrier. I learned long ago that cooking two different meals, one for the kids and a healthier option for me, became tedious. So tonight, I suffered through leftovers of mac and cheese with cut up hot dogs and a protein shake for balance.

Finnegan is having El Mexicano Grill, and I continuously grow more irritated as the delivery guy waits for the man to answer the door.

I don't know why I'm standing here torturing myself, both with the scent of delicious food I can't have and the imminent view of the man, but I hesitate to close my door.

Finnegan eventually opens his door, freezing with a towel held to his head when he spots me across the hall.

The delivery guy is being super nice, chatting as he holds out the food, but it seems Finnegan hasn't even noticed him even though the teen is literally between the two of us.

"Sir? Your food?"

Finnegan leans to the side, grabbing cash from inside, and hands it to the kid with a quick thank you. He doesn't take his eyes off me the entire time, and when the delivery guy darts away, eager to get back to work, or maybe to get away from the weird energy in the hallway, the man standing across from me is fully revealed.

With "Baby Shark" blasting behind me, I take in a shirtless Finnegan Jenkins. I knew the guy was fit because of the time he spent at the gym, but I had no idea he had muscles for days, rippling down his torso. The light smattering of red hair and freckles painted across his pecs only add to his appeal.

"I ordered enough for two," he says, holding the bag of food a little higher. "Would you like to—"

"Mommy!" Knox says, running up to my side, tugging on the hem of my shirt. "Come dance with us!"

"In just a minute, buddy," I tell him, lifting my eyes from my son only to find Finnegan's door closed. "Jerk."

The words are muttered, but somehow Knox still hears me.

"We don't call names, Mommy," he chides.

"We don't, bud," I agree as I step back and close the condo door.

The dance party continues, and I let myself get lost in it. I refuse to taint the memories I'm making with my kids with a sour attitude over nothing I can change at the moment.

Bath time is quick and easy for the kids, and I consider having a dance party every night if it tires them out enough to get sweet sleepy smiles instead of endless requests for water and additional trips to the bathroom when I'm putting them to bed.

Shortly after they're snuggled up with soft blankets and their favorite stuffed animals, the doorbell rings again.

I curse the gods for the interruption, thinking of ripping Finnegan's head off for having the nerve to show up after running away like a baby at the sight of my son. The man clearly has no experience with kids. If he did, he would know to knock softly after the sun goes down because a ringing doorbell is sure to wake them.

I pray they're tired enough to sleep through it as I rush to the door. I can't risk it getting rung again.

"Have you lost your fu—"

My words fall away when I see an unfamiliar man in the hallway.

Finnegan's door is sealed up tight, but my anger at him doesn't ebb.

"Can I help you?" I snap, directing my irritation at the stranger. He rang the bell after all.

"Ms. Kendall Stewart, I presume?" he says with such distaste I want to slam the door in his face.

"Yes?" I hiss instead because I'm saving all of my rudeness for the man across the hall.

"I'm Wyatt Crosby. I own the condo."

I give him a belated smile on the off chance that he's here to tell me he changed his mind. In a perfect world, he'd cut me some slack and tell me I can continue to live here rent free, or at least give me the full thirty days.

"Your brother waived the thirty-day eviction notice," Mr. Crosby continues.

The world is so far from perfect. I'd do well to remember that.

"Yes," I say because I had this conversation with Ezra already.

"Which means you have forty-eight hours to vacate the premises."

"Forty—no. Ezra said I have a week."

"Forty-eight hours," the man says, holding out an envelope.

I stare down at it, refusing to take it because doing so is an agreement to what he's saying.

"Ma'am," he says, waving the thing as if he believes I can't see it although I'm staring directly down at it.

Begrudgingly, I take it.

"Can I get a few more days?"

The man shakes his head.

"Can't you cut me a little slack? I have three kids I have to worry about."

"Your lack of preparation isn't my concern, Ms. Stewart. What I can give you is forty-eight hours to vacate instead of calling the cops. You nor your kids are on the lease."

"Okay," I whisper, near tears before backing into the apartment and closing the door.

I don't bother rushing to the bathroom to climb in the shower to cry this time. I never would've made it anyway.

What I can be grateful for is that the doorbell didn't wake the kids, forcing them to witness their mother breaking down and sobbing in the middle of the living room.

Chapter 8

Finnegan

I'm no stranger to early mornings but hitting the gym before the sun rises to avoid Kendall sucks. The scent of mentholatum mingles with the regular lemony smells of the gym, giving the entire room a hospital smell that leans more toward the geriatric wing.

I smile and nod my head when an elderly gentleman gives me a little wave, but I have to point to my earbuds to indicate I'm listening to something when he tries to chat me up.

I stick to cardio, first the treadmill then the elliptical before finishing up on the stair-climbing machine because I'd likely pull a muscle or drop a heavy weight on my foot if I tried doing those with my head so damned jumbled.

I'm a sweaty mess when I finish and no closer to solving any of the world's problems as I ride the elevator up to my floor.

The now familiar chaos in the condo across from mine greets me when I get closer, and for some reason it doesn't grate on my nerves as much as it did before I knew that it was Kendall over there. Kendall and her kids more specifically.

What does irritate me a little is having that damn shark song stuck in my head all damn night while I tossed and turned. Not getting a good night's sleep always has the ability to annoy me. A lack of sleep bothers me so much that I don't even go out late anymore. In recent years, I've looked for women who have things to do the next day in an effort to get to bed at a decent hour. Mediocre sex wasn't worth the loss of sleep, and I realize just how old I feel as I unlock my door and slip inside.

I grab a quick shower, rushing more than usual just so I can stick my face to the peephole. The condo across the hall typically goes quiet about this time, so I know they have to leave. Sure enough, not ten minutes into spying on the door, it opens. I watch Kendall shuffle two older kids, one boy and one girl, along with a younger boy, out of the apartment. She asks them to wait as she locks the door before they head toward the elevator. She doesn't once look in the direction of my door, and I hate that it hits me in the gut in an indescribable way that I'm not even a consideration this morning.

I couldn't get back inside my condo quick enough last night when the youngest boy walked up to her. I didn't want her to have to explain to him who I was, because I imagine that story would come along with filtered words and things like *don't talk to that bad man*.

I grab a prepackaged frozen breakfast from the freezer and pop it in the microwave, debating on a fattening lunch because these macro-perfect meals I have delivered are seriously getting old. I consider an extra workout this evening because as much as I like to eat, I like the energy working out gives me more. I guess I can consider it a win-win situation.

After eating I dress quickly, wanting to head to work before Kendall gets back. I went weeks of only seeing her at the gym, but now it seems like the woman is everywhere, and that's not even counting her showing up at work yesterday.

If I concentrate hard enough, I can still taste the sweetness of that Mike and Ike's on my tongue, and it puts my head in an area I just can't think about where she's concerned. I avoid complicated like the plague, and spitfire Kendall and her three kids are the epitome of complicated.

I don't avoid single moms specifically; I just don't give the women I pursue the chance to talk much. Kids are seldomly brought up, but then again, the women I seek, or used to seek I should say, since it's been a while since I went out hunting, aren't there to look for a man willing to help with their children if they do have them. They want what I want, a little fun and then a goodbye. No strings. No complications. No next-day call.

Kendall doesn't seem like the type of woman down for that type of situation.

Getting dressed is rote, and eating breakfast carries the very same disinterest as the El Mexicano Grill did last night. I'm a simple man. I like to work, work out, and eat. Sleep is high up on that list as well, and somehow the woman across the hall has managed to taint all those things in a matter of twenty-four hours. Before, I didn't mind losing a little sleep, thinking about Kendall and those tight clothes she wears to the gym.

The bombs she dropped, both the one about her getting kicked out and the baking soda one she left in a trail down the hallway at the office, have left me off kilter. She's getting evicted. That means the noise will stop, but so will the sight of her plump ass in those dark gray leggings she wears twice a week.

I honestly think I fucked myself. The leggings definitely outweigh the noise.

And to make matters worse, I'm swimming in the guilt of that happening because of my complaint.

I wanted the noise to stop. Had I known it was her, I might've handled things differently. Maybe I would've caught her in the hall and asked her to tone it down, but I know that would never have worked. I'd get one look at her and smile like I always do when we run into each other. I'd welcome the noise just so we could keep having conversations over the water cooler and squat bar. I'd eventually invite her to my apartment while her kids were at school, despite knowing she lived right across the hall, a mark in the negative column rather than a pro.

I wash my fork from breakfast and rehang the dish towel on its proper hook before grabbing the things I'm going to need for a day at the office. I'm sliding my phone into my pocket as I open the door, halting in my tracks at the sight of Kendall standing in the middle of the hallway, halfway between our two condos.

"What are—" I begin, but the woman shoves right past me, walking into my condo like she owns the place.

"Show me," she snaps, spinning around in the middle of my living room with one hand propped on her hip.

My cock jerks in my jeans, ready to show this gorgeous woman any damn thing she desires.

Her eyes are locked on mine, hinting at the fact that she's not talking about anything below my waist, so I don't reach for my zipper like the majority of my body is begging me to.

"Show you what?" I ask, because my libido demands clarification.

"The bedroom you offered yesterday."

God, her saying *bedroom* doesn't help this situation at all.

"Never mind," she says, waving her hand dismissively before spinning around. "I'll find it myself."

I'm slack-jawed, not opposed to watching her walk away since it means I can stare at that fabulous ass of hers.

She disappears into one of the guest bedrooms before popping back out and opening the door to the second guest bedroom. I swear on everything holy if she opens the door to my bedroom, I'm not going to be able to resist following her in there and trying to persuade her to perform some tried-and-true stress-relieving tactics.

Was she always this high strung before and I somehow missed it among her smiles and witty replies?

I wouldn't be the first man to get distracted by a gorgeous woman.

"What?" I ask when I notice her standing in the hallway between the two rooms.

"I said, we'll need both."

I smile at her demand, still not having a clue what she's talking about.

"Who's we?" I ask, mildly confused but somehow completely okay with it so long as she's this close to me.

"The kids and me. We'll need both bedrooms."

"For what?" I ask, my brows drawing tightly together.

"You offered us a place to stay. We're going to take both rooms." It's more of a demand than a request, and although she just dropped another bomb right at my feet, my dick doesn't get the memo.

All that damn thing is focusing on is her attitude and that spark in her eyes. My body demands me to light it and set it ablaze.

"I... umm..." I grab the back of my neck as I think of a way to tell her I only did that because she was crying. Now that she's not crying, I can't follow through with that offer.

Her face falls. "Are you backing out? I mean, after what you did, that would be a seriously shitty thing to d-do."

Her voice quivers at the end, and my mind starts to race.

"No. I'm not backing out." What the actual fuck? Am I being controlled by outside forces? I did *not* just make the same offer I did yesterday in a panic.

"Good," she says, a quick smile tugging up the corners of her mouth. "Then you can help me move our things before I have to get the kids from school."

"Kids?" How did I forget the kids? She literally just said *we* need both rooms before explaining exactly who she meant.

I blame her perfect ass for making me lose all reason.

"They get out at three-fifteen. Let's get to work."

She walks right past me, her ass bouncing in those damn gray leggings I'm obsessed with, and stupidly, I know I'll do whatever she requests at this point.

Because I'm useless right now, she props my door open with a stool from the kitchen bar before walking across the hall and unlocking her door. With my eyes glued to her ass, I follow, like that cartoon skunk smitten with the female cartoon skunk.

One second, I'm entranced with the hypnotic movement of her ass, and the next, I'm being attacked.

"What the fuck?" I roar, covering my head with my arms and running for cover.

As I spring into action, I notice two things simultaneously. One, Kendall is smiling at my demise, and two, she's not moving a muscle to help.

"This was a fucking trap!" I scream, realizing now that my attacker is of the winged sort.

I'm being ambushed, and my betrayer finds it hilarious. I grin at the sound of her laughter only to be dive-bombed again.

"Satan!" the bird squeals.

"Fucking stop, Puff!"

How in the hell did Wren's bird make it into this condo?

"Fire! Fire! Fire!" the bird squawks. "Don't just stand there! Help!"

Every chance the bird gets, usually when I manage to straighten and glare at Kendall for just laughing at the attack, the damned thing tries to rip my hair out.

"Kendall!" I scream. "Do something!"

"That's enough, Evie," she says in a stern voice, but the bird dives at my head one more time before flying over to her and landing on her shoulder.

"Evie?" I hiss.

"She doesn't like men," Kendall says with a shrug, a little too nonchalant for the assault that just took place.

"Get out, Satan!" the bird snaps, its wings flapping wildly with the threat of another attack.

"Settle down," Kendall says, scooping the bird off her shoulder with a laugh before walking out of the room.

My heart is racing, and I know it has more to do with the laughter that bubbled from the insane woman than the dive-bombing bird.

I'm in serious damn trouble.

Chapter 9

Kendall

Evie did more than I would ever have the courage to do, and although it was rude, I just couldn't bring myself to stop it any sooner than I did.

Maybe it was the humor in his eyes rather than absolute terror, but it left me feeling lighthearted with a smile on my face despite the tact I had to take this morning.

I'm normally a fairly timid person. I don't like to ruffle feathers or cause drama, but when it comes to my kids, I grow a backbone very quickly.

That's how I found myself standing outside Finnegan's door. I didn't give him a chance to say no when I insisted on taking him up on his offer. He looked more terrified with the idea of us moving in with him than he did being attacked by Evie.

I'm less likely to pull the plug on us moving in than I was in the seconds the man was being mistaken for Satan with flames coming out of the top of his head.

"Don't," the man in question says.

"It needs to be done before I have to go get the kids," I mutter, taking a step back from the heavy cabinet.

"And I said I'll get someone else to help with it."

"I'm strong," I mutter, although I know my limitations.

Ezra opted to hire a moving team to get all my stuff in here because he wasn't willing to exert the physical energy for it to get done. He paid, and I just added it to the growing list of moneys I'd have to repay him. After the shit my brother just pulled, I plan to burn that list and act ignorant if he asks about it. He's left me in a total bind, one that is forcing me to move my kids in with a complete stranger in an effort to keep us from ending up homeless.

"I know you're strong," he says in a way that makes me think he's speaking of more than just physical strength. "But I can get one of the guys to help."

My face flushes at the idea of one of his friends from the office coming here to help him move my things. What do they think of me? It can't be good after the way I acted yesterday. What in the world was I thinking, showing up with a fake bomb and threatening to kill everyone in the room? I'm lucky I didn't get arrested. Surely it has to be a crime to do something like that even if the bomb is fake.

My mouth waters thinking about the Lifesavers still in my purse. I could eat my weight in those damn things.

"What are you thinking about right now?"

"What?" I ask, snapping my eyes back to his.

"You're grinning. What are you thinking about?"

"Lifesavers," I answer honestly. The man works out more than I do, and you don't get the kinds of muscles he has by giving in to temptation very often. He has to know exactly what it's like to lust after unhealthy stuff he knows he shouldn't have.

"I'm not a lifesaver, Kendall. I'm correcting a mistake."

I scrunch my nose. "I'm not calling you a lifesaver. You created this mistake. As far as I'm concerned, moving in with you is your penance for the trouble you caused. I was thinking about Lifesavers, the candy."

His grin only widens instead of him looking a little pissed like I expected.

"Like a little sweet in your mouth, huh?"

"Are you really flirting with me right now?"

His smile drops.

"You lost your right to flirt with me when you got me evicted."

"I didn't know it was you. I don't know how many times I have to say it."

"So that makes it okay that you would call and complain about any other single mother?"

He shakes his head, but the man is smart because he doesn't argue further.

"You're like a tattle-telling child, Finnegan Jenkins, running to the teacher when he doesn't get his way."

He steps around the dresser I was planning to help him move, getting close enough that I can smell the scent of his soap mixed with clean sweat. It's not a terrible smell at all. Honestly, it's a little addictive, but I have better control over myself than to step closer and breathe in deeply.

"I didn't know what was going on over here. I just wanted my serenity back."

"Well, you won't be getting that anytime soon, but I will suggest leaving early and staying out late to avoid my kids. You couldn't get away from Knox fast enough last night."

He shakes his head, taking a step back. "I wasn't avoiding your son. I was trying to keep him from asking questions. You know what? Never mind. I'm going to grab some water and call one of the guys."

He walks out of the room without a backward glance. I won't feel guilty. I won't back out. I have just over twenty-four hours left to clear this condo. I can't pack my kids up and go to a hotel. That would be a temporary solution and using my money that way will only put me further behind in buying our forever home. Nightly hotel rates would drain my account faster than I could fill it.

Believe me, I stayed awake nearly all night last night working through scenarios on how I could avoid moving in with Finnegan. I was strategic, leaving emotion out of the entire thing, and I came up empty. I have no other family, and after what Ezra just recently pulled, I don't know that I'd even call him family at this point. I lost friends along the way, parenting getting in the way of having fun. The friends I did have before aren't the type to open their homes to a family of four.

That left Finnegan. It was only temporary, and I'd do anything for my kids. So, here I am, halfway moved out of my brother's condo.

With Finnegan gone, I pull out my phone and shoot off a text to my boss. I've avoided doing this, but if I want to be on my own and no longer dependent on anyone else, I can't wait any longer.

Me: I'm hoping to get more shifts.

It takes a few minutes for the bubbles to pop up, and I want to scream with the return text I receive.

Sasha: You have to expand your duties at work.

I want to throw my phone across the room, but that wouldn't solve any problems. Plus, I can't do exactly what Kason got into trouble for earlier in the week. Being a hypocrite is the worst.

Me: I'll consider it.

She sends back a smiley face emoji, and it seems a little juvenile with what she's asking of me.

"Are you over your little snit?"

I spin around to glare at Finnegan, prepared to give him more than a piece of my mind, but I have to snap my jaw closed when I spot another guy standing beside him with a wide smile on his face.

"Hi," the stranger says, his eyes darting between Finnegan and me. "I'm Kit Riggs."

I return his smile and shake his hand. "Kendall Stewart."

"Nice to meet you," the man says. "I'm the muscle Finn hired."

"Oh, thank God," I huff out on a breath, relieved he's not one of the guys from the office.

"He works at Blackbridge," Finn says as if he can read my mind. "He was sitting on the sofa during your visit yesterday."

My cheeks flame with embarrassment when Kit chuckles.

I've never been a violent person, but Finnegan makes me want to throat punch him. He's still behaving like the child I accused him of being not long ago, trying his best to get me riled up and force a reaction out of me.

Instead, I grin back at his coworker. "Not one of my finer moments. Please forgive me."

"I thought it was wildly entertaining," Kit says. "Feel free to stop by anytime."

"Can we get to work now?" Finnegan asks, his accent gruff and annoyed.

Since I've already helped move out all the smaller things and the kids' clothes, I step to the side and watch as Finnegan and Kit move the furniture from one condo to the other. They take direction well when asked which room they should put certain things in.

In less than an hour of Kit helping, the only thing that's left is me sorting through the things in the two bedrooms. I know I won't be here long, but now that we have a little more room to spread out, I plan to unpack, hoping it'll help with Kason's attitude problem.

"Nope," Finnegan says, blocking the doorway to his apartment when I walk across with Evie in her smaller cage. Her big cage is already setup in the corner of the room that Kayleigh and I will be staying in.

"What?"

"That bird isn't staying here."

I huff a laugh. "Of course she is."

"She's not."

"Don't be ridiculous," I tell him, but he somehow makes himself bigger when I try to slide around him.

"I'm serious, Kendall. You and the kids, nothing else."

I narrow my eyes. "Her cage is already inside. You didn't say a word when I rolled it in there."

"As far as I'm concerned, you can roll it right down to the street, or it can stay, but the bird isn't welcome. I'm not going to be attacked in my own home."

"She's family," I say.

"She's a bird, and not welcome."

My throat threatens to close.

"Vagabond," Evie snaps, not helping the situation.

Finnegan raises his eyebrow as if to prove his point.

"What am I supposed to do with her? It's not like I can just set her free. She's not a wild bird."

"I have the perfect place for her," he says. "Wait right here."

My mouth is hanging open when he walks back into his condo and shuts the door in my face. He hasn't given me a key yet, so there's nothing I can do but stand in the hallway and stew.

Chapter 10

Finnegan

"I'll have to find someone to stay with the kids," Kendall mutters almost absently on the drive to Blackbridge.

I don't know if she's hinting that she wants me to watch her kids while she works, but I don't open my mouth to offer. I don't know shit about kids, so she shouldn't want that anyway.

"I'm thinking of taking on more shifts, too. I'm planning to get my own house, and the quicker I can do that the better."

I don't disagree with her, not even when she sighs and rubs her hands over her face.

Telling her she could stay with me yesterday was an off-the-cuff spontaneous reaction to seeing her break down and cry in my office. I never expected her to take me up on it, and I was relieved when she left yesterday without agreeing. Her showing up at my door this morning was a complete surprise. Agreeing to hold up my end of the offer was an even bigger surprise.

It's why I couldn't fold on the bird. I can't give her all my power, and it's the last ace I had to play. She gave in a little more reluctantly than I expected, but it also leads me to believe she legitimately doesn't have anywhere else to go. If she did, she would've insisted on my moving her things somewhere else. Standing my ground still leaves me feeling like an asshole. I didn't have pets growing up, but I can't imagine her kids are going to be very happy about their family pet getting her own eviction notice.

Kendall grabs the handle to the bird cage faster than I can, glaring at me as if I'm continuing to ruin her life when she pulls the thing from the back seat.

Evie flaps her wings, appalled that she's being rattled, but Kendall isn't letting her height, or lack of, keep her from doing things.

"Heaven's sake," the bird mutters. "How about a little finesse?"

I bite my lip to keep from laughing, wondering just how things will go between this old-lady-like, proper bird and Wren's foul-mouthed parrot.

I'm honestly near giddy on the ride up in the elevator, filled with eager anticipation at watching it all play out.

Kendall tries to hide on my right side as we enter the front office of Blackbridge, so I step around her, putting her face-to-face with Pam, our office manager.

"Hello again, dear," Pam says with a welcoming smile.

I might have known Pam would react this way, but Kendall had no idea that what she did yesterday would not make the people in the office dislike her. If anything, it endeared her to them.

"Please, let me apologize for my behavior yesterday."

Pam waves off her apology. "It was quite entertaining, dear."

"It was irresponsible. Thank you for not calling the cops."

"We only call the cops for real bombs," Pam says before giving a quick smile and answering her ringing phone.

"Real bombs?" Kendall asks as we step away from Pam's desk and head deeper into the office.

"She was joking," I lie.

Kendall doesn't need to worry about actual bombs. Besides, it's been nearly a year since we had a real bomb threat that carried any weight.

"Right this way," I say, pointing toward Wren's office.

"Hi," Jude says as he approaches. "Who do we have here?"

"This is Kendall," I say at the same time Kendall lifts the cage so Jude can see better and says, "This is Evie."

Jude smiles at Kendall before bending in the middle to get a closer look at the bird.

"Be careful," I warn.

"Hello there, young man," Evie says, manners out in full force.

I glower down at the bird. I get attacked and Jude gets this type of greeting?

Kendall chuckles. "She likes you."

"I'm a likable guy." Jude holds out his hand.

"Kendall Stewart," she says, taking his hand.

I want to growl at him but not because I think he's flirting. Jude is so in love with Parker, other women don't even exist to him in that way. What makes me want to lash out is that the attitude I've gotten from this woman seems to fade away when she's speaking to my friend. It tells me she has a problem with me instead of just being a little angry at the world.

"I know," Jude says with an easy smile. "I heard about your visit yesterday."

I grin, feeling a little vindicated for the embarrassment she's going to feel.

"Yesterday was a little out of character," she says, a wide smile on her face. "It'll never happen again."

"That's a shame," he responds, glancing up at me. "But you wouldn't be the first woman he drove to do insane things."

"You'll have to tell me about that sometime," she says, winking at him.

She fucking winks at him. I can't recall a time when the woman winked at me.

"You should introduce her to Parker," I say, reminding him he has a significant other.

"Your wife?" Kendall asks.

"Not quite yet, but hopefully soon."

"I'd love to meet her."

"I'll set it up," Jude says. "It was nice to meet you, Kendall."

"You as well, Jude."

My head shifts back and forth through their conversation until Jude nods before walking away.

"Lovely boy," Evie says.

"This way," I growl, annoyed that I'm annoyed.

"Such a brute," the bird snaps, but it's Kendall's hummed agreement that bothers me the most.

I knock on Wren's door because the last thing Kendall needs is to interrupt anything inappropriate, and the man isn't exactly known for keeping private things private.

He doesn't answer so I knock again.

"Is he in here?" I ask Jude who has settled on the sofa with a book.

"He's in there," Jude confirms.

I knock again.

"Just a second!" Wren calls, and I swear I'm going to lose my shit if I walk in and he's doing something like wiping off his hands or zipping his pants.

The man went from hooking up with girls he met online on occasion to full-blown sex addict with the introduction of his girlfriend Whitney. Those two are horny all the damn time.

"Hey," Wren says, opening the door. "Sorry."

"I called to let you know we were coming," I complain.

"And I had a list of things to get done for Deacon," he returns, a serious look on his face. "Things I had to deal with before having company."

His tone tells me that he really was working, and once again, I feel like an asshole.

"Wren, this is Kendall." I point to the cage in her hand. "And Evie."

Wren backs away from the door, inviting us into his office.

Puff wolf whistles at Kendall, and when she notices the other bird, the smile I haven't seen much today comes back full force.

"You have an African grey?"

"And, baby, you have the fattest ass I've ever seen!" Puff says, his wings flapping like crazy. "Jesus, woman! What are you feeding that thing?"

Kendall's eyes go wide, and her mouth hangs open, and I can just see us now, heading right back to my condo with that damn bird tagging along.

"That's hilarious," Kendall says to Wren.

"Where are my pearls?" Evie screams from her cage. "I need to clutch my pearls!"

"What do we have here?" Puff says, flying from his perch and landing on the back of Wren's office chair to get a better look.

Kendall holds the cage up, so it's easier for the birds to see each other.

"Hey there, baby," Puff says, whistling at Evie the same way he just did Kendall.

"Puff, this is Evie," Wren says as if the damn bird honestly understands rather than just repeating inappropriate shit he overhears.

"Hey, Evie girl. Wanna come see Daddy?"

"Gross," Evie snaps.

Kendall chuckles. "You're going to be keeping her for me until I can find a place to live?"

Wren looks from Kendall to me. "I thought you were moving in with Finn?"

"I am, but I mean my permanent place."

For some reason, hearing her say that hits me in the chest, and I rub at it as if it's real. A couple of hours ago, I was regretting asking her to move in because she actually took me up on the offer. So why does the thought of her leaving make me hurt?

I shake my head before looking back at my friend. "The bird is violent and attacked me."

Wren huffs, as if what I said is preposterous.

"Do you like pussy?" Puff asks.

Kendall gasps, covering her mouth with her free hand.

"Well, I never!" Evie says, doing her own little version of a bird gasp.

"Simon is Satan!" Puff continues.

"Simon is Wren's girlfriend's cat," I explain, trying to take the sting out of the bird using the word pussy.

"Oh," Kendall says, but her hand is still covering her mouth and it comes out a little muffled.

"Not all pussy is bad pussy," Puff continues as if we're not even in the room. He's hunkered down so he can easily see Evie in her cage.

"I declare!" the female bird hisses. "You're vulgar!"

"Wait until you see what my tongue can do!"

"Oh gosh!" Kendall says, but a laugh bubbles out of her. "He's very vocal."

"Crude," Wren agrees with a smile.

Kendall returns the grin, and I'm getting pretty tired of her grinning at all of my friends and not me, but that makes me think about her accusation earlier. Maybe I am like a kid because I'm seconds away from throwing a temper tantrum right now because her focus isn't on me.

"Think she'll be okay here?"

Wren gives her a soft smile. "She might be shocked by the things he says, but she'll be safe. Puff grows on people. Everyone ends up loving him."

I scoff, but don't open my mouth. The bird has the uncanny ability to annoy just about anyone. We tolerate him at best.

"Okay," Kendall agrees, handing over the cage to Wren.

"Ready to go?" I ask her, needing to cut this goodbye short. If she starts crying again, I have no clue how I'll handle it. I might just end up giving her the information to my damn retirement account.

"Hey, Satan!" Puff says, turning in my direction as if he's just now realizing I'm in the room. "How's Hell this time of year?"

"Satan!" Evie squawks, agreeing with Puff.

"See?" Wren says, assuring Kendall. "They've already found something they agree on. They'll be best friends in no time."

Kendall laughs.

"Har-har," I say with no humor at all. "Ready?"

Kendall looks back at Evie in her cage before nodding and walking out of the room.

Chapter 11

Kendall

I was terrified to come back to this office after the stunt I pulled yesterday, but Pam was super nice as well as Jude.

What looks to be the organization's breakroom has even more of the guys in it than it did before we walked into Wren's office, and that anxiety ramps up again.

"Let's go," Finnegan mutters, walking ahead of me.

I want to escape just as badly but another grinning man walks right in front of Finnegan, making him pull up short.

"What?" the Irishman mutters.

"I just wanted to say hi," the guy says, skirting around the ginger and holding his hand out to me. "Brooks Morgan."

"Kendall Stewart," I say, clasping his hand, then releasing it quickly.

This man is dangerous. He's handsome, clearly charismatic, and has a smile that has the ability to stop a woman in her tracks. I'm not immune, I discover, as he inches closer.

"I heard all about you," he says, his voice low enough to make me look at Finnegan to question what he's been telling these guys about me.

Finnegan shakes his head as if answering my unasked question.

"Quite a stunt yesterday."

"I was out of sorts yesterday," I say as an excuse.

"He making you a little crazy?" Brooks hikes his thumb over his shoulder to indicate his friend.

"Yes," I answer honestly, my eyes still on Finnegan.

That's the absolute truth, but what I don't say is that the man has been making me crazy a lot longer than just getting us evicted from the condo. My mind has been on him since the first day we met in the gym.

"He just moved me into his place, so I imagine I'll be totally insane by the end of the week."

Brooks's smile widens before he turns around to face his friend. "Moved her in, huh? You move fast there, Irishman."

"It's complicated," he tells Brooks before looking past him in my direction. "Don't you need to grab the kids from school?"

"Kids?" Brooks asks. "You're dating a woman with kids?"

"We're not—"

"Yes, I need to get the kids," I say before walking right past them. I don't want to hear the explanation Finnegan gives his friend or listen to him tell him that I'm not worthy of dating. I should hate a man who wouldn't consider dating a single mom with three kids, but I'm mature enough to understand that not all people are willing to take on that type of responsibility. I can't fault Finnegan for not being willing. Hell, I shouldn't even think along those lines. I'm not in his apartment because I want to date him. If I had any other choice, I'd be as far away from that man as possible.

"Have a good day, dear," Pam says when I inch toward the elevator. "Come back soon."

I give her a tight nod and smile, stiffening when Finnegan walks up, placing his hand at the small of my back before guiding me onto the elevator.

"Your hand," I say, once the elevator doors close.

He pulls it away without saying a word, and I studiously watch the lights at the top of the car as we descend into the parking garage.

Our drive back is silent, and I don't bother saying goodbye before splitting off to go to my car. I'm going to be late as it is, and I'm not looking forward to the judgmental looks from the teachers in the car pickup line at the elementary school.

"Kendall," Finnegan snaps just as I'm lowering myself into my car.

I look up at him. "I may not be home when you get back. Here."

I look at his hand to the key there, a million questions I have no right asking on my tongue.

"Thanks," I tell him as I grab the key.

He steps out of the way so I can close the car door, and I drive away wondering where else he could possibly be but home. I settle on it's none of my business just as I'm pulling up to the school, but that question still niggles in the back of my mind as I smile at the kids when they climb into the car.

"Who's ready for an adventure?" I ask when we're halfway home. I figure I need to get as many of their questions out of the way before we enter Finnegan's apartment.

"I am!" Knox hollers, raising his hand as if he's still in class.

"I just want a snack," Kayleigh mutters.

Kason just glares at me as I watch him in the rearview mirror.

"Well, Uncle Ezra took a new job in Las Vegas," I begin.

"Is that by the river?" Kayleigh asks, making me wonder just when the school will start teaching any form of geography to my kids.

"It's a different state," I say.

"We're moving to Las Vegas?" Kason asks, and I want to frown at the excitement in his voice. This kid really hates the school he's in.

"Uncle Ezra moved to Las Vegas," I explain. "We're moving across the hall to live with Mr. Jenkins."

"The big red-headed guy?" Knox asks, with just as much excitement in his voice as Kason had about Vegas.

"That's him," I say, my tone light and airy. My kids don't need to be made aware of my own apprehensions.

"Am I going to have to pack my things before my snack?" Kayleigh asks, her mind always on eating. She's me made over.

"No, sweetheart. Why don't we stop somewhere and grab something to eat before going back?"

She grins, and I know the offer of chicken nuggets, or any form of a kid's meal is all it takes to win her over. She's adaptable.

"That guy is a creep," Kason mutters, assuming his favorite position with his arms crossed over his chest with a deep scowl on his face.

"He is not," Kayleigh argues. "He's nice."

"You've met him?"

"No," Kason answers.

"How do you know he has red hair?" I ask Knox, my anger spiking because Finnegan swore he didn't know there were kids living across the hall.

"I saw him last night when you were at the door. Does he order food a lot?"

Kayleigh perks up with Knox's question.

"I don't know, but he's not going to be ordering food for us. Nothing is changing except where we sleep."

Kason scoffs, but by the time we sit down at his favorite fast-food place, he has a small smile on his lips. I knew bringing them to the place in town with the best kids' play area would help. I don't normally bribe my kids, but a mom has got to do what a mom has got to do.

With full bellies and a little less energy, we head back to Finnegan's place—our place—two hours after I left to pick the kids up from school.

It's still several hours until bedtime, and I stop the kids before they can run off the elevator and down the hall.

"I need you guys to behave and be quiet. Mr. Jenkins is doing us a favor, and we need to make sure we respect his things."

As much as I wanted to annoy him last night, I need to make sure they don't do anything to land us out on our asses. I imagine even the quietest kids would rock this man's world. It didn't go unnoticed just how sterile and perfect his condo was when I first walked in earlier. I hope he got a good, long, hard look because with three kids running around, it won't stay like that for long.

"Hey," I say, grabbing Kason around the waist after he rolls his eyes. "I'll give you back *YouTube* privileges early if you promise to behave like I know you can."

"How early," he barters. "Like right now?"

I narrow my eyes at him. "Yes, but if you so much as antagonize either of your siblings, you'll lose them again."

"Deal," Kason says, holding out his hand because nothing is more concrete than a handshake. I have no idea where he got that idea, but it probably came from a *YouTube* video.

I feel like I should knock when we approach the door, but I pull out my key instead. I don't want the kids to see my uneasiness. I don't want them to feel like this isn't their home, even if it's temporary.

"Wow," Kayleigh says as I return my keys to my purse. "That's a lot of muscles."

My eyes snap up, and I notice two things in the same moment. One, my daughter is a hundred percent right. That is a lot of muscles. And two, how did I miss those specific ones on either side of his waist last night? They're like thick arrows pointing to his—

"Okay, kids, follow me and I'll show you your rooms." I usher them around Finnegan who looks like he's ready to bolt.

"Boys are in here," I say, opening the door to the right. "I'll have all of your things unpacked tomorrow by the time you get out of school. Stay in here."

I close the boys in the room before urging Kayleigh to stop looking down the hall at the shirtless man standing in the middle of the living room.

"This is our room," I tell her, opening the other door. "Stay in here. I'll be right back."

"Where's Evie?" Kayleigh asks.

I turn to her, a small smile on my face.

"Mr. Jenkins' condo lease doesn't allow for animals."

A frown covers my pretty girl's face.

"But," I hedge. "He's trying to work it out so we can get her back. She's staying with a good friend who also has a bird."

I pray I can eventually convince Finn to bring her back. Evie hates men, but she loves the kids.

"She has a bird friend now?"

I nod, loving that she's now smiling again.

"Mom?" Kason asks, sticking his head out of the first bedroom door. "Did you forget something?"

He cocks an eyebrow, but I know better than to renege on a promise to him for even a second.

I hold up a finger before disappearing into the room I'm sharing with Kayleigh. Like the perfect child she is, she already has her homework sheet out in front of her as she digs through her backpack for a pencil. I reach into the top of my closet and pull out Kason's tablet before leaving the room once again.

My son is waiting in the hallway with his hand out.

"It's not been charged, so you'll have to stick close to an outlet this evening. One hour," I remind him.

That's all it takes for him to disappear back into his designated bedroom.

Now I can focus on the man in the living room.

"Have you lost your mind?" I snap as I get closer to him, feeling like I'm losing a little of mine, being this close to him without him wearing a damn shirt.

"I was just asking myself that very same question," he says.

"You can't run around here naked, Finnegan."

"Finn," he corrects. "My friends call me Finn."

I realize exactly where Kason got it from when I cross my arms over my chest and scowl at him. "I haven't decided whether we're friends."

"You're living in my home. I figured we should at least be friends."

"Friends don't talk to a friend's mouth instead of looking them in the eyes," I snap.

"I can't help that you're so cute when you get all snarly."

"Friends don't flirt either," I hiss. "You have to dress more appropriately in front of my kids."

I wave a hand up and down the length of him, indicating the problem.

Gray sweats are fucking dangerous because my eyes follow the wave of my arm. I look down. He looks down.

And yep, right there.

"See?" I snap before lowering my voice to a whisper. "That's the outline of your—"

"Cock," he finishes because I just can't seem to get the word out.

The appendage in question jerks right before my eyes.

"Staring at it doesn't help the situation," he says, his accent deep, and if I'm not mistaken... inviting. "Stop. Staring."

"What?" I jerk my gaze back up to his.

"Stop looking at it."

I can't help but drop my gaze again. The man is working with some seriously heavy-duty equipment.

Finnegan chuckles, a low, husky sound that makes the hairs on my arms stand on end, and not in a bad way either.

Right before my eyes and without a single touch of physical motivation, the damn thing continues to grow.

As if needing to accommodate himself more, he spreads his legs a little further apart, and all it does is tighten the fabric stretched across his groin.

It snaps me out of the dick trance I was in. I back away from him because the several feet between us doesn't seem like enough room to escape whatever orbit of his I ended up in.

"You need to wear more clothes," I hiss before turning back around and walking toward the bedroom I selected.

"I'll grab some socks," he says to my back. "My feet are cold."

Chapter 12

Finnegan

Nothing could prepare me for the terror I wake up to, and that's saying a lot because I've been in some pretty hairy situations in my life.

First, it's the screeching that hits my ears. Loud banging, the sound I imagine a bulldozer would make if it were plowing through the building, is what gets me out of bed. My heart is pounding, not knowing what I'm going to find going on in my condo. I'm moving so quickly I nearly fall on my face, trying to shove my legs into a pair of jeans, because despite giving Kendall a hard time—pun intended—last night, I'm not going to walk around the house in sweats, shirtless, anymore. I don't get to dictate what's appropriate or not for her kids. She's driving the bus on that.

I realize she's also driving the crazy train when I step out of my room, pulling my t-shirt over my head.

The youngest boy is screaming his head off as he chases his sister down the hallway, holding a plastic dinosaur over his head. I'd give him kudos for the lifelike sounding noises he's making, but the screech is so loud, a headache is already threatening at my temples. That and he's moving remarkably fast for a kid with such short legs.

Kendall is concerned about my state of dress, and I mostly understand her reasoning, but this kid is running around in superhero briefs and nothing else.

I would argue the unfairness of the situation, but she looks like she's about to lose her mind when I step into the kitchen. She's dressed in a baggy t-shirt and cut-off jean shorts. It takes more effort than I'd like to admit to pull my gaze from her exposed legs and back where it belongs.

"That kid is naked," I say, indicating the one that has his sister pinned in a corner of the living room.

"That's Knox," she mutters.

"Knox is naked."

"Again?" she hisses, dropping the toast in her hand to the counter instead of on the plate a mere six inches away.

Kendall rushes past me into the living room.

"Go get dressed for school." Her voice is low, carrying the threat of punishment moms are so damn good at. She doesn't even have to say *or else* for the kid to drop the dinosaur—right on the carpet at his feet—instead of carrying it back to his room with him.

"He wasn't naked," she mutters as she re-enters the kitchen. "I was afraid he was bare to his skin."

"He does that, too?" I ask, because I didn't sign up for naked kids.

"He likes the feel of it," she says, shaking her head.

"And I get in trouble for sweats," I mutter.

She makes a choking noise. "We aren't talking about your sweats."

The sound of her voice makes me think she thought about those sweats quite a lot after scurrying away last night.

"They're great sweats," I say, because I just don't know how to quit. "Get a little tight sometimes, but I'm sure you noticed that last night."

I'm not so crude as to go as far as hefting my junk, but only because that's something an immature boy would do. I don't want Kendall to think of me as a boy. I want her to treat me like a man, one that desperately wanted to sneak into her room last night, but instead of putting all three kids in one room so she could have some privacy, she set the girl up in her room. Maybe she did it because she was getting the vibe off me that having her here wasn't such a bad idea.

I cringe as I sit down at the bar and watch her slathering peanut butter on toast. Those thoughts make me feel like a creep. I want the woman. There's no arguing that, but I don't expect sexual favors in return for giving her a place to land, especially after being the reason she got kicked out.

And sneaking into her room and nuzzling her neck seems a little inappropriate.

"You're safe here," I tell her.

She lifts her eyes to mine. "I wasn't questioning it until you just said that."

She rolls her eyes before going back to the toast.

"Is that for you?"

She huffs. "I wish. Knox's latest thing is refusing to eat meat. So, it's plant-based protein for him until he comes around."

"Makes my throat threaten to close up just looking at it."

She snaps her head back up at me. "I didn't bring it into the condo. Are you allergic to peanuts?"

True concern screws up her pretty face, and for a split second, I consider saying I am just to see how accommodating she can be, but I didn't get enough sleep to deal with the fallout when she finds out the truth.

"I'm not allergic, but I appreciate the consideration. It's just a lot. Like, aren't you afraid it's going to get stuck? Like won't get lodged in his throat?"

She looks from the toast and back to me twice before frowning. "I wasn't."

"I'm sure he'll be fine."

Kendall proceeds to scrape half the peanut butter off the bread, scraping it back inside the jar. I take a deep breath to keep from saying something about the crumbs she just shoved back in there. I look away, focusing on the child-sized backpacks lined up on the dining room table instead. Maybe if I don't think about it, I'll forget.

"Mom, I need—" the oldest boy, holding great resemblance to his sister, begins as he walks into the room, but he stops when he sees me sitting there. His eyes narrow in my direction before he looks at his mom.

"Were you two talking?"

"No," Kendall says as I shake my head. "What do you need, Kason?"

Kason and Knox. I can remember that. I'm a pro at names most of the time.

"I can't find my toothbrush."

"Give me a minute," she says, and he walks back out of the room.

"He doesn't like me," I say.

"How do you figure?"

"I've never seen someone snap their mouth closed so quickly at the sight of me."

"He's been told not to walk into a room speaking because he could interrupt another conversation. He's trying to be on his best behavior."

"Sound advice," I say, but I get the feeling that where Kason is concerned, it's more than just having manners.

"I have to help Kayleigh," she says as she drops the toast onto the plate she missed earlier.

The second I hear her bedroom door close, Kason comes back into the room, followed by his little brother. I watch as Knox sits at the dining room table. Kason grabs the plate of peanut butter toast and places it in front of his brother.

Kason then reaches for the hem of Knox's shirt, and I expect the smaller one to throw a fit. I know I would if someone tried to strip me, but Knox lifts his arms, whispering a cute little *thank you* when Kason pulls the shirt free of his head. Kason drapes the shirt over the back of another chair before rounding the counter and heading back into the kitchen.

He opens the fridge and pulls out a half gallon of milk, placing it on the island before looking toward me.

"Bowls?"

I point to the cabinet, watching in awe as he climbs onto the cabinet with skill and grace.

"What are you doing?" Kendall snaps, and I look over at Kason, expecting him to get into trouble. "You're just letting him climb the cabinets?"

Kason grins as if he's a little proud that I'm the one in trouble instead of him.

Kendall walks across the room, grabbing her son by the waist and lowering him back to the floor.

"What if he fell?" she grits out.

I shrug. "He'd get hurt, and then he'd learn his lesson. After that, he'd probably never do it again."

Kayleigh grins at me, nodding her head as if my reasoning makes perfect sense.

"Seriously?" Kendall snaps.

I don't answer her because I get the vibe it's a rhetorical question.

The kitchen is utter chaos of feeding the little people and cleaning up. Well, Kendall's version of cleaning up I suppose. Then she leaves to take them to school.

My once pristine condo looks like a tornado ran through it.

There's some green stuffed toy on the couch along with a bed pillow. The plastic dinosaur is still right where it was dropped on the floor. A glob of peanut butter is on the floor beside where Knox was sitting, and now, removing the shirt makes a lot more sense. Breakfast dishes are in the sink, and when I hazard a look, I see globs of blue, sparkly toothpaste in the hall bathroom sink.

I'm thinking the damn bird is less of an animal than those three kids. I had no clue what I was getting myself into. Since I'd never tell them to leave, I set about cleaning everything up. I close my eyes and walk out when I return the toys to the boys' room and notice streaks of what appears to be blue crayon on the closet door.

I'm washing dishes and taking deep breaths when Kendall returns.

"You're cleaning? You don't have to do that." She tries to hip bump me out from in front of the sink, but I don't budge. I like the nearness of her body. "Seriously, move over. I was going to do that."

"You left it," I remind her.

"Have you ever tried to pick up after kids while they're still around? It's impossible. You have to wait for the tornado to move through and pick up after it's done. Anything else is wasted energy."

"I have absolutely no experience with children, Kendall."

I conceded, handing over the sponge in my hand before taking a few steps away.

"Want to hit the gym?" she asks after scrubbing the remaining dishes as good as I would have. Maybe she isn't a complete slob. The room she was in across the hall was as clean as a crammed room could be.

"Together?" I ask.

"Sure."

I smile, backing away before suggesting the gray leggings. Maybe flirting will be allowed downstairs since she said I can't do it up here. Maybe in the gym, we can go back to the single guy and sexy-as-hell woman instead of the single mom and the jerk who got her kicked out of her brother's condo.

I leave the room with a smile and a head full of hope.

Chapter 13

Kendall

He has to be a mind reader. There's no other reason for him to be wearing those same sweats he was wearing last night to our visit to the gym this morning.

He's a distraction of the worst kind... or best, depending on my mood.

Right now, when my kids are at school and I don't have any immediate issues to resolve, he's the best kind of distraction.

The man isn't even facing me, and I can't keep my eyes off him as I walk on the treadmill. Doing any more would leave me flat on my face.

Seeing the front half of him when I got back with the kids and the ensuing conversation carried over into my mind last night before bed, but the back side of him, the one I have now with his muscular legs and high, tight ass is just as great a view.

I need to remember that I live with this man, and it's out of duress on his part. I shouldn't be focusing on him in any other way than to figure out how to keep him at arm's length until I can move out, not that I want him closer to me after I'm able to accomplish that task.

Maybe it's just me, but I can feel the sexual energy between the two of us all the way across the room from him. It's like waves of energy, begging me to give in. I have no doubt that the man would be down for hooking up, and that might have been possible before, but now it just makes things messy. My life is complicated enough without opening the door my libido is begging to be thrown open.

I'm a grown woman capable of shelving those needs.

Or at least I thought I was because Finnegan catches me watching him do bicep curls in the mirror, and my arousal spikes when he widens his stance much the same way he did yesterday. My eyes drop to the reflection of his lower half, and I have to force myself to pull my gaze away. It doesn't go far, just sliding up his torso and over the ripples of muscle displayed under his sweaty t-shirt until I'm meeting his knowing eyes once again.

He doesn't wink or make any other cheesy move at catching me staring at him. He simply watches me, waiting for me to make my move.

My phone rings then, and I quickly move to answer it, because doing what I'm doing will only lead to trouble, and I have enough to handle on my plate as it is.

"Hello?" I say when the call connects.

"Kendall Stewart?" the woman on the other line asks. "This is Edith McCammon. We were supposed to meet five minutes ago in the lobby?"

"Oh gosh!" I snap, hitting the stop button on the machine. "I'm so sorry! I'm on my way."

She ends the call without a word, and that makes my stomach tighten with worry as I dart out of the gym without cleaning my machine. It's in bad taste, but the woman I'm meeting is the only person I found with adequate qualifications to watch the kids while I work.

I choose to take the stairs because the elevators are slow this time of the morning. I'm out of breath with beads of perspiration on my face when I see her standing in the lobby. She's clutching her purse and looking around with a distasteful look on her face when I approach. I imagine Evie looking the same way if she were a human.

"Ms. McCammon," I say as I approach, wiping away sweat from my brow with the back of one forearm.

She holds her hand out, and I immediately offer mine to her, but before our palms meet, she pulls her hand back, wiping it on her prim and proper skirt as if I've already soiled it.

"Would you like to sit over there?" I ask, pointing to a seating area off to the left.

She told me she only has fifteen minutes for an interview today because she has other appointments. I didn't have the right to ask about her personal schedule before hiring her, so I have no idea what the woman does during the day, but it makes me wonder if she's even going to be a good fit. I've already wasted nine minutes of her time, and she seems annoyed, making me wonder about her experience with kids. I don't know any parents capable of making it on time with any regularity, but being late today was my fault, not hers.

"I require seeing your home first," she says, her face drawn up as if she's already made her mind up about me.

"Right this way," I say before turning and calling the elevator. She doesn't seem the type to be interested in any form of physical activity, so the stairs are out.

It hits me hard that Finnegan was the one who carried the keys to the gym this morning, leaving me without a way to get back into the condo, but my luck must be turning because just as we reach the door, he's exiting the elevator and walking toward us.

"Ms. McCammon, this is Finnegan."

"Good morning," he says as he unlocks the door.

"Your husband?" she asks, still standing in the hallway, looking him up and down.

The woman must have cataracts because she doesn't look impressed, and if there's one thing I know about Finnegan Jenkins is that the man is very impressive.

"Not my husband," I answer quickly. If she doesn't like him then this fact will only help me, right?

"Not married with three kids?" the elderly lady asks. She huffs as if this, too, annoys her. "I don't work with two-parent households."

I shake my head. "He's not—"

"I stated this in my online ad." She clutches her purse tighter as if Finnegan is going to divest her of it. "This is what's wrong with the world today. Parents don't want to raise their own children. Good day."

My mouth is hanging open as I watch her walk away.

"He's not even the father!" I yell after her.

"And that's another problem with your generation," she snips back, her stride not even faltering.

She jabs a crooked finger at the elevator button, shaking her head and muttering under her breath.

"Who the hell was that?" Finnegan asks after the elevator door opens, closes, and carries the only option I had for watching my kids away.

Tears of frustration burn the backs of my eyes as I walk past him into the condo.

"She was going to watch the kids while I worked," I mutter, plopping gracelessly on the sofa.

I want to scream and ask why everything I do has to be so damned hard, but it's not his fault that woman had standards so high that even the royal family would have difficulty meeting them.

Finnegan shrugs as if it's no big deal, as he takes a seat in the recliner I've come to realize is his favorite spot in the room.

"Use someone else. Your kids would hate that woman."

"She was my only option. There aren't many people willing to work nights. They have their own families to care for and finding someone to watch three kids is more difficult than you think."

"You work nights," he says as if I need to be reminded that I haven't been living off energy drinks and coffee for the last year since getting my job.

I roll my eyes at him, once again acting like Kason before I can stop myself.

"And you leave after they go to bed and get home before they wake up, right?"

"Yes, Finnegan."

"Finn," he corrects.

I scowl at him. Calling him by the shortened version of his name brings on a familiarity that will only end up causing problems down the road. Stubbornly, I just can't do it.

"Finn," he repeats.

"Were you trying to make a point or is your goal just to get on my nerves?"

Instead of responding negatively to my insistence on being a pain in the ass and rude, he gives me a wide smile, as if he likes my attitude problem.

I continue to glare because I'm stressed and thinking about him adjusting that attitude in ways I'm sure we would both enjoy will only leave me flat on my back or pinned to the wall by his enormous body.

I brush my hands over the goosebumps those thoughts bring on.

"My point, you feisty little thing, is that I'll be here while they're sleeping. There's no need for you to waste money on hiring anyone else."

I immediately shake my head at his offer. "You just sat there and watched Kason climb the cabinets this morning."

"Does he do that a lot in his sleep?" His brows draw together.

I scoff. "No, he doesn't, but—"

"But nothing," he interrupts. "You'll be able to save money faster if you don't have to pay someone to literally just be in the condo with them while you work."

So you can move out quicker goes unsaid, and although that makes me feel some kind of way, I can't really argue with the man.

"You'd do that?"

"It's not really a challenge, unless they have issues at night."

"They're sound sleepers, and barring any emergencies, you won't even have to see them."

"Then it's settled," he says as he stands. "I'll look after them."

I open my mouth to argue with him, but he pulls his t-shirt up and off before walking toward the hall.

"Going to get a shower then get to work."

My mouth is hanging open as I watch his back muscles flex all the way down the hall to his room.

I may have one problem solved, but he's creating new ones every single damn time I see him without a shirt.

Chapter 14

Finnegan

"I've left my cell phone number on the kitchen counter," she says, her words a little weird with the way she's holding her mouth to apply dark lines to her eyelid. "I want you to call me if there's any trouble."

"I will," I promise because I plan to. I don't know what constitutes one of those emergencies she mentioned last night, but as far as I'm concerned, that could be anything.

Her eyes meet mine in the mirror, and I get lost for a second in just how gorgeous she is. I've stood here for the last fifteen minutes while she applies her makeup, wondering why in the world she's even bothering with it. Her eyes are bright blue, her hair a lush, blond hanging in waves around her shoulders, but she was just as beautiful right out of the shower as well.

Her children have been asleep for nearly an hour, and despite the chaos filling the condo after they got home from school, I found myself smiling. Watching her get them through homework and dinner was akin to watching a cat herder, but she did it mostly with a smile on her face.

"Okay," she says, giving herself one final onceover in the mirror before turning around to face me. "Wish me luck."

"You need luck?" I take a step back, moving out of the doorway when she inches closer. If she so much as brushes against me, she won't be making her shift at the diner she works at.

"I need lots of tips."

I look down at her clothes, the jeans and t-shirt not doing much for her body, but I grin at that, hating the thought of her wearing something as tight as her gym clothes so truckers will hand over more of their hard-earned cash.

"What?" she asks, looking down. "My uniform is at work."

I want to frown, but I manage a flat-lipped look instead.

"I get off at three. Should be home by three-twenty at the latest."

She's a grown woman, but I absolutely hate the thought of her driving so late at night. People are leaving the bars at that time, meaning there are more drunk drivers on the road, but I don't really have the right to chastise her work choices. I can tell just by the way she worries and how she interacts with her kids that she's doing the best she can with the hand she's been dealt. The last thing she needs is another person judging her. She's got enough of that to last a lifetime with just one look from that old lady yesterday.

"Seriously," she says as she walks toward the front door. "Call me if there are any problems."

"I will. Be safe, Kendall."

She stops in her tracks, turning around to face me with a weird look on her face.

"Thank you," she says, giving me a soft smile before she disappears into the hallway.

For some reason I can't explain, I follow and press my eye to the peephole, watching her until she disappears out of sight.

I feel restless in my own home for half an hour after she leaves, wondering if I should text to make sure she made it to work safely. I resist. She doesn't need someone checking up on her. She's been taking care of herself for a long time.

A short conversation before she picked up her kids from school revealed that she had the twins at nineteen, making her twenty-six, a little younger than I normally go for, but my body doesn't seem to care about her age. She didn't let the conversation stray to her ex, the father of her three kids, and I didn't ask. Getting to know that much about her was dangerous, but I already hate the man for deserting them and not taking care of his family.

I'm getting ready to head to bed, early for a Friday night, but as I walk toward my room, a little giggle filters out of one of the rooms.

I freeze in the middle of the hallway; certain I'm losing my mind. Somehow the responsibility of being here alone with her kids is making me create sounds that aren't really there. But just as I start walking again, I hear that tiny little giggle once more.

Does this constitute an emergency? I reach for my phone, but what kind of man would I be if I bother her at work because the kids are awake? It's not like they're in there setting the curtains on fire. Or are they?

I push open the door to Kayleigh's room, certain that's where the sound came from, but the room is empty, the nightlight showcasing flat beds.

The giggle continues as I turn toward the other room, but thinking they could be up to no good, I don't bother to knock when I swing that door open.

Kayleigh lets out a little shriek, and Kason just rolls his eyes. They were both curled over Kason's tablet which is now flat on his bed. Knox is still asleep, and I have no idea how the kid isn't wide awake with the noise they've been making in here.

"You're supposed to be sleeping," I remind them.

Kayleigh looks guilty, but Kason sits up, pulling the tablet into his lap as if refusing to give it up.

"We're bored," Kason says.

"You wouldn't be if you were asleep," I say, repeating something I heard my mother tell me a million times. We didn't have these types of electronics when I was their age, but it wasn't unheard of to be caught with a comic book and flashlight under my blanket as a child.

"It's Friday," Kason says. "We aren't being loud, and we don't have to get up for school in the morning."

"Loud enough for me to hear you in the hallway." And now I'm arguing with a seven-year-old. "You're going to wake Knox up."

"He's a heavy sleeper," Kayleigh says, as if she's validating her right to be up when her mother wanted her asleep.

"Come on," I tell them, swinging my arm into the hallway.

Kayleigh looks sad as she stands, looking back at her twin to say goodnight, but then Kason pops off the bed as well.

"We can watch *YouTube* in the living room instead."

Since I have no idea what rights I have to force them to go to sleep, I just follow behind them, closing the door quietly so Knox doesn't wake up. I've noticed the older two are more capable of entertaining themselves, but Knox only has two speeds—asleep and wild tornado. I think I like the sleeping speed better.

Kayleigh and Kason lie on the living room floor with the tablet in front of them, settling in for more *YouTube* videos.

I sit back in my recliner, and just watch them.

I don't know how long it takes before my eyes close and I fall asleep, but it only feels like minutes before I hear, "And just what do you two think you're doing?"

Startled and a little confused, I open my eyes and stand from the recliner in the same breath.

Kendall is standing on the edge of the living room, her glaring eyes darting between me and the two kids on the floor.

"Finnegan said we could watch *YouTube* all night," Kason says, throwing me under the bus.

"Not exactly," I mutter, my eyes sweeping to the clock on the wall.

It's already three-thirty.

"Bed, now," she snaps, her hands on her hips. Kason reaches for the tablet. "Leave it."

They scurry away, but Kendall doesn't move.

"Seriously?" she snaps, her voice tired as well as annoyed. "You let them stay up all night."

I could argue that let is a very subjective word, considering what really happened, but she doesn't look like she'd be amused by that statement.

"It's Friday, and they don't have school. I figured they'd sleep later tomorrow, and you could get more rest." I added that last part of reasoning because she seems like she could use a few more hours of sleep.

"Kids that age don't sleep later, Finnegan," she hisses, still glued to the same spot she was standing in when I startled awake. "They get up at the same time, only they're cranky as hell because they didn't get enough sleep."

I feel like a complete asshole when she walks away. I know I mentioned I didn't know a damn thing about kids, and this just proved my point. So much for being helpful.

Chapter 15

Kendall

"You wanted to come to the park, Kason. Go play."

Even my words are exhausted, but I try to give my son a smile of encouragement.

"I said I wanted to come because Knox wanted to come. I don't even like the park."

"Since when? You love the park."

"I like the park by our old house. This park is dumb."

I inhale deeply, trying to tamp down my agitation. What I told Finnegan was going to happen happened. Knox was up with the sun, and the other two not long after. Mere hours after lying down, I was back up. Coming to the park felt like the right thing at the time because if the kids wear themselves out enough, I may be able to convince them to take a nap this afternoon, and Lord knows I could use a few more hours of sleep before my shift tonight.

"This is a nice park."

"They only have three swings," he mutters, pulling at the grass in front of him.

"You only have one tush, so as long as a swing is available, and I see all three are, you should be good."

He looks up at the swings, the seats swaying in the light breeze.

"They're orange. The ones at the other park are red."

"Kason," I groan. "Swings are swings. Go play."

"When will we move again?"

If only I had the answer to this question.

"Soon," I tell him, realizing a little too late my mistake.

Soon to a seven-year-old isn't the same soon to an adult.

"Good."

"You don't like where we're at?"

He looks at me as if I'm crazy for even asking the question.

"It's a nice place. You don't have to share the same room with two girls."

"I don't like him," he says.

"Him?" We were talking about the condo.

"The man we're living with."

I go on full alert, my mind racing to consider what in the world happened last night to make him dislike Finnegan so much.

My heart is pounding, threatening to beat right out of my chest when I ask, "Why? What happened?"

He shrugs as I try to remember the last time I had the stranger-danger talk with my kids.

"He tries too hard."

"Tries too hard to do what?"

He's silent for a long gut-wrenching moment before speaking again, and I watch, holding my breath as he twists a blade of grass until it breaks.

"He didn't even tell us to go back to sleep last night. We walked right into the living room and started watching *YouTube*."

"He didn't tell you to watch *YouTube*?" I ask, my eyes narrowing.

Kason looks away, his cheeks heating for getting caught in the lie he told last night.

"He didn't tell us not to," he argues.

"And because you got to do what you wanted, you don't like him?"

He shrugs. "He's not Uncle Ezra."

"No, he's not," I agree. "But it's his condo, and he's doing me a really big favor, so you need to be respectful. If I hear of you two being up when you're supposed to be asleep again, you already know the consequences."

"Okay," he mutters, but the sound of his broken agreement makes my heart ache.

I just want to give them the perfect life. I never wanted my kids to see me struggle, to feel the weight of that like Ezra and I did when we were younger. I feel like I'm making all the same mistakes, no matter how hard I try.

"Go play. I'm going to need a nap this afternoon, and I can't have you running all over the place while I sleep."

He stands and bolts away, deciding that the orange swings aren't that bad after all. I know that he's just hoping I'll forget about the stunt he pulled last night and won't take his tablet away from him. That kid pushes every single boundary put in front of him.

My phone rings twenty minutes later, but after seeing my brother's name flash on the screen, I send it to voicemail, an indication to him that I'm still mad for what he's done.

I haven't been miserable this week staying with Finnegan. If I can keep my head in the right place, understanding that the man is just really nice-looking eye candy, then I'm fine. The kids have everything they need, although they could use a little more space. We're safe and have a roof over our heads.

But Ezra deserting us still makes me feel betrayed, and I'm no closer to speaking to him than I was days ago when I found the movers in his condo, dragging furniture out.

I imagine he's calling because the condo owner refused to give him his deposit back, but I didn't have enough time to fix the dented sheetrock in the living room or repaint the closet doors that Knox drew masterpieces on.

The kids play for another hour before starting to whine about being starving, and I stand from the soft grassy, shaded area I've been sitting in this morning.

"We'll get some groceries."

"McDonald's!" Knox squeals.

"Groceries," I argue. "We're saving money for a house, remember?"

"Chicken nuggets are gooder than a house," Knox mumbles as we walk to the car.

"Better," I correct. "Chicken nuggets are better than a house."

He smiles wide, and I realize my mistake. "I was correcting your grammar, not agreeing."

His face falls.

"We can get frozen chicken nuggets at the grocery store."

He perks up a little at this, but the wide smile isn't there any longer.

"That man can afford McDonald's," Kason says once we're in the car and driving toward the store.

"Then he can have McDonald's."

"He can buy us McDonald's."

"No," I tell him. "That's not his responsibility. I'll buy your food."

Kason sours once more, and I can tell he likes Finnegan even less with my declaration.

The child is part of the instant gratification generation, and I can't really fault him for that. Modern technology has changed all of us, but him picking and choosing how he's going to allow Finnegan to be in our lives is ridiculous. I refuse to get him fast food just to make him like the guy a little more.

"I'm going to need your help today," I tell them as we climb out of the car. "I want to get in and get out."

"I'll help!" Knox declares, jumping up and down with excitement. The child loves to help wherever he can, but I busy myself with grabbing a cart rather than reminding him that picking up after himself is the biggest help of all.

"I'm going to need you to keep an accurate count on the number of items in the cart," I say as I lift him and settle him in the seat in the front. "You two are going to run and get things. I'm in desperate need of a nap."

Both Kason and Kayleigh scrunch their noses at the word nap, but they should have thought of that before staying up all night and getting up with the sun.

"Let's count," Knox says excitedly, bouncing up and down in the seat. Getting him down for a nap is going to be the most difficult.

"Kason and Kayleigh, we need two boxes of mac and cheese."

They nod before darting away to get the items.

"Two!" Knox says, holding up two little fingers.

"Count them once they're in the cart," I remind him.

I'm heading for the dairy section, knowing we need milk, when the twins return. I nod when each place two blue boxes in the cart. I learned long ago that I had to half my request because they were each going to bring the count I gave them.

"Two!"

"Four," I tell Knox, pointing to the boxes in the cart.

His brows draw tight before nodding in understanding.

"Next," Kason says, sounding like he's just as ready to leave as I am.

"Two cans of raviolis."

They dart away again. I grab the milk and sliced cheese, trying to remember what else we need. We were in desperate need of a grocery trip before we left Ezra's apartment, and I just haven't thought about it since. I know we're just about out of everything, but at the same time, I can't take up all the space in Finnegan's cabinets either.

I'm heading toward the frozen food section, knowing I can't forget nuggets when I realize the twins haven't come back with the raviolis yet. I turn back around and head for the canned goods section, praying my kids aren't having a knock-down drag-out fight in the middle of the grocery store.

Neither child is in that aisle, and I move to the next aisle, seeing Kason dart across the other end.

I whistle like I always do to get his attention, but he doesn't hear me. I try to catch him on the next aisle, but the child is running. I'm not going to yell because the store is too crowded for that, so I move a little quicker.

"Momma!" Kason yells, coming up right behind me.

"Where's your sister?" I ask after getting over being startled.

He shrugs.

"Kason," I hiss. "You're supposed to stay together."

"She's the one who stopped to talk to that man."

"What?" I screech. "Where?"

He points, and I rush in that direction immediately.

My own mother got extremely paranoid in the beginning. It was one of the signs that something was wrong. I never wanted to be a helicopter parent, but my heart is racing by the time I make it to the end of the aisle to spot Kayleigh chatting with a guy in a leather jacket.

It's been years since I've seen that jacket, and just the sight of it terrifies me.

"Kayleigh," I snap, no longer concerned for those around me.

She angles her head to the side, looking around the man.

"Hi, Momma," she says, completely oblivious to what it means to speak with this man.

"Kendall," the guy says as he turns around. "Looking good as usual."

I snap my fingers and point to my side, an indication to my daughter to get by my side immediately. Thankfully, she listens without argument.

"Brant," I mutter, giving the man nothing else.

"Saw you walk inside. These must be Ty's kids." He attempts a smile, but it comes out as a sneer because of the jagged scar twisting up his top lip.

"These are my kids," I snap. "And you have no business speaking to them."

"That one there looks exactly like his daddy," Brant says, pointing to Kason.

"Who is he, Momma?" Kayleigh asks, a tremble to her voice because the child is great at reading the emotions of others. Clearly, she can tell I'm not happy about this little run-in.

"I'm your daddy's friend, little girl," Brant says. "Do you know where he is?"

There's only one reason this man would be looking for Ty after so long. My ex wasn't exactly the greatest friend, and he'd screw anyone over if it meant coming out ahead himself.

"He's a piece of shit who abandoned his responsibilities a long time ago," Kayleigh says, and my eyes widen when an elderly lady gasps as she walks by.

"Kayleigh," I hiss.

"What?" she says, her face a mask of confusion. "That's what you told Uncle Ezra."

Brant laughs as if hearing a seven-year-old child speak that way is hilarious.

I scowl at him.

"I don't know where Ty is."

I grab Knox out of the cart, wincing when his shoe gets stuck and falls to the ground, but Kason picks it up.

"Let's go, kids."

"Good seeing you, sweetheart. We'll chat again soon."

"What about the groceries?" Knox asks, looking over my shoulder at the deserted cart.

"We'll shop some other time," I say, trying for a smile, but I can't even manage it.

"Where are we going?" Kason asks as we rush across the parking lot.

"McDonald's," I say, hoping it will ward off any questions they may have.

It doesn't, and I spend the ten-minute drive to the fast-food place avoiding their questions when *one of your father's old friends* isn't enough.

Kason knows the guy isn't a good one after witnessing how I responded to him, and since he's the oldest, he's always felt this responsibility to take care of the rest of us.

McDonald's is packed, just like the grocery store was, but at least they can run around and play some more while I keep my eyes on the parking lot. If Brant is still wearing the same jacket, maybe he's also still driving that same green car, and I calm a little when I don't see it.

My hands have stopped shaking by the time the kids settle in to eat, and we're able to leave not long after. The questions seem to have dried up as well.

I'm calmer, but I keep hearing Brant's warning over and over in my head.

We'll chat again soon.

It wasn't a promise of catching up with an old friend.

It was a warning.

Brant didn't even have to say anything. I know Ty screwed Brant over before he took off years ago, but that's not the worst of it. Brant is only one bad guy in a group of many, and where Brant is, Adrian isn't far behind. Adrian is the worst of them all. It just proves how unlucky I am. In a city of over three hundred thousand people, I happen to run into Brant Jesper, vice president of the Keres motorcycle club.

Chapter 16

Finnegan

In order to avoid the grumpiness Kendall mentioned last night, or early this morning, depending on how you wanted to look at it, I showered when she went to bed and headed to work. I wouldn't get any sleep in my condo anyway, not while feeling like a total dick for letting her kids stay up all damn night.

The office was empty when I arrived, but it didn't matter that it was Saturday. It didn't take Brooks and Kit long to join me on the couch and start mainlining coffee instead of going home and getting some sleep.

We sit, silent and still for a long while, just enjoying each other's company while waiting for the caffeine to kick in.

"You're still on for this coming weekend, right?"

"Huh?" I ask because Kit asked the question while still staring at a spot on the floor rather than looking at whoever he's directing the question to.

"My sister's wedding," Kit says. "You still coming?"

He must be talking to Brooks because this is the first I've heard of a wedding.

"I don't know, man."

Kit rolls his head on the sofa, and I feel just as drained.

"You promised, asshole."

"That was months ago. Maybe I'm just not in the wedding kind of mood."

"There's cake," Kit argues.

Brooks smiles, and I can tell he's in a mood because it's a devious smile. "Beth is so hot."

Kit shrugs.

"Know who's even hotter than your sister?"

Kit narrows his eyes, his brain finally catching up.

"Don't," Kit warns.

"Jules," Brooks says, not heeding the warning.

I groan my annoyance with where this is going. I don't have the energy to get up but staying in the same room when the shit hits the fan isn't smart either.

"She still got that long, dark hair?"

"Brooks," I grumble. "I'm too tired for this shit."

Brooks holds his hand out in front of him, forming a fist as if he's tugging on a woman's hair as he rolls his hips. The energy he's giving barely registers, but I know after another cup of coffee, he'll be hip thrusting and making all sorts of lewd noises.

"What?" Brooks asks, his butt settling back on the sofa. "She's smoking hot."

"And you know Kit has been in love with her since he was a kid."

"A teen," Kit corrects. "And I'm not in love with her."

"You're not?" Brooks asks, seeing an opening. "Then you wouldn't mind if I—"

"Do you want to die?" Kit snarls. "Stay the fuck away from her. In fact, don't even worry about the wedding."

"Oh, I'm going to the wedding."

"Brooks," I groan. "Leave him alone."

"Leave who alone?" Wren asks, walking into the break area. "What are we talking about?"

"Jules Warren," Brooks answers.

"Yeah? She still got that really long hair?"

Kit snarls at Wren as if the man is an actual threat when he has Whitney now.

Brooks cackles, happy to have someone else in the room to give Kit a hard time.

"You still haven't sealed the deal on that?" Wren asks as he makes his way to the coffee pot.

"Why are you even here?" Kit asks, annoyance lacing his tone.

"I work here."

"It's Saturday," Kit reminds him.

Wren shrugs.

"Whitney isn't home, is she?" I ask, knowing if his woman was at home, that's where he'd be right now.

"She went to visit Sarah this weekend," Wren says, and even tired, I can hear the disappointment in his tone.

"The Domme?" Brooks asks. "Are they hitting any special clubs this weekend?"

Wren looks less than impressed with the man's questions, so he doesn't bother answering.

Sarah Revone is Whitney's best friend who lives in California. I know Sarah was instrumental in helping Wren win Whitney over after she took off. They had a big fight over a box of sex toys Wren intercepted and never returned. It seems the massive amount of stalking he did to put himself in Whitney's way wasn't the best plan of action. But he won the girl over in the end.

"Quit antagonizing everyone," I mutter.

"But it's so much fun," Brooks says in a whiny tone. "Speaking of fun, how's it going with the single mom?"

I shake my head. "I'm not getting into it with you."

"You're no fun," Brooks chides.

"I'm not sticking around for this," Wren says, carrying his cup of coffee toward his office.

"Is it true?" Brooks asks a few minutes later.

"Is what true?"

"That single moms are great at sex and have the best snacks in the fridge?"

"It's *his* fridge, you idiot," Kit reminds him.

"That's right! She's living with you. Hey, where are you going?"

I flip a middle finger over my shoulder as I walk toward Wren's office.

"Asshole!" Puff screams the second I push the door open.

Evie squawks and flies to the other side of the room.

"Were they just—"

"Cuddling?" Wren asks. "Yes. They act like they hate each other but I find them snuggled together every damn morning."

"Dick," Puff Daddy snaps as he flies to the same perch Evie is standing on. "Don't worry, baby. He won't tell anyone."

"Unhand me you fool!" Evie screams.

I chuckle and take a seat in the other office chair. "I need you to tell me about Kendall."

"I don't know anything about Kendall," Wren says with his back to me.

"You know everything about everyone."

"Not true," he argues, but he's smiling about my compliment when he spins around to face me.

"I'm watching the woman's kids at night while she's serving greasy food. I need to know more about her."

"They serve food at The Kitten's Cream now?"

My eyes narrow, and he snaps his lips closed.

Doesn't know anything my ass.

"What did you just say?"

He shakes his head, lips clamped between his teeth.

"She works at a truck stop diner on the highway."

He swallows, but still doesn't say a word.

"Are you telling me she works at The Kitten's Cream?"

He shakes his head. "I'm not telling you anything."

"You just said—"

"Are you asking about Kendall Stewart? I thought you meant Kendall... umm... Stew*ard*. My mistake."

"Wren," I growl. "Tell me."

My heart pounds in my chest, a mix of jealousy and desire swirling together inside of me.

The Kitten's Cream is a super nice gentleman's club in the ritziest part of town. I've never been there, but I've driven past the windowless building more times than I can count. It's not one of the places that even has a sign outside. You have to be in the know to realize it's even there. Brooks has bragged more than once about the quality of girls that work there.

If I let myself think hard enough, I can picture Kendall being one of those girls.

But I can't think of her dancing there because I'd lose my fucking mind.

If she thought coming into the office with a fake bomb was bad, she doesn't want to know what I'd do at her work if I walked in and saw her on stage shaking that fine ass for other men.

That thought stops me cold.

Jealousy is new for me in that I haven't felt jealous over a female since I saw Dillon Waite kissing Emmie Grison in fourth grade behind the dunking booth at the fall carnival.

The emotions running ragged through me aren't thoughts of spraying water on his pants to make it look like he pissed himself so Emmie would pick me. My thoughts aren't childish and juvenile at all. They're leaning toward violence, chaos, and mayhem. Death and destruction.

And that's not where my head should be, considering I haven't even kissed the damn woman.

"Can I say that racing into her work and threatening everyone in there would reflect badly on Blackbridge?"

I narrow my eyes at him. "How long have you known?"

"Do you really think I'm going to let a woman waltz in here with a bomb—"

"A fake bomb," I interrupt.

"Any type of threatening device—and not research her?"

"And finding out where she works is part of that?"

"That's standard. You should know that. I needed to see who her known associates were to determine whether they were a threat to us."

"She's a single mother with three kids."

"Who works at The Kitten's Cream."

My jaw clenches. "How long?"

"She's been there just at a year. Before that, she worked at a law office. If she's reporting her tips accurately, she made twice as much in the last six months as she did the entire year at the law firm."

My uniform is at work. I need lots of tips.

She'd said those things to me before leaving Friday night.

Wren turns around, firing up his computer as I try to think of a lie she told me.

I work in the service industry.

That's what she told me about her job. I prodded, but she never gave me more. I asked about her being a waitress and she dodged the question. So she didn't want to lie to me, but she also wasn't exactly forthcoming about her job either.

I work at a truck stop diner out on the highway.

There's the lie. I remember now. I pushed her until she lied. So does that make it my fault, or still hers for not telling the truth?

We didn't know each other well then, but it turns out, we really don't know each other now. The longer I sit here, the more I realize I don't know her at all, other than her being a mother to three kids and sister to a total asshole who deserted her when she needed him the most.

"Is there more?" I hate to even ask, but I'd prefer to get the rest of being blindsided out of the way in one fell swoop if possible.

"Besides her asshole ex screwing over the Keres MC before taking off? No."

"Fuck. Seriously?" The Keres MC was no damn joke. If it's illegal, they're involved in it, and those bastards are a brutal sort. I know there have been several multi-agency task forces created over the years to bring them down, and none have been successful. Adrian Larrick, president of the Keres MC isn't someone to fuck with. "Are you saying she's in trouble?"

"Ty Penman, her ex, hasn't been seen for years. For all the MC knows, the man is dead. She's fine."

His assurance doesn't ease my worry completely, but I know Wren. He dug deep if only to protect Blackbridge when he fleshed out her connection to the club.

"I need a favor."

"I can't get more intel on Keres. Believe me, I wish I could, but the FBI contacted me months ago, and I couldn't help them either. Those guys are like fucking ghosts. Everyone knows they exist and are up to no damn good, but they're impossible to catch."

"No," I say, my mind already back to The Kitten's Cream. "I need you to watch her kids tonight."

"Abso-fucking-lutely not," Wren hisses as if I asked him to eat a shit pie. "I don't do kids."

"You also didn't do cats. Now Simon lives in your condo."

"That pussy comes with more pussy, and that more pussy is the greatest in the world. Feel me?"

"No," I snap. "I don't feel you. I need to go to The Kitten's Cream tonight, and I can't do that and watch the kids."

"She'll see you if you go."

"That's the whole damn point," I say as I stand. "I'll bring them over about ten."

I don't give him time to turn me down before walking out of his office.

My cock thumps in my jeans at just the mere thought of seeing Kendall on stage.

Now all I have to do is build enough control between now and then not to rip her off the stage and claim her.

Chapter 17

Kendall

A nap flew out the window after running into Brant at the grocery store. I couldn't sleep now if I had a silent room and no responsibilities.

I spent the rest of the afternoon with the kids, playing card games, and trying to keep them occupied so they didn't ask more questions about the stranger in the store.

I started getting nervous about Finnegan watching the kids because he didn't show back up until I was feeding them dinner. He stayed in his room until after I put them to bed, but he was right there when I opened the bathroom door to let the steam out so the mirror would clear enough for me to do my makeup.

"How were the tips last night?" he asks, leaning his broad shoulder against the doorjamb.

"Decent," I tell him. "I usually make more on Saturday nights."

"Hmm," he says, his eyes on my reflection.

It's a weird response, but I don't have the time or patience to read much more into it.

"Please don't let them stay up all night again. I'm dead on my feet right now."

"I won't let them," he quickly agrees.

I debate telling him about Brant and the shit about Ty, but he doesn't need to know. Hell, voicing the trouble I could be in may give him reason to put us out on our asses. I looked up Blackbridge Security before showing up with baking soda from the fridge strapped to my stomach. They don't seem the type to be okay with the criminal underbelly of St. Louis, and I know I'm guilty by association even though I only ever saw Brant or Adrian when they were looking for Ty. My ex wasn't even a member of the club, but more of what they call a hangaround—a guy who wanted to be a member but really didn't have whatever qualifications were required to join. I have no idea what the standards are for the Keres MC, but if they needed idiots with gambling and drug problems, then Ty should've been a shoo-in.

"You seem lost in thought," he says, his accent thick this evening.

"Just tired," I say, the lying coming a little too easy.

It should. I lie all the time. Not big lies, but if someone at work asks how I'm doing, good is my go-to answer. When the cashier asks if I found everything okay, I tell her I did because the people that work there don't want to hear how tired I am. They have their own damn worries. The lady ringing up my groceries doesn't care that I spent ten minutes looking for my regular deodorant only having to settle on something else because they can't seem to keep the shelves stocked.

People chat as a form of courtesy. They don't really care.

Finnegan noticing me being lost in thought is just a courtesy. He doesn't give a shit that I ran into a dangerous man today or that Kayleigh spent several minutes chatting with him before I could get to her.

I don't think the Keres MC abducts children, but I wouldn't put it past one of them to snatch my kids, thinking they could make Ty crawl out from whatever rock he's hiding under to get them back.

I meet Finnegan's eyes in the mirror. He immediately looks away.

"Still okay with watching the kids tonight?"

I wait for his answer, wondering just what in the hell I'll do if he says no. I already agreed to *expand my duties* as Sasha called it, and that is stressing me out enough. If I call in sick after she agreed to let me pick up a few more shifts during the week, she may fire me.

"The kids will be fine," he says.

"I know you want us out of here as quickly as possible, so I asked for a couple shifts during the week. Is that okay?"

His face is blank when I turn to face him directly instead of us looking at each other in the mirror.

"More shifts?"

I nod, swallowing as I wait for him to agree. "Not this coming week because the schedule is already made, but the week after that. If you can't, I'll start working on finding someone else."

"I'm here, Kendall. I can do it."

He turns and walks away, leaving me to wonder if looking for someone else isn't best. I know they were a pain last night, and he felt like he couldn't boss them around, but if I have to find and pay for another babysitter, that's really going to throw a wrench in my plans. At the same time, I don't want someone keeping an eye on my kids that's going to spend the entire night being annoyed by it. If the kids do need something, they'll pick up on that crappy attitude, and my kids have had enough of that already in their short lives.

I finish my makeup before heading to the living room to grab my keys and purse.

"Be home around three-thirty," I call out.

"Be safe," he says without turning from the kitchen sink.

He said the same thing to me before I left last night, and I don't know why, but it hit me in the chest. It's not often that I get concern from someone else. Usually, it's me doling that out to my kids. It was nice. So nice it made me want to turn around and thank him, but I was near tears. A sad *thank you* was all I could manage.

The drive to work is spent behind a long row of cars that seem to be going nowhere fast, and because I never like to get there early, it puts me clocking in ten minutes late.

"Is this going to become a habit?" Sasha asks as I tie my apron around my waist.

"No," I tell her. "Traffic was horrible."

"Weekend traffic is always horrible," she says, and it's true. St. Louis tends to be bumper-to-bumper at all times, except when the club closes. Then it's mostly drunks, cops, and people up to no good.

"Sorry," I tell her.

Sasha is actually a great boss. She looks out for everyone, but she also doesn't hesitate to call someone out on their shit. She runs a very tight ship, and I've seen her fire girls for chronic tardiness.

"How many extra shifts are you looking for?" she asks, continuing our conversation from last night that was interrupted due to a fight over prime seating around the main stage.

"Two if possible."

"The girls that work weekday shifts are hybrid," she says, as if I need the reminder.

"I know," I tell her, hating the way her smile starts to creep across her face.

Hybrid means they waitress like I've been doing for the last year, but it also means that if they get busier than the schedule anticipated, those same girls also dance.

"And you're sure that's what you want?"

I give her a small smile and a quick nod, but hell no I'm not sure. I want a job where I don't have to walk around with half my tits out and literally all of my ass out except for the tiny strip going between my cheeks. I might as well already be naked, but even wearing this without taking off more scares me to death. Fear is the only thing that's kept me off stage because the money some of these girls pull in each night is beyond tempting.

"You don't seem sure."

"I can do it."

She frowns. "And will that same enthusiasm carry over to the stage?"

Her dry question makes me smile.

"I can't be sure. Won't know until I get up there."

"I can't have you embarrassing the entire club if you freak out."

I understand where she's coming from.

Despite the ridiculous name, The Kitten's Cream is high end. The women who grace that stage are damn near considered celebrities by the men who pay to watch. More than one woman has been swept off her feet right into a brand-new Mercedes by the patrons. I get offers each and every night that are hard to turn down, considering the position I'm in right now with my living situation. These men are loaded, but the women on stage are too, depositing thousands of dollars a week into their bank accounts. I don't do too badly just waitressing, but on the stage is where the big bucks are.

"I'll be fine," I tell her, hoping that saying it will make it true.

"Maybe we'll start you in the booth first."

"I don't—"

"We can market you as the shy girl who can't shake it for an audience. The men will be scrambling for a private show."

"I—" I clamp my mouth closed when she cocks an eyebrow at me.

Unwilling to lose my job, I just nod.

"That may be better."

The private booths are actually little rooms along the back wall. They're lush and clean, and more importantly, they're monitored by a security team. Each move, every roll of a dancer's hips is watched, but that means the guys are watched as well. One hand in the wrong place, and the guy touching is in trouble. If the girl allows it, she's written up as well... Like I said, Sasha runs a tight ship.

"We're entertainers, not whores," she has said on more than one occasion while chastising someone who broke the rules. *"What you do in your spare time is none of my business, but you'll abide by the rules at The Kitten's Cream."*

One girl argued that the man who licked her nipple was her boyfriend. It didn't matter. She was fired, and he was blacklisted.

"Get to work," she says, satisfied with my responses.

It took some time to get used to the low lights in the club, but I'm a pro with moving about the dimly lit place now. I turn on the small lamps on the tables in my section, an indication to patrons that they're now allowed to sit there, before heading to the bar to check-in with the bartender.

As I get my night started, I pray for excellent tips, all the while knowing that the real tips are to be made on stage, and until I bite that bullet, I'll be living with a man I hardly know.

Chapter 18

Finnegan

"I'm telling Momma about this," Kason threatens as I lift my hand to knock on Wren's door.

"I'm going to see your momma," I snip, not at all feeling guilty for adding the same level of attitude to my voice that he just used. Who says a grown man can't be petty? I'm killing it right now. "She'll know where you're at."

Wren's door opens, and despite his earlier misgivings, he smiles down at the kids instead of running away like I did the first time I saw little Knox beside his mom.

"Kason, Kayleigh, and this is Knox," I say, pointing to each of the older kids before pointing at Knox's back.

He barely woke up when I pulled him from bed to bring him up here, and he's already back asleep, snuggled against my chest.

"That one can't party if he's sleeping. Let me make him some coffee," Wren says, smiling wider when I glare at him.

"He can't have coffee!" Kayleigh laughs. "He's not old enough!"

The twins follow Wren inside, and I follow behind them.

"Where do you want him?" I ask Wren.

"Guest bedroom," Wren says, already chatting with the other two as they follow him into his kitchen.

I head to Wren's guest bedroom, noting that it's in the same spot as one of mine. His condo is a little smaller, but most of the layout is the same.

Knox doesn't even so much as grumble when I place him on the bed and cover him with the blanket.

I realize I'm going to catch hell from Kendall when I walk into the kitchen to see Kason turning up a huge glass of chocolate milk.

"They're never going back to sleep," I mutter.

"You don't sleep at sleepover parties, Finn. He was looking a little sleepy, so I have to make sure he stays awake."

Kason turns, giving me a huge chocolate syrup smile. Of course, he would like Wren. The man is about the same age as them maturity wise. I choose to ignore how I acted before Wren opened the door.

"I'm going to head out," I tell them, wanting to get this over with.

Wren, perfectly in his element, gives me a quick wave. The kids are too focused on what Wren's going to do next to even notice my departure.

***

"Kendall," I tell the man as he looks down at the tablet in his hands.

"We don't have a Kendall," he says.

Relief washes over me at finding out that Wren was either wrong, or he told me that she works here just to piss me off.

"Okay," I say, turning back around to leave. I've never been a fan of strip clubs. The women are sexy as hell, there's no doubt about that, but I'm also not one to waste money, and it's a waste to spend loads of money on women pretending to like you.

"She goes by Ginger."

I stop in my tracks, all my elation falling to the stained concrete floor at my feet.

"Excuse me?"

"Kendall goes by Ginger." He frowns when he looks up at my red hair. "Are you going to be trouble?"

"No," I tell him.

"I don't want to have to kick your ass because your girlfriend gets hit on by someone else."

"You won't," I assure him. I'm not exactly agreeing not to start trouble, but rather letting him know he couldn't kick my ass if I was tied to a pole and blindfolded.

He grins, not catching my meaning at all. "What were you wanting?"

"A private dance."

"Gold or platinum?"

"Platinum," I answer, wanting to know what each level entails, but my blood pressure just can't manage hearing it right now. I'll find out soon enough.

"Can't," he says, his meaty finger swiping up the tablet.

"She booked?" It wouldn't surprise me. I find her the sexiest woman I've ever seen. I can't fault other guys for feeling the same way even though it makes me want to scream the place down.

"Not on the schedule."

"She's here. Her car is outside," I argue.

"Give me a minute," he says before walking to the side and speaking quietly into the headset he's wearing.

He looks me over more than once while he's chatting, and I'm wondering if he's calling backup because he's reading me right about not causing trouble. I'm vibrating with energy, my cock already half hard at the thought of seeing her dance and the thrill of kicking some guy's ass for seeing that very same thing.

"Payment?" he asks as he steps back up to me.

I hand over my credit card, waiting for him to slide it. I don't even check the price when he turns the tablet in my direction so I can sign off on the purchase.

"I'll escort you," the man says after he hands back my card. "There are rules."

"Okay," I tell him as I follow him along a dark hallway. I've yet to see inside the club. The front is separated by a thick, dark glass, making it impossible to see what's going on inside, and the hallway we're walking down is regal with red carpets and gold sconces on the walls, but there are no windows into the club.

"No touching."

"Of course not." This news makes me giddy. Now if only I can gouge out all the eyes that have seen Kendall naked.

"No hip thrusts. If the girl complains that you're grinding your dick on her, you're out. No refunds."

"No grinding. Got it."

"Oh, she can grind on you all she wants, but you just can't do it back. The dances are monitored."

"People are allowed to watch?" That creeps me out.

"Security is watching to make sure our girls are safe. Don't ask her to break the rules because she won't."

"No touching, no grinding. Got it," I say, repeating the rules.

"No licking either."

"Licking?" I make a grossed-out face and he smiles. "That happens?"

"Not often, but I thought you'd need the warning."

"I look like a licker to you?"

The guy doesn't answer my question. "You're in room three. She'll be there in a minute. Music preference?"

"Something slow and sensual," I say automatically.

"You got it," he says before disappearing back down the hall.

I open the door to the room and step inside. The chair in the center of the room looks like a throne, but I feel less like a king and more like a fool when I sit down in it. I plan to confront a girl I hardly know about a lie she didn't have to tell, and although I've run this through my head a million times, I know her answer doesn't even matter.

I'm going to leave with a hard-on and blue balls. I shrug as if answering an unasked question. It's not like I don't walk around with blue balls already because of her, so nothing is really going to change.

My pulse ramps up when music fills the room, but the door doesn't open. Is it possible that she can see me in here and decided not to come?

The song plays through, continuing on repeat once it's done. Just as I'm about to stand and leave, the door cracks open. She doesn't automatically enter, and all I can see are her red-tipped toenails and part of a very high heel.

I shift on the chair, wanting to go to her, but not wanting to get kicked out of here before all of this plays out.

Her eyes are downcast when she finally pushes the door open, and she closes it, back plastered to the thing.

I wait for her to look up, not wanting to miss her reaction when she sees me.

When she finally gets the courage to lift her head, her eyes widen, her face a mix of what can only be described as terror with a hint of elation.

"Finn," she whispers, her hands coming up to her throat.

I don't know that she's ever used the shortened version of my name until now, and I like it. My dick likes it. Hell, every part of me likes it.

I don't say a word. She knows why I'm here. At least it's clear I've bought a dance, and she's smart enough to know we're not meeting in this room because of chance. I'm here because I know she lied about where she works.

Her eyes dart to the corner of the room, and although it's too dark in here for me to see it, I imagine one of the cameras that security has is mounted there.

The song begins for the third time, the low bass seeming to make her remember why she's here, and I have to shift again when she starts to prowl toward me. I drop my eyes from her mouth to her hips as they sway closer, and I feel like I should request that my hands be tied to this stupid fucking chair because it's going to be impossible to keep them off of her.

I haven't seen the back of her, but telling from the thin straps at her hips, there's not much to the bottom part of her wardrobe. For sanity's sake, I pray she doesn't turn around. I've been staring at her gorgeous ass for a while in athletic clothing, seeing it mostly bare with a tiny strip of fabric disappearing between her cheeks would probably be my undoing.

I open my mouth to speak, having no damn clue what I could say right now, but she shakes her head, pressing her finger to her lips.

Then she begins to move. First, it's just a roll of her hips, but the momentum of it moves her trim torso and eventually her arms. Her knees brush against mine during her undulation, and she might as well have stroked my cock because that's exactly where I feel it.

Maybe I'm an asshole for actually letting her go through with this dance. No, I'm definitely an asshole because I never considered stopping her, even before I walked through the front doors of The Kitten's Cream.

She smells of sweet flowers when she leans in, placing her hands on the back of the chair, and I suddenly realize why there's a no licking rule. Her ample breasts are mere inches from my mouth, and it waters for a taste of her.

I manage to tilt my head back, looking up into her stunning face—an effort to keep my sanity—and I find her eyes closed, mouth whispering the words to the song as if she's picturing herself being anywhere else but here. Shame slams into me. This was the wrong way to go, and it doesn't even matter what she did at my place of work, this is different.

I've never shied away from explaining what I do for a living. Maybe she did because she's embarrassed. Maybe she was afraid I'd judge her.

I frown deeper. It's not that I'm mad about her dancing. I'm a little agitated at her dancing for others. It speaks of a possession I have no right to, but it doesn't stop me from feeling it.

My fingers jerk to help her when she stands on some part of the underside of the chair in an effort to get closer. I should stop this, but my brain is not the one in control right now. My body craves her, firing off shots of arousal with every brush, and despite agreeing not to thrust against her, my hips jolt unbidden when she settles a little on me.

"Ah fuck," I mutter, sweat beading at my temples as I try to stay in control.

It's then that she looks down at me, her body moving against mine, her lips only a few inches away.

I swallow, locking eyes with her because looking back down at her mouth would put an end to all of this very quickly.

My mouth drops open, gaining her attention, and my balls ache like they've never done before.

A slow smile spreads across her face as she drops another inch lower.

Maybe I'm imagining it, but it's as if I can feel the heat of her core against my erection, and then all doubt fades away when she grinds, a whimper of pleasure escaping her lips.

I give her a slow smile as she drops down again, the apex of her thighs making maddening circles in just the right spot that threatens to make me embarrass myself.

"Damnit," I mutter, my fingers aching from my grip on the arms of the chair in an effort not to touch her.

Her body serpentines up and down mine over and over, her body brushing, her breasts swaying.

I'm hypnotized by it, enthralled at her skill level, desperate to feel us together skin on skin rather than being separated by so many layers of clothes.

She leans away, her arms reaching behind her, and I know what comes next. I know in seconds, the bra barely managing to keep her in will be gone.

"No," I hiss, not wanting to see them for the first time this way.

It hits me that she's doing this because it's her job. I put her in this situation. She's never gotten this close to me back at the condo or in the gym. I'm making her do something she wouldn't normally do with me, and that makes the worst kind of guilt settle inside of me.

I stiffen when she pulls her hands away, bra still in place and places them on the back of the chair. I keep my eyes locked on hers, trying to read any level of hatred for me, but she keeps her eyes cast to the side.

When the song ends, she backs away and leaves the room.

I, of course, have to wait a few minutes, because even through my shame my cock stayed hard. But once it deflates, I'm out of there. She has several more hours until her shift is over, and I know I'll pace my condo until she gets home. We're going to have a long talk once she arrives, and I don't know if that's going to be with me apologizing or demanding she quit her job because I don't want her doing with other men what she did for me tonight.

Chapter 19

Kendall

If running away after what happened tonight was an option, I probably would have, but my kids are at his place and even my bone-deep embarrassment for him seeing me that way won't keep me from my kids.

With any luck, he'll be in bed asleep. I have a million questions, like why did he follow me and just where in the hell were my children while he was rock hard buying lap dances.

My body tingled all damn night after he left. I still had goosebumps on my arms when I found Sasha and told her there was no way I could work the private rooms or get on stage. I left work tonight knowing I'm going to have to find another part-time job to make up for that money because I wouldn't be getting those extra shifts now.

I wonder why I even went through with the one tonight, but I know exactly why, and that fact hits me in the face the second I walk into the condo.

Finn, as I'll think of him now, considering that I ground myself on his dick earlier, is sitting in one of the dining room chairs in the middle of the living room. The very same song that was playing during my dance is halfway through, and I absently wonder how many times he's listened to it tonight while waiting for me.

I would walk right past him, maybe snarl about him being an asshole, but he's shirtless, his muscular abdomen on full display. He's no longer in jeans like he was earlier. Those devilish gray sweats are low on his hips with his body curved on the chair, his ass nearly over the edge.

"What are you doing?" I snap, my mouth suddenly dry from my rapid intakes of air.

He cocks an eyebrow. "Waiting for my dance."

I drop my purse and keys on the console table, mildly agitated at his expectation, but I also can't deny the thrill that runs up my spine.

He followed the rules at the club, but I doubt he'll do the same in the middle of his own home.

I have a choice to make, and it doesn't take long.

"I'll go change into something more—"

"What you're wearing is fine," he interrupts, his eyes hungry, sweeping down the length of me like I'm naked and not wearing a t-shirt and leggings.

The song starts over, and I move my hips as I walk closer. I was more embarrassed to do this in front of him back at the club than I am now. Probably because I've been trying hard not to see him as a sexual being in order to maintain my sanity. Knowing I'm going to lose the battle anyway, I inch closer, my fingers playing with the hem of my shirt and giving him a peek at my bare torso, before teasingly letting it drop again.

The chair he's sitting in is just a regular chair, whereas the ones at the club are made specifically for lap dances. On those, there are places to put your feet so the dancer can determine how close she gets to a patron. The chair he's in has rungs, and I'm not certain they'll hold my weight.

So, I do what I wanted to do back at the club but couldn't and stay within the rules set forth for the dancers. I straddle his body.

His hands don't hesitate to grip my hips, his body rolling to the music under mine. His cock, more defined now that he isn't restricted by denim, presses to me, feeling just as good now as those brushes did at the club.

"Mmm," I moan, looking him right in the eye.

He's the one controlling this dance now, and I move my hips how his grip demands, watching with awe as his eyes go from olive to emerald with heat.

Although I knew this was going to be more than just a dance, I still gasp when his lips brush my throat. I freeze, unsure how I should respond.

"Don't stop," he groans, his fingers tightening on my hips.

When I lean back to reposition, his hands move up my waist, taking my shirt with it.

The bra I'm wearing now is full coverage, unlike the one I had on earlier, but he still seems just as enthralled as he did before. The way he watches me makes my skin light on fire. Eyes, filled with desire, sweep over me as I pull the shirt completely off and toss it to the floor.

"The bra too," he demands, leaving it up to me to unhook the clasp at the back.

Knowing that this is where things were going to lead because of our interactions at the gym before he managed to blow up my life, I unhook my bra, holding it to my chest for a long moment while letting my hips continue to roll against his.

Urgency to expose myself washes over me when his tongue skates the lower curve of his mouth. Trembling with need, I drop the garment, and his eyes lock on my breasts. I feel his gaze there like a tangible thing, needing his mouth on me more than I've ever needed anything.

As if reading my mind, Finn leans forward, brushing his soft lips over my skin but studiously avoiding the place I need him the most. My nipples furl, demanding to be noticed.

"Finn," I plead, my body aching all over in desperation for him.

He obliges, first with a quick swipe of his tongue, but then he draws the taut tip into his mouth. I feel the sucking right in the center of me, and I whimper for more, more, more.

My fingers curl into the muscle at his shoulders, and the groan he releases reverberates through my entire body.

It's never been like this for me, and that's more bad than good because I know I'm going to be left still wanting him. He can bring me all the pleasure in the world, and instead of feeling sated, I'm only going to want it all over again. It's like uncorking the best bottle of wine and trying to assure myself I'll only have a single glass. Come morning, I'm left with regret and a headache, the empty bottle beside me.

Finn will be no different, and since I can't escape the man who sleeps right down the hall from me, I know this won't be the last time. With his mouth on me, the warmth of his tongue laving my skin, we've already gone too far.

I can only hope to survive him at this point because the train wreck is coming.

With his palm flat on my lower back, he urges me deeper into him, my center brushing over his rigid cock.

We groan in unison, both enjoying the contact our bodies are making, but it's not enough. My eyes flutter closed as I picture him sliding through my arousal to find the center of me. I whimper, needing exactly that as my hips jolt, seeking friction and fullness.

I can't recall a single time I've ever been this hot for a guy, and it doesn't bode well for my slightly crazy, very addictive personality. I don't have to sink down on him. He doesn't have to fill me up for me to know just how good going that far with him will feel.

Instinctively, I know Finn will be a good lover. He'll be generous, not only with what he's been blessed with but also in his tentative care to my own pleasure.

He's not rushing me, trying to get to the finish line. The man is taking his time, savoring, enjoying the build-up just as much as I am, and it's delicious, decadent, and making me feel things I've only read about.

Gooseflesh covers every inch of me, making my nipples draw in even tighter, and he groans against the tip of one breast, his hand coming up to cup the other one in his massive hand as if he just can't get enough. It's like he wants to be everywhere at once, and not having every inch of me in his mouth is a point of contention for him.

"Finn," I whisper. "We're wearing too many clothes."

I grin when I feel his smile against my skin.

"Let's fix that problem," he says, pulling me right off him as if I weigh less than a feather.

My feet hit the floor, and I'm grateful for the grip he keeps on my hips as his eyes stay locked on my exposed breasts. If he weren't holding me, I'd likely fall over because my legs literally feel like jelly. I'm weak in the knees, and I never understood the saying until now.

My body screams at the lack of contact after experiencing the brush of him against me in all the right places.

His mouth meets the tip of my deprived breast as his fingers work my leggings down. In an effort to help, I kick my shoes off, letting them land wherever they choose. I don't hear them crash into anything, so I call it a win.

"You're riding my cock tonight, Kendall."

Chapter 20

Finnegan

A slow smile spreads across her flushed face with my words, her teeth digging into the corner of her lower lip.

"Should I let you come?" I ask, my eyes locked on her even with the distracting jiggle of her amazing tits in my face.

"Let me?" she asks, her brow drawing in. "What makes you think you can stop it?"

She's playful, and as much as I love seeing her like this, the anger from her lying to me is still simmering deep inside my gut.

"You lied about where you work."

She tries to take a step back, and I realize my words came out harsher than I intended. I have no desire to stop what we're doing, and I know I'm skating a fine line confronting her before she slides down the length of me.

The scent of her arousal swarms around me, and my mouth waters for a taste of her there, but I'm a patient man. I'll lick that glistening sweetness from her skin soon enough.

"I'm not in the habit of telling strangers all about me," she says, her body tightening as she tries to inch away.

"Because you're ashamed you dance naked for men?"

She stiffens further, her muscles locking under my grip.

"I don't dance for men." Her eyes narrow as she glares at me.

"What do you call tonight?"

"I—" She sighs, and I just know another lie is going to escape her fuckable lips.

Releasing one hip, I slide my fingers over the flat of her lower belly, arrowing them lower. I let my gaze follow my fingers, nearly moaning out loud at the sight of her delicate pussy. Her perfect outer lips split at the top, the swollen tip of her clit exposed, her arousal too strong to control that part of her.

I swallow, eager to feel that little bundle against my mouth, on my tongue, scraping on the root of my cock as she seeks her own pleasure.

I thicken further which is a damn feat because I'm already a steel pipe in my sweats.

She twitches when I split my thumb and forefinger on either side of that part of her, exposing that little treasure slowly. She wants more. Despite the argument fighting to rumble from her throat, the need she's feeling takes precedence, and I watch in awe as one dewy drop of arousal begins to drip from her slit. The tip of my cock weeps in solidarity, and I know that the time for explanations, lying, and getting to the truth will come later. Denying each other what we both need is stupid, and painful, my cock reminds me as it throbs with desire.

With my grip on her hip, I move her back a foot so I can crouch low in front of her. This isn't what I had in mind when the scene played on repeat in my head as I waited for her, as the bass of the song I can no longer hear throbbed in my chest. I was going to either take her bent over the back of my couch or I was going to pull her down on my cock and let her do all the work.

Tasting her, although an appealing thought, wasn't on my mind then. Getting all the pleasure and not giving an ounce of it was all I could focus on. I wanted to use her. I wanted to fill her up so much that her little eyes squinted at the corner, to plant inside of her so deep that she rose to the challenge and tried to sink further down like I knew she would.

With her standing naked in front of me, her skin flushed with arousal, her pussy literally dripping with need, I'd be a fool to waste the opportunity to taste her. As I lean in, I tell myself this is for me, not her. The pleasure she'll get is secondary to what it does for me.

Tiny hands flex on my shoulders, fingers digging into my flesh as I blow cool air over her pussy. She whimpers, the keening sound ten times sexier than the song playing on repeat. I haven't even brushed her pussy yet, and she's already trembling. As I flatten my tongue, preparing to lick up the middle of her, I look up, my cock throbbing more when I notice her watching. God, her eyes on me as I prepare to taste her for the very first time is my undoing. I take a deep breath, planning on not being able to breathe for a while with my entire face buried in her delicate flesh, and latch on.

She jolts, as if struck by lightning, and that keening noise turns into a low, guttural moan.

Letting my mouth do all the work, I lift one of her legs over my shoulder, giving me better access, and wrap my arms around her body. Trusting I've got her, I smile when her body relaxes, giving me more of her weight.

Something pings in my chest with her trusting me, even if it's only to bring her pleasure. I could lift her with no problems. I could move her body exactly where I want it. She's thick in all the right places, all the places that make my cock start controlling my actions, but compared to me, she's a delicate little thing. I've imagined pinning her down, holding parts of her body this way and that, situating her into the perfect fuck toy, more times than I can count, but right now, with my face buried against her pussy, tongue lashing at her clit, I find she's controlling my head with the simple grip of one hand.

I growl against her wet, heated flesh, a little angry and very aroused with the turn this has taken.

Her hips roll, and I can easily tell it's her seeking, trying to satisfy her own needs rather than a continuation of her dancing to the music.

Desperate to feel her convulse against my tongue, I double my efforts, skillfully using the bump of my nose on her clit as I tongue her entrance to my benefit.

"Finn," she pants, and just like the couple of times tonight when she said it before, my cock threatens to erupt with nothing but the stimulation from my sweats to set me off. "Coming!"

The warning is nice, but I knew she was there before the word rolled out of her perfect mouth. Her core flutters against my tongue before the real pulsing of her orgasm begins, and I just know I'll relive this moment for the rest of my life.

The scent of her deepens as her orgasm rolls through her body, starting right in the middle of her before reverberating through her torso and limbs.

Making a woman come is pleasurable for me, so I make sure it happens every time I have this sort of encounter, but there's something different settling inside of me when Kendall does it. I'm desperate to feel that flutter, to hear the low moan within seconds of it happening, so I triple my efforts, licking, sucking, tonguing at her until it happens again.

My attempt at a third time is thwarted by the tips of her fingers literally breaking my skin in an effort to get away from me.

Without releasing her, I pull my mouth away, looking up to find dreamy eyes and parted lips staring down at me. My own mouth seems swollen, and when she runs her fingers over my bottom lip as if she's praising them, they tingle at her touch.

"Want you inside of me," she whispers, her words slow, a sleepiness to them that makes me imagine her saying the very same thing when she wakes in the middle of the night, desperate for me to fill her.

Standing, I guide her to the sofa, pushing my sweats down my thighs as I go. She chuckles, her eyes locked on my lower half when my clothing gets caught on the end of my cock, but she's helpful, reaching down to grip the base of me with one hand while pulling the fabric free. Her touch is cool compared to the heat of my rod, and I revel in the difference for a moment, standing still and waiting to see what she'll do next.

Her hand looks miniature compared to mine, making my cock look even bigger. My chest puffs up a little at that, and she shakes her head when she looks up at me.

"Gloating?"

"Didn't say a word," I say, my words husky and still filled with unsated need.

"You don't have to."

She grips me once again, and maybe she's to the point she can take a breather, but I'm desperate for more than a little touch of her hand. She's had two orgasms, the second one right on the tail of the first. I've gotten no form of relief.

"Kendall," I groan when she seems just content as can be to explore my length and compare it to the size of her hand.

I kick my sweats free of my feet and turn to sit down on the sofa. Fucking her in my bed would only lead to me being tortured with the memories of her there while she's down the hall in her own room. I don't need the headache that will bring. I have no idea how things are going to go once this is over and we have a serious talk.

"It's just so—"

"Ready, Kendall. It's ready. Slide that pussy down it, babe."

"I figured you wanted my mouth with how often I find you staring at it," she teases, both with her words and the trickle of her fingers down my aching shaft.

"Fuck," I grunt, knowing that it's impossible to make that decision.

Staring at her mouth was more about wanting to know what her lips taste like. Letting my mind drift to her using it to taste me was too damn dangerous to consider.

"Hard choice?" she asks, gripping me tight again.

My balls tighten, drawing up as she lowers to her knees between my splayed legs.

God, she's going to make the decision for me, and I fucking love it.

Her hot breath skates over the glistening tip as she watches my face, and now I understand her reaction when I did the same to her earlier. It's absolute bliss. Literally, the best fucking thing I've ever felt.

Her tongue sweeps out, tasting the precum from the tip, and God I was wrong. I was so fucking wrong because this is the best thing I've ever felt. Unbidden, my hips jolt, causing my cockhead to brush her lips. I groan with need, doing my best not to grip her head and choke her with my dick.

"Kendall," I growl, not a fan of being teased.

"Yes?" she asks, her eyes on me as her tongue snakes out to get another taste.

"I'm fucking begging," I whisper, my fist gripping the couch cushion at my hips because I know if I touch her, I may cause her pain, in desperation for more.

"Poor thing," she says, licking at me once again.

Her eyes widen when I move, gripping her under the arms and hauling her onto my lap. I take her mouth as I use one hand to lift her body and line myself up.

"No," she snaps, just as the tip of me splits the lips of her pussy.

I freeze, my chest heaving with the exertion it takes not to just release her hip, knowing gravity will have her sheathing me in seconds.

"No?" I ask, my balls exploding from pressure a real possibility.

"I have three kids already," she snaps, moving as if she's going to pull completely away. "I don't think my body would even survive your baby."

Like I've been submerged in icy water, her words hit me right in the face.

How did we go from desperate for each other to having children?

"What?" I ask, beyond confused.

"We need a condom. Knox was a birth-control baby. So even though I'm on it, I don't trust it."

"In my sweats pocket," I say, my body getting back on board after realizing she's wanting to avoid a pregnancy not expecting to get pregnant like I originally imagined.

"Terrifies you, doesn't it?" she asks as she climbs off me, her eyes locked on my flagging erection.

I chuckle because what else could I say right now?

When she stands with the foil packet in her hands, she doesn't hand it over even though my palm is out. She settles back between my legs, just like she was when she was teasing my cock.

"You know," she says, bouncing the condom wrapper against her lips as if she's contemplating her decisions. "Condoms aren't always a hundred percent effective either. Maybe we should stop."

I see the game she's playing now that my arousal has waned a little.

"Okay," I agree quickly, reaching out one hand to tangle my fingers in her hair as I grip my cock with the other. "Make sure you swallow."

Her mouth hangs open, but it's clear she's doing it because I've surprised her, not in preparation to drink me down as I quicken the strokes down my cock.

"You're going to jack off into my mouth."

"I'm going to come," I tell her. "I'd prefer you riding my cock, but if you're worried, this will have to do."

She smiles, lifting further up on her knees, and rolls her mouth over the top of my dick.

She doesn't tease or taunt me with soft touches. Her fucking cheeks cave in from the suction, and once again she easily gains the upper hand.

"Fuck, fuck, fuck," I chant, so close to coming that I don't know if I can even get the warning out, but then the heat of her perfect fucking mouth is gone.

My eyes pop open, a glare I can't control turned in her direction.

"I like option two," she says, lifting the condom wrapper to her lips and using her teeth to tear it open.

I lift my hand to take it from her, but Kendall surprises me again when she pinches the tip of the condom before rolling it down my cock. I groan, my need growing exponentially with every swipe of her hand as she situates the protection.

I don't want kids, and it's clear she doesn't want more, but the thought of sliding into her bare makes me hate the latex layer already.

"There," she says, giving her handy work a long look.

My cock jerks, rebelling against just waving in the air when there is something else we could be doing.

"Get up here," I command, reaching down for her exactly like I did before she climbed off me.

"So pushy," she chides as she straddles my hips.

"Just eager," I correct, knowing she feels the exact same way when she reaches for my cock, lining me back up where I so desperately want to be before I can do the very same.

"Mmm," she moans, rubbing my cock through her arousal. "Let me do this, Finn. It's going to take some getting used to."

I smile wide, wanting to remind her that it's not my fault she's been with pencil-dick assholes before.

We groan in unison when she lowers, taking the very tip of me into her slick heat.

"So damn big," she says, her words coming out on a whimper.

"Keep complimenting me like that, babe, and it's going to end way too soon."

Leaning forward, she presses her lips into my throat, and I tilt my head a little further to give her all the access she wants. I feel her breath as she chuckles.

"Sex has never been so—Oh God."

"Good?" I ask, thrusting my hips up some to give her a little more.

It's the sweetest torture working myself inside of her.

"Easy," she says.

"Easy?" I huff, my jaw clenching when her hips still with several inches left to take. "This is beyond easy. I need more, Kendall. Fuck, give me more."

She pulls back, her eyes locked on mine as her fingers once again dig into my shoulder. "Easy as in I'm not lost in my head thinking about tomorrow. Easy as in—"

Her mouth hangs open, her eyes unfocused as I lift my hips and seat her fully on my cock.

"You were saying?" I have to distract myself and talking seems like the easiest way, because if I focus solely on the clench of her body, I'm going to have to make excuses for why I didn't last long enough for her to even get anything out of this.

"This is the only thing that exists right now—my pussy stretched so deliciously around your cock. God, how does it ache and feel like the best thing ever at the same time?"

"So good," I manage before clenching my jaw once again.

Good isn't the best descriptor.

Amazing, phenomenal, perfection work so much better, but my mouth can't seem to form those words.

I'm to the point where saying something like *pussy good, give me more* is about all I can handle.

She shifts, rolling her hips from side to side as she acclimates to my thickness. She might as well be up on her feet bouncing on the damn thing for how good it feels.

She presses her forehead to mine, her eyes locked on where we're joined. Is there anything this woman does that doesn't turn me on?

"Look at you," I praise, looking down at the same connection. "Stretched so wide. Fuck, your pussy is amazing."

"Who knew you were a talker?" she asks, her mouth hanging open after the last word as I use my grip under her ass to lift her a couple inches.

She groans again, and the rumble of it swirls around us, the acoustics in the room better than I ever realized.

"God. Damn. Sweetheart, so good."

"How am I already close to coming?"

I hiss, wanting to hear it but hating that her confession makes my balls tighten. I want this to last forever, but it seems a few minutes is all we're going to get.

"I'm going to bounce you on my dick," I warn, my fingers flexing against her ass before I can get an agreement from her.

Her lips meet mine, and it's a great fucking kiss. Her lips are soft, her tongue seeking, and I give as good as I get, but my hands are working independently from my brain, lifting her and urging her to fall in a frantic rhythm. Her breaths escape her nose, those little whimpers from earlier gaining some strength as she pulls away.

"Jesus. There, Finn. I'm there."

I grind her against me, my cock jerking inside of her without warning.

"Fuck it," I snap, flipping her so her back is to the sofa, ass hanging over the edge, and I pound into her, my hips snapping forward.

Her eyes roll back, body curving away from the furniture, and I'd think she wasn't having a good time if she didn't reach down and hold her legs open wider for me.

I resist jerking the condom off and painting her with my cum, but just barely.

I groan out my release, stabbing into her once more, planting my cock in her as far as it can manage. Her body quivers around mine, her core taxed and fluttery along my length.

Four maybe five minutes tops since she rolled that damn condom down me, and this was still the best sex of my life.

I lean over, my cock shifting inside of her so I can take her mouth in a fiery kiss. Our breaths are harsh, mingling as she smiles against my lips.

"So good," she pants, biting the corner of her lip once again when my cock jerks at the praise.

"Agreed, baby," I say, nuzzling her nose with mine.

It seems to break her out of some trance, and I don't know if it's just the sound of my voice or the pet name, but she wiggles until she's free of me. I can't formulate words as I watch her walk away, that perfect ass of hers looking ten times better with my handprint there. She may have bruises come morning time from the grip I held her with, but I doubt she'll complain. If she does, I'll offer to kiss it better.

"Finn!" she screams, and I'm on my feet ready to protect her from whatever is making her so terrified.

She meets me back in the hall, the door to her bedroom open as she runs out of the one the boys have been staying in.

"Where are my damn kids?"

"With Wren," I tell her, my brows drawing together.

"Why aren't they here?"

I want to ask if I've fucked her stupid, but the scowl on her face doesn't leave much room for teasing.

"They're at Wren's, and thank fuck for that, because you're noisy when you're getting fucked. You would've woken them up."

She narrows her eyes again before darting into her room. I know I have a stupid grin on my face as I stand stark naked in the doorway and watch her pull on clothes.

"Don't get dressed," I tell her. "We still have hours to get to know each other better."

"I'm getting my kids," she snaps, her eyes locking on me for only a second as I stroke my awakening cock, but then she huffs and looks away as if she's disgusted with what she sees.

"What's that attitude for?"

"You," she hisses. "Can you go get dressed?"

"Me?" I chuckle. "You didn't have a problem with me a few minutes ago when your pussy had a death grip on my dick."

She spins, pulling a t-shirt over her head, and her eyes narrow further. "We aren't talking about that."

"We're not?" I reach for her. I'm perfectly okay with not talking.

She smacks my hand away. "We're going to pretend like it didn't happen."

"Can't, baby. Not with the sweet smell of your pussy still on my dick, on my tongue."

"Get dressed so we can go get my kids," she snaps as she shoulders past me out the door.

I sigh, frustrated as hell as I follow her to the living room. I snatch up my sweats, grinning like a fool when her eyes follow the other condoms as they fall to the floor.

"Get that thought out of your head," she says, studiously avoiding the sight of me as I tug my sweats back on. "Once was it."

I huff a laugh, knowing she had too grand of a damn time to keep to that promise, but saying so won't win her over right now.

"Are you planning to drive with no shoes and no shirt?" she snaps when I walk across the room and pick up my keys.

"Wren lives in the building, Kendall. They're only a short elevator ride away."

She huffs, lifting her head in an indignant way as she once again pushes past me to the front door of the condo. I reach out, gripping her by the hips as I press the front of my body to her back, leaning in low to speak in her ear.

"I like it when you're all huffy and rude, baby. Keep it up and we're only going to end up naked again."

She stiffens in my arms, rolling her head to the side so she can look up at me. I turn her, ready for the softer side of her. I lick at my lips in preparation for a kiss when she lifts up, bringing her mouth close as she cups my jaw, her palm flexing against the scruff there.

"In your dreams," she says sweetly before pulling back and walking out of the condo.

I grin like a fool as I follow her to the bank of elevators.

Chapter 21

Kendall

I'm just as growly as Finn was this morning when he came into the kitchen and tried to press his lips to my throat. Well, he wasn't growly until I pushed him away from me and gave him a look that said I didn't want him anywhere near me.

The man has no tact whatsoever. Surely, he saw Kason and Knox at the table. Maybe he just didn't care.

Kason saw him, and when Finn muttered something about me being an unreasonable woman before walking away, I watched Kason narrow his eyes as he watched Finn leave the room with a scowl on his face. I turned away before my oldest son could shift that anger toward me.

Wren kept them up all damn night. Well, Kason and Kayleigh were still awake when I showed up with Finn at Wren's place looking well and truly fucked if the look on Wren's face spoke the truth. The man grinned at me before looking over my shoulder at the broody asshole plastered to my back. He knew exactly what we'd been up to. Despite Finn pulling a t-shirt on, he opted to ride the elevator with the outline of his cockhead pressing against those damn gray sweats.

My body throbs, sore in the best way possible for what we did last night, and I can't imagine how I'd feel if I actually gave in to his request and went at it for another round. I would've had to crawl to Wren's apartment to get my kids, and that would earn me more than narrowed eyes and a nasty scowl from Kason.

Grumpy Finn stalked out of the condo without another word mere minutes after I rejected his affections in the kitchen earlier, and after breakfast, I convinced the kids to take a nap. Knox didn't sleep, but he sat quietly with Kason's tablet as the twins tried to catch up on what they missed.

After their nap, and regretting not lying down myself, I got them dressed and headed out for a little shopping.

I was utterly distraught after leaving the private dance room last night. I knew I'd never be able to do that for men I don't know. I didn't even come out of a single part of my uniform for Finn, and I still felt like my nerves were exposed. I don't fault anyone working in any part of the sex industry. Women have beautiful bodies, and if they're comfortable sharing some parts of those—or even all—I say go for it. I just can't go that far myself.

Lily, another one of the dancers caught me crying in the changing room, and on a series of sobs, I dropped all my problems at her feet. I told her about losing the apartment, and not having anywhere to go. I cried through telling her about my need for more shifts, but how impossible it was for me to take those shifts considering what would be expected of me. I even mentioned Finn and how damn sexy he was. She didn't see that last part as a problem, but she gave me advice on what I could do to earn that extra money without having to sacrifice the time I have with my kids.

That lead to the shopping trip with the kids, who are all now sleeping for a late afternoon nap because shopping is exhausting, apparently.

I should be lying down as well, considering I have a shift tonight, but I'm taking Lily's advice, and sorting through my purchases before getting on my computer.

The front door opens and closes, the atmosphere changing around me just with Finn's presence in the condo. I consider shoving my purchases back in the bag but doing so would only draw more attention. He doesn't walk straight to his room or flop down in his recliner like I expect, and in a matter of seconds, he's standing on the other side of the table, his eyes glued to the lace, cotton, and silk spread out over the top.

"That is a lot of underwear," he observes, a sly smile that does things to my body I won't admit spreading across his face as he visually inventories the garments.

"Gotta do what I gotta do," I say with a sigh, trying to remember the counts in my head so I'm ready for later.

"Like change your panties every ten minutes?"

He inches closer, his eyes locking on the white cotton in the center of the table. He crooks a finger, picking it up, and we both stare at the dangling fabric.

"I can't picture you wearing these. In fact, you weren't wearing panties last night."

A thrill runs up my spine, and I stand statue still in an effort not to clench my thighs together. Before, it was the sight of him and all his glorious muscles that turned me on. His accent played a huge part in my fantasies as well. Now, after knowing what he's like in bed, it takes actual restraint not to suggest going back to his room. I want to mention him holding his hand over my mouth because I can't control the sounds I make when he's inside of me.

And I need to quit.

"They were requested," I lie, my eyes darting down to the table because I just can't look at him.

I'm not ashamed, but explaining that I plan to sell used panties online makes my cheeks heat with embarrassment.

Lily gave me all the info I needed and explained how to shop sales to save money. She gave me tips on how to get more fans and what I needed to do to keep them once they reached out.

"Requested?" he says, letting the fabric slip from his fingertip.

"I sell them."

"Your used underthings?" he says, sounding confused.

"Panties, Finn. I'm going to sell them online because—" I snap my mouth closed. I don't owe him an explanation. I don't need to justify my choices to anyone.

He moves then, but not away like I expect. Instead, he lines up behind me, pressing his erection to my lower back as his hands come around my stomach. He doesn't inch his fingers inside of my clothes, doesn't toy with the hem of my shirt, but it's as if my body doesn't know the difference. He might as well be two knuckles deep inside of me for how ready I am for him.

His warm lips brush my neck, and I have to clamp my teeth between my lips to prevent a whimper of need from escaping. His teeth nip at my earlobe, threatening to make me crumple to the floor.

I should be pushing him away. I told him last night what happened would never happen again, but I know better. Maybe he does, too, because instead of trying to step away, I lean more of my weight against his chest, wanting to purr and rub on him like an affectionate cat.

"Tell the man who gets the ones you're wearing just how they got so fucking fragrant."

Then he's gone, leaving me horny and my panties definitely wet.

Chapter 22

Finnegan

Maybe not sleeping while worried about kids in the other room is a rite of passage. I was sure I'd be fine when Kendall left for her shift, but I tossed and turned. For hours I blamed being responsible for them as the reason I couldn't sleep, but deep down, I know that it was Kendall that kept me from falling asleep.

I wasn't so much worried about her rejecting me or never having my mouth on her again. That's a given.

It was the fact that she was at work, her fine ass body on display for other men, that made me uneasy. I thought about putting my foot down and insisting that she stay home, but that would do more bad than good. She's not the type of woman to obey when issued a command, and it made me think of demanding she come on my cock and watching her fight not to. That would be a lot of damn fun, actually.

She wasn't smiling when she got home from work and found me sitting in my recliner with the television on mute. She swept her eyes over me once before retreating into her bedroom.

Sleep didn't find me then either, hence the reason I'm mainlining coffee today and in the foulest mood ever.

Not getting good rest isn't really the issue. I could probably go days without sleep and still manage to keep a smile on my face. It was her being so close after getting home and yet still so far away. I thought a hundred times about grabbing her from her bedroom, but she shares that with Kayleigh, and I'm not going to wake a child up because my dick is hard and in desperate need of her mother. That just seemed like the wrong thing to do. I thought about making enough noise that she'd come out and tell me to be quiet, planning to urge her to do the same when I dropped to my knees and tongued that greedy little pussy of hers, but just the thought of doing that made me hard and I couldn't risk one of the kids walking out and finding me like that instead of her.

So, no sleep and no pussy made me a cranky guy.

I had to get out of the condo early today because there was no telling what I'd do after she returned from dropping the kids at school.

I was torn between kissing and having my way with her and growling like a crazy man and making her describe in detail just what she did all night at work. The latter was winning out as I got dressed, and that was the worst of the two choices. I'm not a man to care about what a woman does when she isn't under me. Not once in my life have I been upset with the thought of someone showing too much skin. As far as I've always been concerned, there was no such thing as too much skin. I've always been of the mind that if a woman is comfortable showing anything on her body, then more power to her.

Kendall? I want her dressed from neck to toes, and I waver on the idea of a ski mask. I don't want anyone looking at her.

I've never been this possessive, never wanted to sit outside someone's work and pick the patrons off one by one with a sniper rifle because they may have seen her thick ass just walking by in that damn string bikini bottom she calls a uniform.

I'm losing my fucking mind at the prospect.

I hiss more in agitation than pain when I pull the cup of coffee from the machine before it's done, and the scalding liquid runs over my hand.

"Motherfucker," I snap, reaching for a paper towel.

"Problems at home?" Wren asks with a grin that has no place in the office on a Monday morning.

"Fuck off," I grunt, cleaning up my mess instead of walking away. I'm not a savage after all.

He chuckles, the sound grating on my nerves.

Letting my mind wander back to Kendall, I turn to face him. "I want you to tell me about Ty Penman."

"Can't," Wren says, stepping to the side so I can toss the used paper towel in the trash.

"Don't give me that shit."

"I'll tell you what I told you before. If Kendall wants you to know about her ex, then she'll tell you about him."

"You knowing who I'm talking about tells me you already know."

"I never said I didn't know. I'm saying I'm not telling you."

"That's incredibly petty, don't you think?"

He shrugs. "Why do all of you guys come to me?"

"Because we know you research them."

He makes a sound of acknowledgment, but doesn't give me anything else before walking away.

I leave my coffee sitting on the counter and follow him, not planning to give up on this.

Late last night or early this morning, however you want to look at it, I decided that Kendall is just too precious to just let slip through my fingers. Maybe I was still riding the high of my orgasm, my body begging for more, but even after my shower and getting dressed it didn't fade. In order for me to open myself up to more with her, I need to know what I'm facing.

The man has three kids with her, and although he's a piece of shit that's apparently no longer in the picture, I can't imagine a man staying gone forever when he has children. I know I couldn't, but I also never would've walked away from a woman who carried my child. I may not stay in a committed relationship with the mother of my child, but I sure as fuck wouldn't disappear and leave him or her behind. I just don't have it in me to do something like that.

Wren closes his door before I can get to it, and I growl my frustration when I turn the knob only to find it locked.

I call him a slew of names, pound my fist once on the damn thing, and walk away.

Kit, Brooks, Jude, and Quinten stare at me from the couch. It's not like they weren't there earlier, I just somehow managed to focus all of my attention on getting information from Wren.

"What?" I snap, glaring at them on my walk back to retrieve my coffee.

"You seem more surly than usual," Brooks answers.

"I'm not in the best of moods," I explain as I take a seat beside Quinten.

Kit grins at me as if there's not a damn thing wrong in his world, and somehow it makes my hackles go up. I don't want to be around happy people, and the urge to ruin his damn day swarms around me.

"Why are you fucking smiling?"

Kit's smile doesn't falter, and Brooks chuckles, clearly in the know.

"His wish came true this past weekend," Brooks says.

"Weddings are always fun," Jude says, reminding me that Kit's sister Beth got married this weekend.

"Oh, I bet he had fun," Brooks adds.

"You don't know a damn thing," Kit snaps, but that silly smile is still on his face.

"I know you disappeared from the rehearsal dinner, and the reception," Brooks discloses. "And funny enough, Jules was absent during those times as well."

"I have no idea what you're talking about." The smile grows wider as if Kit is remembering just how his weekend went.

"So, it's a mystery why I saw Jules sneaking out of your room yesterday morning?"

Jude and Quinten chuckle.

"I don't kiss and tell," Kit says, his attention suddenly on the magazine in his lap.

"You don't have to *tell*, my friend. We shared a hotel room wall."

I feel a smile tugging up the corners of my lips. Kit has been fawning over his sister's best friend since high school, maybe even junior high. If he locked that in this weekend, then I'm happy for the guy, despite my girl going to work to show her body to other men.

Not my girl, I remind myself. May never be my girl at the rate things are going.

Do I even want a woman that has three kids? That's a lot of responsibility, and although I kind of figured I'd end up married with children eventually, getting all of it practically overnight was never a consideration.

My cock kicks, remembering what she said about carrying my child, and I have no idea how to even work through any of it.

"I'm going home," I say as I stand.

"Sudden illness?" Brooks asks, his tone teasing and light.

"Yeah," I agree quickly, washing my cup in the sink before hauling ass from the office.

I spend the drive back to the condo, tapping my fingers on the steering wheel and doing my best to drive the speed limit. There's an urgency inside of me to get to her even though I have no idea what I'm going to do when I see her. The elevator ride is slow as fuck but ends, eventually. I prowl past two guys wearing leather cuts, praying they aren't my new neighbors. They seem like the type to party hard, and shit will come to blows if they keep the kids up.

Thinking they came from my apartment, I hustle faster, debating on whether I should turn back around and beat their asses, or go to Kendall. The closing of the elevator doors makes the decision for me, and I fumble with my keys to unlock the door.

My heart caves in at the sight of Kendall sitting on the sofa with tears streaming down her face.

"Did they hurt you? I'll fucking kill them."

She snaps her eyes up at me, her dark eyelashes showcasing the redness in them.

"Was one of those assholes Ty?" I snap, feeling like I can still run down the stairs and catch them before they exit the building.

"That was Adrian Larrick and Brant Jesper."

I freeze at hearing the names. I recognize the names. As much as Wren refused to tell me more about Ty Penman, he did mention that the dickhead did screw over the Keres MC the other day. He also assured me that whatever beef they had with Penman wouldn't bleed over into Kendall's life. He was wrong.

"And why was the president and VP of the Keres MC here?"

Maybe I have it all wrong. Maybe Penman is gone but somehow Kendall is still involved with the MC. Maybe she's under their protection? I don't know a damn thing about this woman.

"They're looking for Ty," she says, a sob bubbling out of her throat.

I go to her immediately. Although she's lied to me in the past, I don't see her lying to me about this.

"Why are they after him?" I ask, holding her to my chest.

I feel like the king of the world when she wraps her arms around me and buries her face in my chest.

"Ty stole something from them, and they want it back."

"What exactly?"

She shakes her head, answering that she doesn't know.

"Whatever it is, it's causing them to lose money. Adrian said Ty owes hundreds of thousands of dollars and that number goes up daily. They want me to pay his debts."

I know just getting paid back is never enough for those types of men. If they feel betrayed, they'll ever only be satisfied with blood, and I hate to think they'll go after Kendall for her ex's mistakes, but they're already doing that by insisting she pay them.

"Have they been bothering you at work?"

If they have been causing her problems there, then maybe I can convince her not to go back. Her being here at night with me would solve so many damn problems, and maybe I could actually get some damn sleep.

"No. I ran into Brant the other day at the grocery store."

"And you didn't bother to tell me?" I hold her tighter when she wiggles like she wants to be released.

"I didn't owe you that then."

Then? Does that mean she feels like she owes me more now? The thought calms me a little.

"My ex was a shitty man. First, he was loud and angry all the time, and eventually just yelling wasn't enough."

"He hit you," I determine.

"He hit everything but me," she whispers, her head against my chest. "I knew it was only a matter of time before he turned his fists on me or the kids."

Ty Penman just arrowed to the top of my shit list.

Chapter 23

Kendall

Finn held me against him for hours, asking questions I didn't want to answer but felt like I should.

I cried and sobbed, reliving all of that pain and trauma, and when it was time to go get the kids, I felt lighter but emotionally drained. The gods must be looking out for me because the kids were unusually calm this evening, eating, doing homework, and getting baths without an argument.

I put them to bed on time for the first time in as long as I can remember, and now I find myself curled right back up in Finn's arms on the sofa.

The television is on, playing repeats of *Coco Melon* episodes, but neither of us are paying attention to it. When I look up at him, I find that his eyes are closed, and if he wasn't steadily running his fingers through my hair, I'd guess he was asleep with how little he's moved in the last fifteen minutes.

Movement catches the corner of my eye. Looking over, I see Kayleigh standing there with a wide grin on her face. Before I can lift myself off Finn's chest, she darts away with a giggle.

Having to explain and answer questions about what's going on between Finn and me from my kids would be impossible because I don't have a clue myself. I can't tell my children that sometimes adults seek comfort in each other but that doesn't mean they're together.

I climb off the couch, and shuffle away from Finn without a word.

There's no way I can get involved with another man. All my life, I've only ever been disappointed with them, and now I have my kids to consider. They see everything, hear everything, and ask way too many questions. I stuck around with Ty for much longer than I ever should have, and vowed when he left that I'd never put myself in a situation where my kids could be hurt physically or emotionally. The giggle that followed Kayleigh back to our shared bedroom tells me that she's not upset with her discovery. That says she likes the man, which also means when we leave him behind, she's already going to be upset. I've already broken that vow I made years ago.

I want to cry again as I walk to the bedroom because I know I'm going to miss him too. For all of his grumbling and the looks he gives the messes the kids leave behind, I catch him smiling too. He grins when Knox mispronounces a word. He even chuckled tonight when Kason shoved past him to be the first in the bath. Those are just things with the kids, and I refuse to think about the things he does to me. I can't focus on the butterflies in my belly when he looks at me, nor how he felt Saturday night after my little living room strip tease.

Thankfully, Kayleigh is pretending to be asleep when I close myself inside our room. It means I get to postpone all of those questions, but I have no doubt she'll hit me with them first thing in the morning.

***

Although I fell asleep fast last night, I don't feel rested.

I jolt in the bed when I notice Kayleigh's is empty.

There's a difference in Finn staying here while I work and being responsible for sleeping kids, and being swarmed by three of them first thing in the morning.

I change clothes quickly, dressing for the day before heading out of the room. I cringe at the sight of Kason and Knox's open bedroom door. One glance tells me that they're elsewhere in the condo.

Despite imagining walking in and seeing them swinging from the light fixtures, I find Finn standing tall in sweats and a t-shirt, plating food for them. All three kids are sitting at the table, legs swinging as they wait to eat.

I just stand and watch them for a minute, wondering what he had to threaten them with to keep them from bouncing off the walls. My kids are utter chaos in the mornings, their energy reserves refreshed from sleep and uncontrollable. Since I don't want them acting out at school, I allow them to burn some of that off before leaving for the day.

Knox's eyes grow wide as he watches Finn add a few pieces of cantaloupe to the plates.

I let myself dream for the briefest of moments at the picture before me. I let myself imagine Finn being their father and having the prefect life I always dreamed of, rather than the shitty ex whose troubles still continue to taint our lives.

It disappears almost as quickly as it arrives because my life will never be picture-perfect. Having a man like Finn inside of me isn't the same as keeping him in my life. Taking my body is one thing. Him stepping up as the father these kids have never had is another, and wishing for anything that resembles it would be fruitless. I disappoint myself too much already as it is.

"What's all this?" I ask, walking further into the room.

Finn grins at me, telling me that he knew I was near.

"Breakfast," he says, adding a couple of strawberries to the plates.

"You made all this?" I point to the eggs, fruit, and sausage on the plates.

"No. They didn't want tofu, so we compromised." He points to a bag on the counter from a nearby diner.

He may not have cooked, but he ordered it all and had it delivered, and that's just as awesome.

"You didn't have to do this."

"They wanted frozen chicken nuggets," he grumbles. "Who eats nasty frozen chicken nuggets?"

I scoff. "No one eats frozen chicken nuggets, Finn. I heat them up first."

The kids giggle, and it earns a smile from the man dishing out the food.

He turns his head, leaning in for a kiss, and I skate around him, denying him what I desperately want as well. We have a long damn talk ahead of us, and it's not going to end with our mouths locked on each other. Besides, my kids are right there, bearing witness to all of it.

"Knox isn't going to eat that," I whisper as I reach for the bread and peanut butter.

"Just watch," he says, somehow carrying all three plates to the table without spilling a drop.

"This has the super powder on it?" Knox asks as he picks up his fork and nudges a piece of sausage across his plate.

"I added double," Finn says, walking away.

My mouth falls open when Knox spears the sausage link and bites half of it off. He chews for a second before saying, "I'm going to be as big and strong as Finn!"

I smile, but tears sting my eyes. What I was worried about with Kayleigh last night has already filtered over to Knox as well.

I'm glad Kason is still holding out, watching Finn with a sneer as he eats.

Sensing my unease, Finn does something I never expected him to—he gives me space.

"I've got some calls to make," he says, his hand brushing my hip.

I'm glad the contact is below the counter line so the kids can't see. I nod.

"Thank you for feeding them."

He gives me a quick nod before leaving the room.

I set about packing lunches for them, making a mental note to get something a little more substantial than a banana and bread since Knox may be expanding his palette. Due to kids with peanut allergies in school, I could never send his favorite sandwich.

The kids chatter among themselves while they eat, and I may be losing my mind when they each stand and carry their plate to the sink. It's not like I don't have them do this daily, but this morning, I don't even have to remind them.

"Teeth," I tell them as they walk out of the room.

Despite sleeping late this morning, we're still able to leave the condo on time.

As eager as I am to get back to the condo after dropping the kids off, I'm equally hesitant to be alone with Finn. We need to talk. We both know it, and I'm wanting to avoid that conversation.

I sit in the parking garage of the building and search for houses on my phone. The longer we stay with him, the harder it's going to be to leave, and I already find myself wanting to cling to the man. He's stable and kind and unlike anyone I've had the pleasure of spending time with in the past. He's rugged and gruff, but not an actual bad guy which has always been my kryptonite. Those traits are what kept me taking Ty back. I've always had a thing for the bad boy.

Finn is all of that but not at the same time. The man is a damn anomaly, and that can't bode well for anyone. With Ty, I knew what to expect. Finn is a mystery.

And that's a problem as well because I've always been addicted to puzzles.

Chapter 24

Finnegan

The minute she leaves with the kids, I'm on the phone.

"It's too fucking early," Wren grouses when he answers the phone. "Plus, Whitney's back. I'm not even working today. Shoot me an email, and I'll—"

"You were fucking wrong," I snap, uncaring what his plans are for the day.

He chuckles, the sound grating on my nerves even more today than it did yesterday.

"I'm never wrong."

"I need all the info on Ty Penman," I snap.

"And I told you—"

"You told me she was safe, and yet I come home yesterday just as Adrian Larrick and Brant Jesper are leaving my condo, Wren. She isn't fucking safe."

"What?" he snaps, and I hear his covers rustling.

"Baby, what's wrong?" Whitney asks, her voice equally concerned.

"Can you bring me my laptop?" he asks, the phone held away from his mouth. "What time?"

"They were here midmorning. I left work and came straight home."

"Thanks, baby. Put on some clothes. I have work to do."

The sound of a hand slapping flesh echoes through the line, and I clench my teeth. If he's fucking around when I need him, I'll spit fucking nails.

But before I can tell him as much, I hear his fingers working over his keyboard.

"She said that Ty took something from Keres, and he's racking up a debt daily that they expect him to pay."

"The jump drive," Wren says. "At least that's what dark web chatters says it is. A client list maybe?"

"I don't have a clue. Maybe you can track Ty down and we can offer him up."

"Can't," Wren says. "The feds have him."

"What?"

"Want to come up? I'm not talking about this shit over the phone."

"You programmed these phones. I thought they were—"

"I'm not talking about it over the phone," he repeats. "Plus, I don't have more for you, really. Nothing that would help with your problem. I told you Keres is fucking untouchable."

"I need you to dig deeper. This isn't about some contract with the feds, Wren. We're talking about my girl."

There's silence on the line as he considers what I'm saying.

"Give me a couple hours," he says, and the line goes dead.

I shower and dress for the day, but I have no damn plans to go to work. Maybe I can convince Kendall to come with me. My skin is already itchy for letting her take the kids to school without some form of detail or insisting that I take them.

She's not in her room when I walk out of mine, and my heart starts to pound. I'm heading back down the hall to get my phone to have Wren track her when the front door opens.

I release a sigh of relief when I see her. Her brow draws together when she sees me standing in the middle of the hallway.

"Are you being nosy?" She asks it with a smile, but I hear the hint of annoyance in her tone.

I look to my right, realizing I'm standing right in front of her bedroom.

"I was on my way to grab my phone to call you when you opened the door. Did you have more than dropping the kids off on your schedule this morning?"

Her eyes narrow. "Policing what I do now as well?"

Why is she so riled up this morning?

"You had two criminal thugs come to the door yesterday, Kendall. I was worried when school drop-off took longer than normal."

Her face falls, her head shaking. "I'm being a bitch. I'm sorry. You got the kids breakfast for me this morning."

"I got the kids breakfast for them," I correct.

"Well, it helped me out."

"A secondary concern."

I don't know why I say it, but I need her to know that as much as I love being with her, spending time with her, talking with her, flirting with her, all the things *with her*, I also understand that she's a package deal. I went from wanting to spend time inside her to wanting to protect her and her kids about the minute I realized that she was in trouble with St. Louis's deadliest motorcycle club.

"I want you to come to work with me," I tell her as she just stands there, trying to figure out what my angle is.

"I can't. I have too many things to do."

"And I have a very busy day at work, and I'm not leaving without you."

"I still haven't showered. I need to work out."

"How about I give you a workout in the shower? Two birds, one stone."

And as much as I want to protect her, the animal needing to claim her is never ever far either.

She chuckles as if I told a corny joke, but her face freezes, her smile fading away when she sees that there's less joke to my words than she initially realized.

"You've already showered," she says, pointing to my still damp hair.

I give her a wide grin. If she's actually considering my offer, I'll spend all day in the damn bathroom with this woman.

"I forgot to wash my feet," I tease.

"I'm still embarrassed about the fake bomb, Finn. I can't spend the entire day at work with you."

"They all like you," I remind her. "Pam has a panic button she could've pressed if she thought she was really in any danger."

I watch as she chews on the inside of her cheek, trying to decide what to do.

"I wasn't joking about needing a workout and a shower. I won't feel normal all day if I don't."

"And I wasn't joking about the in-shower workout either."

Her eyes sparkle, and that tells me all I need to know.

Work can wait.
It's time to get soapy.

Chapter 25

Kendall

I blink at the man, fighting a smile.

Despite Kayleigh catching us snuggled together on the couch last night, I don't feel an ounce of shame for being that close to him. There's just a conversation I need to have with my kids. I need to let them know on some level what's going on between Finn and me, but at the same time, I don't really know.

He was there for me when I was upset after Adrian and Brant left, and he's primed for sex at the drop of a hat. Both things I can appreciate.

But that doesn't indicate anything other than he's horny and a decent guy for comforting a crying woman.

Reading into it more than what it actually is can be very bad for me. I have three kids to worry about, and letting my heart run away with ideas of this man being more than nice and able to hand out orgasms like he aced a class on it in college is dangerous.

As much as I consider myself an adult, I don't want those tiny fantasies crushed, so I don't open my mouth to have a serious conversation with him. How can I when he's grinning at me with the promise of those intense orgasms glinting in his pretty green eyes?

Deciding a conversation after is my best bet, I place my hand in his and let him guide me to his en suite bathroom.

He leans past me, turning on the showerhead and pressing his lips to my neck before whispering, "Get naked."

His warm breath skates over my skin and I feel sexier than I ever should in leggings and a loose fitting t-shirt.

The heat of his body leaves me, but I don't look over my shoulder to see where he's going. I do what he demands, taking my clothes off. I fold them neatly with hands trembling with excitement and place them in a pile on his bathroom counter before stepping under the heated spray of the shower. I groan as the forceful flow hits achy muscles on my back. Not getting a decent night's sleep in as long as I can remember is really taking its toll on my body. If I could find a decent job that didn't require me to work nights, I'd jump on it in a heartbeat.

"Goddamn," Finn whispers as he steps into the shower with me. "The only thing missing from the fantasy I had of this is bubbles teasing your nipples."

I grin at him, trying not to gape at the sight of water droplets clinging to his body. The man is a work of art. He's muscled, dotted with freckles, and dark red hair covers his pecs. My eyes trace the line of that hair down the center of him right to his very erect cock.

My fingers twitch in an effort not to reach out and grab him. Finn is driving this train, and I have every intention of letting him, knowing just how good things are with him when he's bared to his skin.

With a wide grin, he holds up a strip of three condoms before placing them beside his shampoo/bodywash. I grin at the sight of the single bottle. Of course, he's the type of no-nonsense man who would use only one product to take care of all his shower needs.

"I should've pulled my hair up," I say, pointing to the bottle. "If I use that, it will wreck my hair."

"The plan is to get dirty in here. I can run to your shower to get what you need after."

A shiver runs up my spine at the thought of my things sitting right beside his in here, and I shove it away immediately. The man isn't offering to share his space with me forever, just as a consolation for getting dirty with him.

"Now where were we?" he asks, his hands at his sides, eyes roaming over my skin. "Ah, yes, bubbles."

I'm filled with impatience as he squeezes his shampoo/bodywash into his hands, lathering them for a long moment before he touches me. The first brush across my nipples is like a cattle prod to my spine, and I jolt, my sensitive nipple furling tightly.

"Mmm." His sound is low and appreciative as he shows the same attention to my other breast. "Even better than I imagined."

I smile, loving that he's spent time away from me, thinking about doing this with me. It makes it easier to wrap my head around doing the same.

"Feels good," I groan when his entire hand cups my breast, testing the weight in his palm.

"You're fucking perfect. You know that, right?"

I'm far from perfect, but I preen at the compliment.

"I mentioned a workout, and this is going to be more cardio, but I promise a full-body workout. Lips, beautiful."

I lift on the tips of my toes and give him my mouth, groaning when he doesn't waste a second, sweeping his tongue along mine.

The heat of the water at my back does nothing to ward off the goosebumps that pop up along my arms and legs, and God, never in my life has kissing a man felt like this.

That's the dangerous part of it all. He's deadly. His body, his mouth, the skill he uses when he touches me—all of it doesn't bode well for when I have to walk away. I accepted long ago that I could never have a man that not only fucked me right but also treated me right out of the bedroom, or the shower as it may be. Until Finn, I was certain no such creature existed, but here I am, my very own unicorn under the palms of my hands as I trace the muscles of his back.

Instead of sobbing for my imminent loss, I take all that I can from him, tilting my head to the side when his mouth traces the column of my neck, hands gliding over my soap-slicked ass.

His cock pulses against my stomach, just as excited as I am about being in here together.

"Jack me, baby. I have to get the first one out of the way if you want me to fuck you right."

He shifts back, giving me access to his cock, and I bite my bottom lip as I take him in hand. His skin is just as heated as mine, and we both watch as I stroke my hand up and down the length of him. His groans echo off the shower walls as his mouth seeks mine, and I smile against his lips when he jerks in my grip a second before hot cum paints my stomach.

"You weren't joking," I say as he pulls back and reaches for a condom.

"Been needing that since the last time I had you naked," he says, his eyes going a little glossy as he rolls the condom down his obviously sensitive cock.

"You're already ready to go again?" I ask in disbelief.

"Almost," he answers as he sinks to his knees on the hard shower floor.

I open my mouth to say something else, but the thought drifts away on the steam filling the room as his mouth meets my sensitive flesh.

That's the beginning of a very long morning with him. He wasn't being overeager when he brought three condoms in the shower because we used every one of them. He wasn't lying about it being a full-body cardio experience because by the time we turned off the water and stepped out, sweat was mingling with water droplets, and my legs were shaking like I'd just run a marathon.

I rode his cock while he sat on the edge of the tub. I sucked his cock in the same reverse position he licked me and brought me to my first orgasm of the day. He bent me over, forcing me to brace my hands against the wall as he fucked me from behind. The man, lifting me in his arms, urged my legs around his waist and bounced me on his dick like I didn't weigh but a pound.

The sex with him was so damned good that I couldn't look at him as we toweled off, in fear of smiling like an idiot and ruining the moment.

Most importantly, something I'm trying not to read too much into, is the fact that he held me in his arms and kissed me while we both came down.

Good sex I'm certain I can handle.

The sweetness afterward is what's going to be a problem.

I don't argue with him when he insists I join him at his office after we get dressed. Honestly, agreeing to go is twofold. One, I don't want to be in this condo alone, not after the impromptu meeting with the president of the Keres MC, and two, I don't want physical distance between the two of us.

I know this feeling, that little hint of obsession starting to fire up inside of me. I've pushed all those feelings away for years, knowing that they only brought me trouble and heartache, but I just can't seem to fight them fully back where this man is concerned.

So, I know that I'm going to end up doing something stupid, something that's only going to bring on more pain and heartache. Since the ball has already started rolling, I can only pray that my kids don't get caught in the crossfire.

Chapter 26

Finnegan

I'm no stranger to distractions. It seems there's always something popping up while we're working to throw the day off course, but I haven't been interrupted all day. There hasn't been drama knocking on my door or something going down with one of the other guys that would pull my head from my work.

Today, Kendall is my distraction.

Her quietly reading earlier made it to where I couldn't focus.

Her going to Wren's office to visit with Evie got me on my feet following her.

And now, her breathing softly, taking a nap on the sofa in my office is the most distracting of all. She isn't snoring or talking in her sleep. It's the simple fact that she's resting, and I'm not.

Okay, it's not even that I'm not resting because what happened in the shower this morning rejuvenated me so much, I could probably stay awake and be fully functioning for days and be fine.

She's on the couch alone when I should have her resting in my arms. I ache for the brush of her hair on my face while I have her back pulled against my chest. I could even get behind her breath washing over my throat if she were lying on my chest, leg thrown over the top of mine. I need to touch her, feel her skin against mine while we're not actively engaged in sex. I don't push for it because she seems like the skittish type, but I long for something more.

I could sit here, since I can't seem to focus on anything else but her, and go over the many reasons why that's the worst idea in the world, but all I can do is wonder when things changed and what it is about her that has me feeling this way.

The sex is out-of-the-world good, literally the best I've ever had, but I've never wanted to take a woman home to meet my parents. I've never pictured what a vacation would look like, especially not one where three kids were included. I never imagined wanting to move out of my luxury condo and into a regular house with a yard. Hell, yesterday, I thought about a damn dog and cute names for the nonexistent thing.

I well and truly lost my damn mind, and there's only one person in the entire world to blame for it.

Kendall Stewart has me tied in knots, and the scariest thing is, I'm not sure I want to be unraveled.

I press my hand to my face as a gentle knock comes to the door. I stand in a rush to answer it because Kendall has to be exhausted if she's sleeping in the middle of the day. She jolts on the couch, her eyes blinking up at me before I can answer it.

She apologizes softly as she sits up, and I answer the door.

Deacon, my boss, looks at me before looking over my shoulder to see Kendall there.

When he frowns, I know what he's thinking. Hell, I know what it looks like. Kendall is disheveled, her hair matted on the side she was sleeping on.

"You woke her up," I say in a low voice, explaining away where his mind went.

"We have a job," he says.

"I have to take her to get her kids." I look down at my watch. "It's less than half an hour before they're released from school for the day."

Deacon frowns.

"I can go get them on my own," Kendall offers.

Deacon and I both look at her, letting her know that's not a good idea. Deacon wouldn't force her to go with someone from the office, but she's not going to get as lucky with me.

"I think it's best if someone goes with you," I tell her, hoping she doesn't get all riled up.

It would only turn me on, and I don't think Deacon would be too impressed if I spring an erection with him nearby.

"You have to work," she says, standing from the sofa and running her hands down the front of her to straighten her clothes. "I'll be fine."

"Wren is available," Deacon offers.

Kendall looks between the two of us before quickly nodding in agreement.

Deacon looks between the two of us again. "Five minutes."

He walks away, and I catch Kendall before she can follow him out of the room. She blinks up at me, her eyes still tired despite her nap. There are a million things I can say, each one as terrifying as the next, so I don't say a word. I simply lower my mouth down to hers and kiss her lips.

The kiss is soft and sweet, full of promises I don't know if I'll ever have the courage to say out loud, and it ends too quickly. She pats my chest, kisses my cheek, and walks away.

I spend the next couple of minutes fighting an erection before I'm able to meet Deacon in the breakroom. By the time I get there, Wren and Kendall are gone.

"Wren is going to bring them back here, so don't worry."

I nod at him, walking toward the elevator.

***

"A residence?" I ask as we pull up in front of an old rundown house. From the passenger seat, I peer up at the house in desperate need of a lot of work.

"It all checks out," Deacon says as he shifts the truck into park. "Financials and all."

Blackbridge is the best at what they do. If we take a job, it's because there's no one else around as capable as we are. It also means Deacon is able to charge a mint for every single call we get.

"You're sure?" I verify, because this house doesn't look like it belongs to someone we'd normally work with.

"Yep. It belongs to some rich social media guy. People swear the house is haunted, so he bought it for pennies on the dollar and plans to film some *YouTube* series in it or something."

"And you brought me along to fight off ghosts?"

I don't believe in ghosts, so it doesn't bother me, but I'd much rather be in the truck with Kendall going to pick up the kids. Man, has my life changed from not even considering kids to wanting to be around them.

"He found an old safe in the basement. Can't get into it. That's why you're here, dummy."

"Wait," I say, racking my brain for why all of this sounds so familiar. "This job is for Mystery Man Medano?"

Deacon sighs, rolling his eyes and shaking his head at the same time. "Not you, too."

"Me too what?"

"Anna is obsessed with watching this guy's *YouTube* station. Apparently, you are too."

"I'm not," I say with an indignant huff. "If I'm obsessed with anything on *YouTube*, it's gun range videos."

That and you can never go wrong with funny cat videos, but I'd never tell my boss that.

"Good, because I don't need you going all fangirl over this guy. I'm already going to catch shit for not letting Anna tag along. I'll probably be sleeping on the couch for a week as it is."

I chuckle, knowing better. Anna may be a little disappointed, but I doubt she'll be mad enough to sleep alone. That punishes the both of them. As we walk up the front path, I can see why Deacon doesn't want his wife here. The yard is overgrown, probably teeming with all sorts of things that bite. The front porch looks like it will collapse at any given point.

It's just unsafe.

"Look," Deacon says, pointing to the area immediately off to the right.

"Are those fake weeds?"

"Yep," Deacon confirms. "Seems there might be a little staging going on here."

"Imagine the disappointed subscribers," I mutter, wanting to get this job done so I can get back to Kendall.

Deacon huffs. "Nothing on social media is exactly as it appears."

I tighten my grip on my tool bag as Deacon bangs his fist on the warped screen door. I guess you can't even call it a screen door as it doesn't have any screen in it.

"Are we up to date on our tetanus shots?"

"Yes," Deacon says without humor in his voice. "I made Jude verify earlier after Wren pulled the address up on satellite view."

"My man!" a guy says when he pulls open the door.

He can't be any younger than twenty-two, and he's the definition of dude-bro from his hipster clothes to his haircut, the one that looks both shaggy and somehow expensive at the same time. His shirt is too small for his frame, showcasing a tribal tattoo on his bicep. I snort at the sight of it, betting this guy whined to the artist the whole time he was getting it done. He's all gym muscle, probably never seen a day of physical hard work in his life.

Deacon holds out his hand to shake, but the guy claps it and pulls Deacon to his chest, smacking him on the back in a familiarity I know isn't actually there.

Deacon backs away, that tiny muscle above his right eye twitching as he puts some distance between the two of them.

The guy inches toward me, and unlike my boss, I don't have the patience.

"Touch me and die." My threat is as thick as my accent, but the guy just grins in my direction like I've told a joke.

"Come on in but watch your step. There's camera equipment and cords all over the place."

I follow Deacon, my eyes darting across the room. The air is thick with recently burned wood, and I see another area of staging when I glance in the living area to see the walls around the fireplace scorched. The lengths some people will go to get views, but I guess you have to get creative when it's your source of income. At least he's doing something more than what I know a lot of middle-aged guys are doing—dancing and taking their clothes off for all the thirsty women on the internet.

I grin, thinking of ways to tease Deacon about Anna following this young guy and being obsessed with his videos. I have no doubt the dude-bro does videos without his shirt on.

"The safe is down in the basement, but first, the paperwork we discussed."

Deacon takes a clipboard from the guy, and I take another one.

Reading through the form, I see that we're agreeing to no claim of the video or royalties that might be earned for the video.

I look to Deacon. "I'm going to be recorded?"

Deacon smiles, knowing it will irritate me. "That's the agreement."

I scowl. "And what are you charging?"

"Ten thousand," Deacon says with a smile. "And financials have already been taken care of."

Translation—the job has already been paid for, now sign the paper, and get to work.

Deacon signs, and I do the same.

"What do you suspect to make off this?" Deacon asks as we descend the rickety stairs into the basement.

Dude-bro turns and grins when he clears the last steps. "More than I paid."

He points to the corner of the room, and I want to cry with the damage done to the antique safe. I can tell it's over a hundred years old just by the brand and design, and this is one of those kinds of safes that the house was probably built around rather than it being carried into the house after construction.

BRANDON D. GILES is printed across the top to indicate who the original owner was.

"What in the world did you do to it?" I ask as I walk closer, lifting my hand to trace some of the damage.

"All sorts of things," the guy says with laughter in his voice. "I have personal protective equipment for you over here. I won't be able to post videos if you aren't wearing it. *YouTube* has stupid rules about safety."

Frowning, I turn around and face the guy as I drop my tool bag and open it. I pull out my safety glasses and hardhat, donning both before glancing at Deacon. I give him a look that makes my dissatisfaction clear before turning back to the mangled safe. It looks like they tried to set it on fire, using some sort of explosives if the dent in the concrete under it is any indication. There are scratches all over it. The brand logo is nearly unreadable.

"Maybe keep the cussing to a minimum. The fewer bleeps I have, the better ratings I get."

I'd never cuss at a safe, but I have a few choice words for this guy.

Taking a deep breath, I whisper an apology to the safe because it feels like it's warranted. I have great respect for these things. They've survived the Great Depression, several wars, and even now, it's holding strong against a guy willing to tear it to pieces to find out what's inside.

Getting on my knees, I run my hands all over the thing before sweeping my fingers up the underside. There, my fingertips run over a small metal tag, and I have to grin.

I pull out a small mirror from my kit and hold it so I can read the combination. It's easy to memorize, and in a matter of seconds, and much to dude-bro's chagrin, I twirl the lock and grin when the locks give way.

I back out of the way before opening the door because the reveal of what's inside isn't up to me. It's not what we were hired for.

"That fucking easy?" he snaps, and I'm waiting, mentally daring him to argue the price with Deacon. "We saw that code, looked at it the same way and the numbers didn't work for us."

"Did you think to consider they were backward in your mirror?"

The guy narrows his eyes, and I pause, thinking he's going to get pissy, but he tilts his head back and barks out a laugh that echoes around the concrete room.

I begin to pack up my things, taking off my hard hat and glasses, stowing both in my tool kit.

"Are you guys going to stick around to see what's inside?" dude-bro asks as we start back up the stairs.

"No thanks," Deacon answers.

"Did you see what they did to that thing?" I complain as we walk toward his truck.

"It's a shame," he says as I toss my bag in the back of his pickup.

"That safe is probably worth more than whatever he's going to find inside," I mutter.

"Probably, but it's good for a few million views, I'm sure."

I brood in the front seat on the way back to the office, texting Wren to make sure Kendall and the kids are okay, getting further annoyed when he responds back with a simple yes.

The man is all about the details one minute, and the next, he doesn't offer any more than what's asked. The only consistent part about it is that he does whichever he knows will annoy you the most at the time.

Chapter 27

Kendall

"Maybe this was a bad idea," I mutter to Wren as we walk into the Blackbridge office and the kids scatter in all directions like they've been here a million times.

Wren chuckles. "Naw, the guys love kids. The only one who doesn't really like kids—"

He snaps his jaw shut, but his eyes darting away from me answers the question I don't even have to ask. Finn doesn't like kids, and he's not here. That's what Wren was going to say, and that, ladies and gentlemen, is the sound of the other shoe dropping.

Great sex with the man is just that, great, but I don't come alone. I'm a package with three very wild, very boisterous kids. Not liking my kids is a sure sign we're not compatible.

"He hasn't said he doesn't like your kids specifically," Wren says, reading my face. "It's just he's never—"

"It's fine," I tell him, even though it's anything but fine.

I'm more upset about the loss of what I let myself imagine having with the man than anything else. He's allowed his own viewpoint. It's fine that he doesn't want kids or a woman who comes tied to three.

I'm upset at myself for letting my mind even picture a future. I blame the sight of him fixing their plates when they insisted on chicken nuggets. I read too much into him persuading Knox to eat meat. I was too hopeful at the sound of Kayleigh's giggle when she walked out and found us cuddled on the couch.

I let myself dream, and I should know better.

Dreams are meant for people other than me, for those who haven't been crushed under reality over and over.

"Kendall, please—"

"Wow!" Knox screams as he runs to Jude, a man I'd met here before. "What's that?"

I let the interaction between my youngest son and the other man distract me, because if I don't, I may cry, and that's not a conversation I want to have with Wren or my kids.

"It's a gas mask," Jude says, holding the thing out so Knox can get a better look.

"For your brother's stinking toots?" Knox asks, his nose scrunching up.

"More like deadly bombs while facing enemy combatants."

Knox frowns. "Deadly?"

"These are meant to protect," Jude says, his eyes widening when Knox's little chin begins to quiver.

Knox looks in my direction. "I don't have one. Am I going to die?"

I narrow my eyes at Jude, judging the man for not considering what he says despite not having kids himself.

"You don't need—"

"Holy cow! Is that a real bomb?!"

I spin around. Kason is standing in front of Kit Riggs, the weapons expert for Blackbridge Security, who has a fucking grenade in his hand.

"Seriously!" I yelp, rushing to my son when Kit stupidly holds the thing out for Kason to take.

"Just don't pull the pin," Kit warns, and of course my son, the one to test every single damn boundary put before him, pulls the fucking pin.

I lunge, but I'm not fast enough. The pin drops to the ground, and I'm still several feet away.

Nothing matters, not my feelings, not the pain I'm going to feel. Those dreams I barely let filter into my head are meaningless because it's all about to be over.

The grenade bounces in Kason's hand and he squeals, a thrilled sound because the kid doesn't understand he's about to die, but then it transforms as it falls to the ground.

Skidding to a halt right in front of him, we all look down, and the damn thing is literally a transformer. Once in the shape of a grenade, it's now a little army tank.

"Holy fuck," I gasp, my heart about to pound out of my chest.

"Fuck is a bad word, Mom," Knox supplies helpfully, drawing a chuckle from several men in the room.

Kit looks up at me. "Did you really think I'd hand him a real grenade?"

I gape at him. "Knox is upset because he's now worried about Armageddon, so yeah, I thought it was possible you'd hand my seven-year-old a grenade."

"I have two older brothers who have three boys each. I'm not an idiot," Kit says, his brow drawing tighter when his explanation doesn't calm my racing heart any. "Kendall, I'm sorry."

I nod because it's all I can manage right now.

"Where's Finn?" Kayleigh yells from the other side of the room.

"Did you want cream and sugar?" Wren asks my little girl as he pulls a cup from the single cup coffee machine.

"What are you giving her?" I snap as I walk closer.

"A cappuccino," he says, winking at me.

"A—"

Wren holds up the used coffee pod, and at least he's not a complete idiot like the others because it reads *HOT COCOA* on the top.

"I like marshmallows in my cappuccino," Kayleigh says with a wide grin, clearly in on the joke.

"Coming right up," Wren says with a wink in my direction and a wide grin for my little girl.

"Momma," Kayleigh says, turning to me while Wren does her bidding. I swear the child is an expert at batting her eyes to get what she wants. She's going to give me hell when she gets older. I just know it. "Where's Finn?"

"Finn is cracking a safe," Wren answers, and I'm glad, because working was all I'd be able to offer the guy.

"Did you say cracking a safe?" Kason asks, running across the room.

"I did," Wren answers. "Are you familiar with Mystery Man Medano?"

Kason squeals, bouncing up and down on his feet. "I love him. Is Finn cracking his safe?"

Excitement curls around every part of my child. I had this conversation with Finn at the gym a while back when he told me he cracks safes. Kason is obsessed with the guy, watching his *YouTube* videos on repeat until he comes out with a new one.

"He is," Wren answers, and Kason grows calm.

"My mom's boyfriend is cracking Mystery Man Medano's safe in that haunted house?" Kason's eyes go wide, an even bigger smile on his face as he turns to me.

"He's not my-we're not-that's—" I stammer, unsure what to actually say.

I'm still stuck wondering what I did to give Kason the idea that Finn and I were an item when Kason squeals like he did two years ago when he got his first bike for Christmas.

"Mom! Do you have any idea how cool that is? Is he going to be on the video?" Kason turns back to Wren who winks at me before looking back down at my excited son. "Do you have *YouTube*? Can we check to see if it's uploaded? Mom can we go home and get my tablet?"

"We're not going home just yet," I tell him, not giving him the full reason why. Thankfully, the kids were at school yesterday when Adrian made his little house visit, and I was calm enough to shove my fear down by the time they got out of school. "We're meeting Finn here."

Kason listens to my explanation and turns back to Wren. "Do you have a computer?"

Wren looks up at me, not answering until I nod.

"I do have a computer. It's in my office."

Mentioning his office reminds me of Puff Daddy.

"Wren, I don't—"

"I'll grab my laptop and meet you on the couch," he says, and smiles when Kayleigh, forgetting her hot cocoa, and Kason book it to the sofa.

"Thanks," I tell him.

"No problem."

I carry the deserted cocoa to Kayleigh, who smiles with a roll of her eyes at herself for forgetting about it before thanking me for bringing it to her.

"Are you excited for the Mystery Man video?" Jude asks Knox who is still eyeing the gas mask like he plans to shove it down his pants just so he's safe when the enemy combatants use poisonous gas on him.

"All that stuff is fake," my youngest mutters.

Jude looks up at me and I just have to shake my head. The kid picks and chooses what he believes, and I'd be concerned about his doomsday attitude if he also wasn't scared about getting shrunk by a machine and ending up stuck in the yard. That fear made me realize that maybe five is still too young for him to enjoy the same movies I liked as a kid. Thank God, I didn't let him watch *Stand By Me*. He'd probably never go swimming again.

Kason and Kayleigh have watched Mystery Man Medano open that safe probably a hundred times, and they're so engrossed watching it over and over, that they both miss Finn's arrival to the office.

"Hey," Finn says, walking toward me as if I'm his single focus, but he stops short of kissing me, giving me an awkward pat on the back like a weirdo before stepping away. "What are they watching?"

His accent drifts through the air, reaching the kids. Kason snaps his eyes up first, nearly shoving the laptop to the floor in his bid to get off the sofa. Thankfully, Kayleigh catches it before I'd be forced to buy Wren a new one. I get the idea that I wouldn't get away with a purchasing a regular three hundred dollar one from Target to make up for it.

"Finn! You met the Mystery Man?" Kason asks, running up and stopping so close to Finn's legs that he has to hold his head way back to look in the man's eyes.

"I did."

The unpleasantness playing in Finn's eyes tells me that it wasn't the best meeting.

"I saw you on the video!" Kason says. "You're a movie star now!"

"I guess so," Finn agrees, winking at me when he notices me smiling at their interaction.

"Did you see what was inside?"

"I didn't stick around for that part."

"Come look," Kason says, and I nearly fall when my son grabs Finn's hand and all but drags him across the room.

"It was just some papers," Kayleigh says, ruining the surprise.

Kason sneers at her but doesn't hesitate to turn the laptop so Finn can watch himself find the combination on the safe and quickly, without flare, open the thing up.

"Just paperwork?" Finn asks, a satisfied grin on his face.

"Stocks and bonds dating back before World War I," Wren clarifies.

"No shi—really?" Finn quickly corrects, his eyes darting to me in apology.

I want to laugh, to tell him that Jude terrified Knox with death talk and Kit handed out a grenade, but I'm stuck watching the man who Wren all but said didn't like kids, wondering if that's the case, why is he smiling at my kids, as they tell him the details of the video despite him being there for most of it, with patience.

Chapter 28

Finnegan

"If you're waiting for me to tell you you're the greatest thing on the internet, it's not going to happen," I mutter, walking around my condo, picking up toys.

"That wouldn't even help, but feel free to express those opinions," Wren says with glee.

"I need for you to make it stop."

"I can't. You saw what happened with Flynn and Remington. Plus, if you didn't want the attention, why did you lift your shirt on camera?"

"It was hot as fuck in that basement, asshole," I snarl. "I was wiping sweat away. I didn't even realize I did it until I watched that stupid video."

"Now you're an internet sensation. Deacon and Pam should be the ones angry, not you. They're the ones having to wade through another wave of calls for ridiculous jobs. You wouldn't believe the women calling about you cracking their safes, and I won't go into detail the mentions of cobweb removal."

"I know you have the ability to wipe *#BlackbridgeSpecial* from the internet."

It's been a week since I opened that damn safe, and it took all of three hours of it going live for shit to hit the fan.

"I can't do it. Don't you think I've been asked by several people already?"

I huff my disappointment, knowing that if Wren was able to rid the internet of the stupid hashtag, Deacon would've insisted he do it long before now. There's busy and then there's too busy. We topped too busy months ago, and things haven't slowed down since.

"Plus, I have bigger things to worry about."

"Yeah? And what could you possibly be worried about?"

"Do you know how hard it is to convince Whitney to have kids?"

This information stops me dead in my tracks on the way to the boys' room to put away a bucket of Legos.

"I didn't know you were even thinking of having kids."

"That's the whole point. I got fucking baby fever out of nowhere. One minute, I'm making Kayleigh hot cocoa at the office and the next, I have thoughts like having one of these little things all the time doesn't seem so bad. By the time I made it home, I was in full daddy mode and not like my normal *call me daddy* mode, like real, let's have a fucking baby daddy mode."

"That sounds complicated."

"Not really. The convincing has been fun. Now we have to wait for the birth control to be out of her system, but I tell you man, I'm going to fill her—"

"No," I snap. "I don't want to hear about you filling anything up. I have to go."

I end the call just as I hear Kendall's key in the front door lock, and I can't imagine what I look like, standing in the middle of the hall with a scowl on my face, holding a bucket of toys.

"You left again," I hiss, my cock already hard at reminding her that she's not supposed to leave without me.

I toss the toys in the boys' room, thinking they can clean the mess when they get home because I have other things to worry about, the first, reiterating to my woman that Keres is still a danger despite us not having heard anything from them in the week since their last visit to the condo.

"I had to take the kids to school. You were sleeping so soundly, I didn't want to wake you."

I've slept soundly for a full week because Kendall has taken to sneaking into my room after the kids go to sleep. She wears me out, then falls asleep in my arms. It's been utter heaven.

"Besides," she continues. "I'm going to have to leave the house alone when I go back to work."

I barely keep the snarl from my face. She took the last weekend off, and I had stupidly let myself imagine that she quit her job at The Kitten's Cream. I know she hasn't done shit with the bag of panties I saw spread out on my dining room table. I guess maybe I should've asked instead of assuming.

I prowl closer to her, not bothering to hide the outline of my thickening cock in my sweats.

"I'm sleeping so good because your pussy is the best medicine. I'm—"

"So, you're saying it puts you to sleep?" She rolls her eyes. "If you don't like it then—"

She squeals, a perfect, happy sound followed by a chuckle when I lift her off her feet.

"Your tight pussy grips my cock like a fist and drains me dry. You literally suck the life out of me. It leaves me sated and utterly exhausted. Holding you at night is the best thing I've ever had, Kendall."

Her eyes dart between mine, and I can still see that wall she has there. The only time it drops and she lets me in is when she's naked and we're minutes away from getting dirty. If she's wearing clothes or not in my bed, she's all caged up again, and I don't know how to fix that.

"If you leave without me again before the shit with your ex is solved, I'm going to spank your ass."

She shakes her head. "Can't do that. I don't want marks on my ass when I go back to work."

"Why are you going back to work?" I ask, lowering her back to the ground because I'm the one that needs a little space right now.

She laughs like I told a joke, but then her face softens when she sees that I'm not finding any of this humorous.

"I have to work, Finn. The Kitten is the best place to earn quick money. I need to move out."

"What?"

"I'm sure you want your space back. You looked beyond annoyed when I walked in with that bucket of toys in your hand."

I didn't know she was planning on moving still. I know it's only been a week in my bed, but fuck, I was ready to ask her to move her shit into my room permanently.

"I was annoyed, but not at picking up after the kids. I was irritated that you left alone again this morning. I'm agitated that some of the people who saw the viral video of that damn safe cracking have now figured out where we live."

"We?" she asks, her brows drawn together in confusion.

"Me and the guys. We have legit fucking stalkers now. That's why they locked down the floor, requiring the key card here."

"That also makes me safe from Adrian and Brant."

"If you're here, you're safe," I clarify. "If you leave, they can grab you in the parking garage."

"I won't be scared forever," she snaps, as if she's angrier about that fear than me feeding into it by wanting her with someone when she leaves.

"Baby," I whisper, closing the distance between the two of us. I cup her jaw so she can't look away from me which is her MO anytime I try to get serious or talk about the future. This woman is the queen of shutting that shit down. She usually does it by crawling in my lap and grinding on my dick, but that's not really possible since we're both standing up. "I don't want you to be scared, but sometimes bravery is stupid, too."

Her eyes soften only for a second before she pulls away.

"I don't need an escort to drop off and pick up the kids."

I want to growl at her, demand she stop being so stubborn, but maybe I'm the one overreacting now.

I won't tell her to think of her kids' safety because fuck, that seems like I would be playing on her love for them, and there's nothing worse than someone using children as pawns, but I'm legit worried for her. I've seen things and read reports of the brutality that Keres is capable of, and if she's right about Adrian still looking for Ty Penman after all these years, then that fear is warranted.

"Okay," I agree even though I don't feel like it's the right thing to do.

I've learned enough about Kendall to know that she doesn't back down. She doubles down, and going by the look in her eyes, this subject won't be the one she finally caves on.

"What are your plans for the day?"

"Cleaning this disaster area," she says, looking between the kitchen and living room. "This afternoon, I have an appointment to go look at a house."

"Today?" The words come out snappy, filled with disbelief.

"I said I was looking for a place."

"But I thought you were a ways away from being able to buy."

"I found something on the southside."

"Where exactly on the southside?"

She narrows her eyes at me as if she's already preparing for my argument.

"Does it matter?"

"Of course, it matters," I snap. "I don't want you living in fucking College Hill or Benton Park West."

"Have you been to either of those neighborhoods lately?"

"I avoid them at all fucking costs. I don't want to get robbed."

"I'm not talking about this."

"What neighborhood?" I growl, keeping my distance, because if I get my hands on her right now, after I fuck some sense into her, I don't think I'd be able to let her go.

"Doesn't matter."

"Let me go with you."

"I don't need your protection," she says, sounding as equally annoyed as I feel angry.

"I'm great at inspecting houses. My dad did that for a living, remember?"

She nods, acknowledging that she's listening now and when we chat in bed before going to sleep.

"I need to do this on my own."

There's that stubborn streak I used to think was so damn hot. Right now, it's a huge pain in my ass.

I want to tell her that she never needs to be alone again. I want to show her the bunk beds I have in the online shopping cart from one of the downtown furniture stores because it's time for Kason and Knox to get a little distance from each other. If anything, so they'll stop chatting and staying up after they're supposed to be in bed because it delays Kendall crawling into my bed. I want to tell her that we need to talk to the kids, so she doesn't have to sneak out every morning before she wakes them up.

But apparently, we aren't even close to being on the same wavelength. I stopped to look at dogs at the animal shelter after Kayleigh mentioned being jealous of a girl at school who got a new puppy, but Kendall is making appointments to get the hell out of Dodge.

I hold my hands up and back away.

"You're choosing to do this on your own." She looks away from me as if she just can't stand the sight of me. "You don't have to. Call me if you want me to tag along later."

I head out of the living room toward my bedroom. It's clear I won't be able to talk any sense into her and standing there and arguing about it will only make things worse. Against all my better judgment, I get dressed and head to work. Kendall, of course, must be hiding in her bedroom so she doesn't have to see me before I leave.

It isn't until my irritation boils over on my drive to the office that I decide that we're going to have to have a serious heart-to-heart. I can't be willing to go all-in with this woman when it seems she has one foot literally out of the door. I need to know exactly where she stands, and maybe her knowing where my head is at with it all will help as well. I'm done skating around each other, letting things progress naturally between the two of us.

It would kill me if she left. My condo will never be the same without Kason's snide comments, Kayleigh's laugh, and Knox running around every morning in his underwear. I've gotten used to it. Hell, I look forward to it.

I'd miss all of them if they weren't there. She needs to know that. If she walks away after that, I guess I can accept it, but I don't want her making these strides because she thinks I need space. Space is the very last thing I want from her.

Chapter 29

Kendall

You're choosing to do this on your own.

Those were Finn's words before he walked away to get ready for work. I hid like the coward I am, wondering why he can't just leave well enough alone. I'm in his bed, in his arms, every night. At least I have been for the last week, and when I'm there, I feel utterly satisfied. With sleep dragging me down after he does wicked things to my body, I can let myself be content, but when he pushes while I'm awake, I can't help but let my heart get involved.

I'm used to doing things on my own. I learned long ago that depending on others just leaves me brokenhearted and alone in the long run. I can't help but open my legs, my arms, and my heart, when he's got that devious look in his eyes, but my legs are the only part of me that should be involved. That's how I feel anyway.

I need to stop reading more into what he does, like helping with the kids and always being there when I need to chat. He's present, something Ty never was, and it's seriously messing with my head. That's why I made the appointment today to look at a house, but as I drive through the neighborhood, I hear Finn's voice in my ears. I didn't tell him the house I found in my price range since I have the urge to get out sooner rather than waiting to save more money for a larger down payment is in Mount Pleasant. It's one of the top five worst neighborhoods in St. Louis, but I can't afford one of the better places and escape with my entire heart intact.

People loiter on street corners, some houses look like they're nearly falling down, and a good majority of the businesses are still closed even decades after the financial crash. It hasn't bounced back like so many other places, and that's beyond concerning.

Traffic to get from the condo to here has taken much more time than I allowed for, and despite having hopes I could attend this meeting and still make it to the kids' school in time for pickup has dwindled to nothing as I pull into the cracked, concrete driveway.

I debate even getting out of the car at the sight of the rundown place. I knew it was going to be a fixer upper just by the ad online. There was no way for the realtor to hide the warped front porch or the stained carpet, but the price is a steal.

With a sigh, I pull out my phone and do something I never thought I'd have to do. I shoot off a text to Finn to see if he can grab the kids from school since I won't make it in time. When he responds that he can, I place the call to the school to add him to the pickup list. The woman on the phone seems a little put out that she'd have to relay a message for me but agrees that she will. Finn's condo is in a nice neighborhood. The school district is supposed to be excellent, yet I catch hell for needing to make a transportation change. Maybe she's having a bad day. It makes me concerned for how things would be at the school my kids would have to attend if I buy this house. As if giving me an ominous warning, a tree branch breaks free from the decayed tree to the left of the porch and falls to the ground.

Still unsure if I should get out of the car, I can't help but think about the people I have in my life.

Ezra moved away, and he's the only living relative I have. My friends peeled off one by one after I spent so much time with Ty. My ex was a total dick to everyone, and looking back, I can now tell that he was systematically separating me from everyone I knew. He either wanted to be able to control me easier or he was just a bitter asshole who didn't want me to have any joy in my life. Since he left, I've focused on the kids and nothing else. Losing friends hurt, and I didn't want to put myself in that position again.

I guess I can count Finn because I know he'd do anything to help me but leaning on him too much will ultimately push him away as well. People who give and never receive don't stick around long, and I don't have anything to offer the man besides sex. Even that will grow old when it's paired with three rambunctious kids taking up more of my time than anything else.

Movement on the porch draws my attention, and I give the realtor a small wave, clenching my jaw at wasting time sitting here because now I have to climb out and look at this house. I lost my window of escape, but I can make this quick. If I only spend a few minutes here, I can possibly still make it to the school for the kids. Finn will be less bitter if I'm able to handle my parental duties on my own.

"Good afternoon," I tell the woman as I climb out of my car.

Her face is pinched as if she regrets being here as well.

"Kendall Stewart," I say, holding out my hand.

She claps mine and I want to pull away at the feel of her clammy skin against mine.

"Megan Dobbs," she says, her voice tight and a little shaky.

Maybe she's new? I don't see well-established realtors taking on a property like this, so that makes sense.

"Shall we?" she asks, sweeping her hand toward the front door.

I've never been in a position to buy a house before, but the woman doesn't mention a thing about the house. She doesn't try to point out the positives or mention the reduced price since it's been on the market for so long.

As soon as I step into the house, I know why.

A man I don't recognize is standing on the far side of the small living room, a handgun pointed in our direction.

"I'm so sorry," the realtor sobs. "They threatened me."

Megan screams when another man comes from out of nowhere, slamming the front door closed right before he grabs her.

I'm stuck, frozen in place as I watch the man zip tie her hands behind her back before stuffing a dirty rag in her mouth and tying a strip of cloth around her head to hold it in place. I watch, stunned, as her tears trail down her face, disappearing into the fabric. That man then disappears into one of the rooms down the hall with Megan.

The only thing I can think of is escaping, and I turn to run out the front door. I know what will happen if I stay. These men will rape us and then murder us. The man with the gun becomes inconsequential because staying is sure death. If I can skip the assault and get right to death, then that's my play.

"Kendall," the man growls. "Run and you'll never see your kids again."

His voice doesn't sound like a threat to my person, but one involving my kids, and it stops me cold, shivers working their way up my spine before radiating down my arms and legs despite the heat in the house.

"Give me your phone," he snaps, evil rolling off of him in waves when I turn back around to face him.

"Now," the other man snaps as he rejoins us in the living room.

With shaky hands and terror filling my bones, I pull my cell from my back pocket and hand it over. The man who tied Megan up steps up to take it, but he doesn't touch me or begin to tie me up.

"She's terrified," the man says, and I try to place his face, but I don't think I've seen him before. His face is covered in pock marks as if he struggled with severe acne as a teen.

"She should be," the man with the gun says. "Now go."

I turn to leave, thinking the man is talking to me, and as overcome with guilt as I am to leave Megan here, I have three kids to think about. I'd like to think I could be a hero and save the day in this situation, but I just can't. I wouldn't fault Megan for leaving me behind either. The problem is it's not even a tough choice.

"Not you, stupid bitch," the man across the room snaps.

The other man smiles at me, cupping my jaw with dirty fingers. "See you soon, sweetheart."

And then he's gone, the dragon tattoo on his neck flashing ominously as he walks out of the house.

"Just you and me, doll. You gonna give me trouble?"

"What do you w-want?" I stammer.

"We'll get to that. Why don't you have a seat?" He points to a nasty couch that wasn't in the online pictures. I never would've showed up if it had been.

I move across the room as he demands, sitting on the couch, but I keep my eyes on him the entire time. I have no way to combat a gun, but I also don't want to be taken by surprise if he lunges at me either.

"How much money do you have?"

I blink up at him, hating the way he has inched closer until he's towering over me. I want to mention that excessive intimidation because just having the gun right now and the threat to my kids is enough to keep me compliant, but he doesn't seem the type to heed the reminder.

"Nothing on me, but a hundred or so in my purse." The cash I have on me is my emergency money in case I break down or end up somewhere I can't use a debit card.

He chuckles, a grating noise that echoes off the walls of the mostly empty house. "So not three hundred grand?"

I stare at him, wondering if he's high.

"Of course not," I snap. "Do you really think I'd be looking at buying this shithole of a house if I had over a quarter of a million dollars?"

A smile slides across his face, and it's misplaced in this moment, but what the hell do I know about crazy?

"What about the jump drive?"

"The what—fucking Ty," I mutter.

"Look, everyone," he says to the empty room. "She's pretty and smart."

The situation just got even more dangerous, going from a robbery or potential sexual assault to this man holding a gun on me because he works for the Keres MC.

"I don't have the jump drive or three hundred grand. I haven't even spoken to Ty in years."

"You two have three kids together. You want me to believe he just took off and hasn't reached out?"

"How much quality time do you get in with your kids?" I snap, growing irrationally angry because Brant and Adrian had the same argument when they showed up at Finn's condo last fucking week.

All humor slides off the guy's face, and I know it doesn't bode well for me.

"I'm going to get what I'm looking for one way or the other, lady. I promise you that."

I stare up at him, my back molars grinding together. I'm going to die today all because my piece of shit ex took something that didn't belong to him. My kids are going to suffer because I made the worst choice in the world when I was a teen. Picking Ty Penman over that stupid football player because he was the bad boy is going to get me killed, and when I break it down that way, I realize I only have myself to blame.

Chapter 30

Finnegan

I tap my fingers on the steering wheel as my truck inches a couple more feet forward.

I want to growl at how inefficient this damn pickup line is. There are much better ways to handle this and stopping the teachers from leaning in to have a conference with parents would be a very good place to start.

Even with the windows rolled up, the sound of chattering children fills the cab of my truck. It doesn't make me want to walk away like it did in the past. Right now, I'm smiling and trying to determine whether any of the loud voices belongs to one of mine. Well, not *mine*, but Kendall's. I mean, mine in the sense that I'm picking them up today.

I inch further, rolling down the passenger side window since I'm next in line.

"Can I help you?" the teacher asks, grinning when she steps up to the side of my vehicle.

She bites the corner of her lip. Women do this a lot when they see me. I'm a big guy, and there's something about that that draws women in. Maybe it's their perception that I'd make a good protector, but honestly, I don't really know. I don't care either. Her perusal, her chatting with each parent is annoying me. The only woman I want with her eyes glued to me is being a stubborn brat and looking at a house to buy. My condo isn't perfect, but I'm also not so attached to the damn thing that I wouldn't consider moving to a bigger place.

"I'm here for Knox, Kason, and Kayleigh Stewart."

Her face falls.

"Kendall called to let you guys know I'd be picking them up."

She looks over her shoulder, her confusion doubled when she turns her face back in my direction.

"I have my ID," I say, picking it up from the console to hand it to her.

"The Stewart kids have already been picked up."

I huff an incredulous laugh. "Impossible. Check again."

She shakes her head. "I loaded them myself, sir."

Her tone grows annoyed, and I get it. No one likes to admit to being wrong.

"Who picked them up?"

"The man she called and said would get them." She looks to the car behind me, and I want to clamp her chin and force her attention back on me. She spent minutes chatting with each parent while every other subsequent parent in line waited. She can damn well give me a few minutes.

"What was his name?" I snap, drawing her eyes back to mine.

"I don't recall."

"Was it Finnegan Jenkins?" She just stares at me. "Did he say his name was Finnegan?"

"I didn't ask his name."

"You didn't ask, or you don't recall?"

Her eyes narrow, and I can tell she's growing more and more agitated and defensive.

"You let three kids get picked up by a fucking stranger and didn't even bother to ask his name?"

"Sir, we don't use that type of language here."

"Fucking unbelievable," I hiss. "What did the car look like?"

"It was a light-colored sedan," she says, but her tone doesn't make me think she's a hundred percent sure about that either.

I pick my phone up.

"You can't use your cell phone in a school zone."

I glare at her as I press Wren's name on my contact list and hold the phone to my ear. With my free hand, I put the truck in park.

"I need you to track Kendall's phone," I snap before he can even get a greeting in.

"I told you. I'm not—"

"Some strange man picked the kids up from school, Wren," I hiss. "Track her fucking phone."

The teacher has backed away, and is chatting with other teachers, pointing in my direction.

Cars honk behind me, and I ignore them.

"Wren," I growl when he doesn't respond.

"Working on it, Finn. Hold tight."

There is nothing tight about me right now. I'm fucking falling to pieces. I try to convince myself that it's an honest mistake. That the teacher somehow put the kids in the wrong car, but that would require whoever picked them up being a complete idiot and not realizing that they had the wrong kids. Grasping at straws isn't helping my anxiety.

"There are no cameras outside the school aimed at the pickup line," Wren says. "Come back to the office and regroup."

"Where is her phone?"

I never thought I'd be in a position to have to tell the woman I'm falling for that her children were abducted, but I don't want to do that over the phone.

"Have you had any luck tracking Ty Penman? Did he pick them up today?"

"From what I can tell, he's still in Federal custody."

I know this. Wren and I have talked about Ty more than once over the last week, and his status hasn't changed. What we do know is that Ty is not only in Federal custody, but the man is also a key witness in a case they're building against Keres. He hasn't handed over that fucking jump drive to the feds either. It seems he's still trying to play both sides of the fence, probably looking for a huge payday, either from them for giving up Keres, or in hush money from Keres so they can keep operating their criminal enterprise.

"Got it," Wren snaps. He gives me the address location where Kendall's phone was last pinged, and it's only then that I put the truck back in drive and take off.

Wren assures me he will contact the police and keep looking for the kids in whatever ways a hacker may use to track someone before I hang up.

After-school traffic is ridiculous, and I scream more than once at idiots who have nothing but time on their hands as they drive through town. I'm a fucking ball of nerves by the time I pull up to the address Wren gave me. Talk about the shittiest house in one of the shittiest neighborhoods.

Her car is not in the driveway or parked across the street, so I pull out my phone and call her. It rings several times before going to voicemail. I don't leave one because just what the fuck would I say? *Call me when you get this. Your kids have been taken by a stranger.*

Eeriness and helplessness wash over me as I open my door and climb out. The front door isn't completely closed, and that helplessness turns to fear as I push it open further.

The air in the house is heavy, and I pull my gun from my waistband holster at the sound of someone in one of the rooms.

I wish for a chance to just rewind the whole damn day. I should've talked to Kendall this morning or gone back to my condo after my epiphany in the truck on the drive to work. Waiting to tell her how I feel allowed all of this to be possible.

I use the door frame as a block. Considering how big I am, I make a pretty easy target, but I don't find an intruder or a completely empty room. A crying woman gasps and cries harder when she sees me, her whimpers of fear muted by the gag in her mouth.

I inch forward, my gut twisting and turning because something clearly bad happened here, and my girl is nowhere to be found.

"I'm not going to hurt you," I say, not holstering my weapon because I haven't cleared the rest of the house.

I turn away from her, moving quickly and efficiently through the rest of the tiny house and even checking the doorless shed in the backyard before going back inside.

"My name is Finnegan Jenkins," I tell the woman as I reapproach her, weapon now tucked safely away. "I'm looking for Kendall Stewart."

The woman's eyes widen, and this time she doesn't flinch when I reach for the gag in her mouth.

"Thank you," she whispers.

"Do you know Kendall?"

She begins to sob. Normally a woman crying would tear me up, and I'd do anything to try to calm her, but my girl is gone, and I don't have the patience.

"Lady!" I snap. "Kendall Stewart?"

"I don't know!" she screams. "I don't know what they did with her."

"So, she is in danger?"

The woman nods, her face disappearing into her hands.

I should call the police first because this woman has clearly been the victim of a crime, but my first call is to Wren.

I relay what I have found.

"Ping her phone again," I urge.

"It's there. Your cell is right on top of her. Let me call."

Ringing echoes through the house, and I move like my ass is on fire, hope rolling over me, but it all crashes when I locate her ringing phone in the bathtub.

"Fuck," I mutter. "She was here. Her car is gone. Call the police and get them to this location."

I hang up the phone and go back to the woman, only to find her standing in the open doorway of the house, staring at the driveway.

"You can't leave until you speak with the police."

"They took my car," she whispers, more tears streaming down her face. "You aren't going to leave me here alone, are you?"

Red-rimmed eyes beg me, and I would in a heartbeat if we had any leads on where Kendall and her kids are. I will haul ass out of here if Wren contacts me with any information, but I can stay for now.

"What kind of car did they take?"

"An older model champagne-colored Ford Taurus," she explains. "It's not much, but it's paid for."

I shoot that information to Wren. "Do you know the license plate?"

She shakes her head.

"What's your name?"

"Megan," she swallows. "Megan Dobbs."

I relay that information to Wren because he can get her plate number through the DMV.

"What else can you tell me about them?"

She shakes her head, crumpling to the nasty floor, and that's where she stays, sobbing uncontrollably until the cops arrive.

Chapter 31

Kendall

"If the gun wasn't enough," the guy in the passenger seat says after looking down at his phone, "maybe this will keep your ass in line."

Although I'm driving my own car, I look over when he turns his phone in my direction. On the screen is a picture of my three babies in the very clothes I sent them to school in this morning. Tears burn the backs of my eyes, and I open my mouth to beg, but he growls.

"Watch the fucking road!"

I gasp when I look back out the windshield, slamming my foot on the brake to keep from rear-ending the car in front of us that has slowed for a traffic light.

"Why are you doing this?" I cry, wondering if my anguish is going to be noticed by someone around us. Would them calling the cops help or hurt this situation? Probably hurt, I realize, so I wipe away my tears, and try to look and act as normal as possible. Knowing my kids are with someone I don't know, someone aimed at hurting us because of their father and not Finn, it's the hardest thing I've ever done.

"You know why," he snarls as if I've somehow personally wronged him when this is all on Ty.

"Do you hurt children and innocent women often?" I snap, hating that he has the power to scare the life out of me.

"I do what I'm asked."

"For Keres?"

I feel his eyes on me as traffic begins to move again.

"I don't know what you're talking about."

Of course he'd never admit to working for Keres. Hell, the MC may have outsourced the job to keep their hands mostly clean. Who knows how Adrian operates his club these days? They managed to skate away scot-free from all the other investigations according to the information Finn shared with me, so maybe this is how they do it.

My words must affect him because the man begins to thrum with agitation as he tells which turns to take. It's left and right and right and left, so many turns that once we get to an unfamiliar area of town, I can no longer keep track of where we are.

"You don't have to do this," I whisper.

"You sure talk a lot for someone who claims to love her kids. Keep fucking talking. It'll only take one fucking text for me to create your worst nightmare."

With this, I snap my mouth closed. My hands continue to shake on the steering wheel as I drive. I wordlessly obey when he tells me to turn. I'm not willing to risk my kids' safety with stupid questions or snide comments.

Eventually, we pull up to an industrial part of town, and this area looks worse than the neighborhood I drove to earlier, but it's quiet and devoid of anyone loitering around. It's the perfect place to end up with a bullet in the head because no one would be around to hear the shot.

The man doesn't point his gun at me as he climbs out of the car, walking toward an old, rusted metal door. He knows he doesn't have to. With my kids' lives at stake, I'll do anything he wants.

Surprisingly, the electricity is still on in the warehouse, but he doesn't turn on a light until he shoves me through the door of what looks to have once been the manager's office. The single light in the middle of the building probably can't be seen from the outside, once again making it the perfect place to hide for anyone not wanting to be found. I doubt the police or even a hired security company would wander this far into the industrial park, and since he made me park my car behind a set of dumpsters deep into an unlit alley, I know even if someone did happen by, it wouldn't be seen unless they drove that way themselves or decided to go for a walk down a long alleyway.

My phone was left behind, and that makes me lose even more hope. If this man had held on to it, I figured Finn would get Wren to track me once he realized I was missing. I doubt the man put a tracker of any sort on my car because he wouldn't have had a reason to since we were together mostly all the time.

I had only thought I felt hopeless before, but until now, I never knew true despair.

"Sit the fuck down," the man snaps when I just stand in the middle of the room.

I have no idea why I'm looking around. It's not like getting free from him would solve anything. The other guy, the man with the dragon tattoo on his neck, has my kids, and I believe this evil man when he says one text would activate my worst nightmare.

"I said sit down," the man snarls, shoving at my back until I sprawl forward, my hands hitting the concrete floor.

I scream as pain radiates up my arm and I roll to my back and clutch my wrist to my chest.

He inches closer, and I scramble to get away from him, somehow managing to press my back to the wall.

He stops, seeming satisfied with my new position, and grins.

"It's broken," he says, looking at my wrist.

I don't bother breaking eye contact with him, but I know he's right. It throbs, my heartbeat pounding in my wrist, and I can tell just from clutching it that it's already beginning to swell.

"Now, how are we going to get all that money?"

I shake my head. I've been over this more than once since he first pointed his gun at me.

"I don't have three hundred grand." I swallow. "I have thirteen thousand."

He narrows his eyes. "You said you have a hundred."

"I never said I had a hundred grand."

"A hundred dollars," he snaps. "Are you fucking toying with me?"

The threat in his eyes is clear. He doesn't like to be fucked with.

"In my wallet," I clarify. "I have a hundred dollars in my wallet, but I have more in the bank."

"Let's go get it," he snaps, inching even closer.

"I h-have a limit of thirty-five hundred. I can only get that amount tonight."

His upper lip twitches, and I can't tell if he's pissed or considering the money I'm offering.

"Thirteen grand is still a lot of money." He says it in a way that tells me he's going to fuck up.

Fuck up as in probably screw over the Keres MC which doesn't benefit either of us. He probably took this job with the understanding that actually finding the three hundred grand and jump drive was a long shot. He never anticipated having that kind of cash in his hand. His eyes narrow as he does the math, and I imagine thirteen grand is a lot more than Keres offered him to carry out this job. It's very bad for the kids and me because he doesn't seem the type to leave behind witnesses.

"I wouldn't," I warn.

"Wouldn't what, bitch?"

"Adrian Larrick will kill you if you steal so much as a penny from him."

His jaw clenches, but I can tell he's actually hearing what I say. Maybe the man isn't completely unreasonable after all.

"Is it thirty-five hundred every twenty-four hours or does it restart at midnight?"

I shake my head. "I don't know."

"Don't fucking lie to me!" he roars, his scuffed boots getting close enough to kick me if he decides that's the best way to relieve some of his anger.

I curl tighter, still keeping my eyes on him. "I've never taken that much money out. I don't know. But we can go now and then try again at midnight."

Even those two withdrawals wouldn't drain my account, meaning I'd have to be with him for a very long time before he gets all the money, and my kids would have to be with the other guy that long as well.

"Or we can wait until morning, and I can go inside the bank and make a full withdrawal," I offer.

"So you can alert the fucking police?" he snarls.

"I'd never do anything to compromise my children's safety," I remind him.

He nods as if considering what I'm telling him, but then he begins to pace around the room, extremely agitated with the decision he has to make. I keep silent and as small as possible with my back still to the wall.

Sunlight begins to fade in the sky, and I watch it disappear through the high warehouse windows as he mumbles to himself. The office we're in has one solid wall which my back is against and three walls of windows, no doubt for the boss man to be able to look into the warehouse to make sure his workers are staying on task. The warehouse surrounding this one room is filled with what looked like machinery on the way in. The layers of dust and trash scattered all around the floor told me that it hadn't been used in quite some time. No one is going to show up for work in the wee hours of the morning and discover us here. I was on my own with this man, and as time crawls by, he just gets more and more agitated.

I keep my eyes locked on him, trailing him from one end of the office to the other and back again. I realize the true danger I'm in when he starts to scratch at his arms, and I recognize the movements. Ty got that way when he was trying to stop using drugs. What started out as having a good time—social use if you will—turned into a full-fledged habit by the time the twins were born.

Like Ty, this man is turning into someone that would do anything for a fix, even steal the money I offered meant for Keres, to stop the bugs from crawling under his skin.

"We'll wait for the streets to clear," he says. "Later we'll head to the ATM."

I want to sob even harder with his plan. With the way he's acting, there's a good chance he'll get that cash and kill me just so he can find his dealer.

He spins to glare at me, and I try my best to quiet my cries, but it's nearly impossible. Instead of hurting me, however, he makes a few more threats before walking out of the office.

Chapter 32

Finnegan

"I'm not saying there isn't anything to find," Wren says, his voice low with his eyes locked on his computer screen. "I'm saying I haven't found anything."

I rub my hands over my face. I've done this so many times since I got back to the office, the skin on my cheeks hurts.

Wren's confession hits me hard. He isn't the type to keep from interjecting humor into the most serious of situations, and yet he hasn't muttered a single joke since I arrived. Even the birds, Puff Daddy and Evie, are huddled together as if they too can sense the seriousness of the situation.

"Keep looking," I tell him, even though I know he hasn't stopped in the hours since I called him from the school.

An Amber Alert has been sent statewide with the description of the realtor's car, but that was found abandoned an hour ago in the parking lot of a grocery store a few blocks from the school. I thought Wren was going to lose his shit when he got excited to track the abductor from there only to discover no camera in the area.

My initial thoughts were that this had to do with Ty's bullshit and the Keres MC, but the more brick walls we hit, the more I begin to think that it may have something to do with Blackbridge because these guys are sure going through a lot of trouble to avoid digital detection.

Wren couldn't find the car pulling into the parking lot, and although he's watched videos of every car leaving the parking lot, he didn't find a vehicle with three kids inside.

With each tick of the clock, I feel like I'm closer to losing my damn mind. I don't even know if the kids and Kendall are together or if they've been separated. The latter makes more sense because I know the abductors would get a hundred percent compliance out of almost any mother with the threat of harm to her children. Hell, I'd do whatever they asked if they had me in that very same position.

"Hello," Wren snaps after hitting a button on his phone.

"Wren?" an unfamiliar male voice asks.

"Speaking," my friend says, his hands still flying over his keyboard.

"This is Officer Ray Olsen with the St. Louis police department."

"I'm in the middle of some—"

"Looking for the Stewart kids?"

I spin around to face the phone, and Wren's fingers freeze on the keys.

"That's right," my friend says.

"We have them here at the station," the man says.

"And their mother?" I ask.

"I only have the children. I have very little information about what's going on, but I also have a procedure to follow. With their mother unavailable, I'm going to need to contact social services."

"No," I snap. "I'll come get them."

"And you are?" the officer asks, not very quick to release kids that were abducted right back to an unidentified person.

"Finnegan Jenkins. I'm their... I'm their mother's boyfriend."

"I'm sorry, sir, but—"

"We live together," I interrupt. "After what those kids have been through, they need familiarity. I can assure you that they'll be safe with me."

Wren nods as if he agrees, and I turn to him.

"Do what you have to do so I don't have any issues when I get there," I tell my friend before hauling ass out of the office.

A dozen or so worried faces look up at me when I leave the office.

Deacon pushes off from the counter, striding toward me.

"They found the kids," I say, and several of the women begin to cry with joy. "I'm going to go get them from the station. Wren may need some help to persuade the cop on the phone that I'm not going to hurt them."

Deacon stalks toward Wren's office, and I know if he's involved, it'll get handled.

"What can we do?" Jude asks as he stands from the sofa, his hand still holding Parker's, who was sitting beside him.

All of these people have been congregated in the breakroom for hours, waiting helplessly for any word about the situation.

"The kids are probably starving. They're going to need to be comfortable and distracted."

"We're on it," Anna, my boss's wife, says as she steps forward.

Whitney, as well as Parker and her best friend and Quinten's woman, Hayden, all stand from the sofas they're sleeping on.

"I've got to go," I tell them. "But thank you for being here."

I let my eyes roam over every person in the room, my heart swelling with gratitude, but then I bolt.

I don't bother obeying traffic laws on the way to the police station. If I get pulled over, I'm sure I can convince the officer to give me an escort to get the kids.

I'm stopped by a stern-looking man as I enter the police substation where the kids are.

"Can we talk?"

My eyes drop to the name tag on his chest, noticing it reads OLSEN. This is the guy that called Wren.

I nod, following him to the corner of the room, my eyes darting all over to locate the kids.

"Are they hurt?"

He shakes his head. "They aren't hurt. What I was able to determine is that the kids were picked up at school by some guy with a dragon tattoo on his neck."

I file this information away because Wren may be able to identify him with it.

"That man took them to the park. The oldest boy told us that they played for a while, and he didn't think anything of it when he noticed the man had left. You know kids, they don't pay much attention. He said the little boy complained about being hungry, so they went to find the man and couldn't. It was nearly dark before a woman walking the track around the park noticed them alone and called the police."

"They were there until dark? The fucking Amber Alert went out at four-thirteen."

The cop frowns in solidarity. "You know how people are. Their phone chimes and they just rush to turn the alarm off. I doubt hardly anyone pays much attention. The woman who called it in admitted that she does the very same thing, but despite not knowing the details of the alert, she knew it wasn't okay for children that young to be out that late on their own."

"I need to get my kids," I tell him.

"I spoke with Deacon Black and then referred that call to my supervisor. I have clearance to release them to you, but I hope you understand why I'm cautious."

"I appreciate your diligence, Officer Olsen."

He nods before guiding me through a thick door that reads *POLICE PERSONNEL ONLY*.

Kayleigh is the first to see me, and she screeches as she jumps up from her seat at a small table, running across the room. She flings herself into my arms but isn't really interested in the hug I have to offer. Her little hands press against my chest, and she looks up at me with a wide smile.

"We played at the park for hours, and Kason even pushed me on the swing!"

I look to her brother, and even though they're the same age, I can tell Kason is more aware of what's going on than Kayleigh is.

"Hey!" Knox says, pulling his eyes from the mostly blue crayon drawing he's working on. "We got chicken nuggets."

The Happy Meals have been consumed and long forgotten.

"You guys ready to head to the office?" I ask as Kayleigh wiggles out of my arms.

"Yes!" Knox says, and he abandons his drawing.

"Let's clean up in here before we head out."

I turn to find a woman handing a booster seat to Officer Olsen and I could hug and kiss them both for taking Knox's size into consideration.

"Figured you may need this."

"Thanks," I tell him, taking the booster when he holds it out for me. "What I have with Kendall is new, but I'd never let anything bad happen to those kids."

We both stand here and watch as the three kids clean up their dinner trash, and Kason is extra attentive in helping Knox gather his crayons and stuff them back into his backpack.

"My wife is a nurse and she swung by to see them. They don't have any physical injuries, but that oldest boy has a lot of questions. Still no word on their mother?"

I swallow a lump forming in my throat. "No."

I haven't until now considered that although the kids are safe, things may not be so good for Kendall. I haven't even called her brother Ezra to let him know what's going on. Thinking of him makes my head go to a dark place, one that includes burying their mother and having to watch a man who took off to Vegas take custody of these kids. I honestly don't think I could ever let that happen. I wasn't lying about what I have with Kendall being new, but I'll be damned if I lose her to some piece of shit and then walk away from her kids, too.

"I'll be praying for her," Olsen says as he claps me on the back in solidarity.

"Ready?" I ask the kids, not even managing a fake smile when they approach.

"What about ice cream?" Knox asks, his eyes bright and hopeful when I buckle him in my truck.

"That's a great—"

"Mom would say no because it's late," Kason says, interrupting me.

I nod at him, noticing how he looks older now than he did when I saw him yesterday before bed.

"He's right," I tell Knox, scrunching up my nose. "But tomorrow, I promise."

Knox scowls at his older brother but keeps his comments to himself.

With such precious cargo in my care, I drive much more calmly back to the office, and despite feeling his stare burn into the back of my head, I don't make eye contact with Kason.

Kayleigh is excited to be back at the office, but Knox is already half asleep when I pull him out of the truck. I walk with the youngest in my arms to the elevator.

When we arrive on the Blackbridge floor, everyone swarms into action. Whitney takes Knox from my arms, telling me she's going to lay him down in my office. Kayleigh easily gets distracted by something Anna offers, but Kason sticks right with me.

"Where's my mom?" he asks, his eyes telling me that he isn't going to move until I give him answers.

"She's—" I open my mouth to lie to the kid, to tell him she's running errands, but he's not a fool. "The man who picked you up from school was a bad man."

"I figured that out when he mentioned Ty."

It's not lost on me that he doesn't refer to him as his dad.

"Another bad man took your mom."

He nods, as if he had already suspected that in his own head.

"We're doing everything we possibly can to find her."

He looks over his shoulder, noticing all the men and women fawning over his brother and sister.

"Doesn't look like it."

"Wren has been going nonstop, Kason. We won't stop until she's found. I promise."

He considers me for a long time before nodding and walking away. I've been grilled while testifying in Federal court on a case before and didn't even feel the level of scrutiny I just felt from that seven-year-old.

I lock eyes with Deacon who draws Kason into the conversation he's having with Jude, Kit, and Quinten. He gives me a slight head nod, letting me know the kids are taken care of.

I arrow myself back to Wren's office.

"He's fucking working!" Puff Daddy snaps. "Leave him the fuck alone."

"Sorry," Wren says. "I had a telemarketer call. I wasn't exactly friendly when I answered the phone. Like who the fuck even buys a goddamned extended warranty anyway?"

"Find anything?"

Wren shakes his head, his hands still working over the keyboard.

"Couldn't find the clit with two hands, a flashlight, and a map!" Puff says, and I find that with the bird back to true form it calms me. This office is always wild and lively, and the quiet, I now realize, was making me even more antsy.

"Puff," Wren warns.

"I swear!" Evie snaps. "Such a scoundrel!"

"Say it to my dick!" the male bird responds.

I shake my head, watching them, but snap my head around when Wren's computer dings.

"About fucking time!" Puff yells. "I thought you were losing your touch."

"What is it?" I ask, getting closer.

"An ATM," he says, his fingers working fast. "I have to hack—"

"I don't give a fuck what you have to hack. Just do it."

Wren, not waiting for my response, pulls up a grainy video two seconds later.

I want to rejoice at the sight of her, but then I notice she's favoring her right arm and using her left to key in the information. I know for a fact she's right-handed.

"She's hurt," I whisper.

"Her wrist," Wren predicts. "The alert was delayed because that ATM is a fucking dinosaur. The withdrawal happened eight minutes ago."

Wren pulls up a map, a red flashing dot, pinpointing the location.

"That's a really shitty part of town," I hiss.

"The worst. Minimal cameras, but I'll track what I can. Whoever has her isn't going to take her very far to get her money. I'd gamble they're within a few miles of that machine."

"Does it say how much?" I ask, waiting impatiently as his fingers continue to work. A few miles to cover is still nearly impossible especially in an area that's notorious for hating cops. Even if people have information or saw something, they're not going to be very forthcoming with that information.

"Thirty-five hundred. Her daily limit."

"Fuck," I mutter.

"She has nearly ten grand more, so with any luck, they're going to hold on to her to get the rest."

"Probability of them using the same machine?" I ask, getting ready to go park across the fucking street if I have to and wait.

Wren types even more. "According to my crime mapping program, four-point-two percent."

I frown. That's a shitty percentage, but it's still not zero, and that's what we were working with without this recent update.

"Hold on," Wren says when I turn to leave. "Holy shit. Look."

The screen switches from camera view to camera view, and I've seen him do this enough to know he's tracking the car. They're still in Kendall's car and hope fills my chest as I watch it, turn after turn.

"They're in the industrial district."

I'm on the move, knowing every single minute is precious.

All the guys are on alert when I leave the office, and the look on my face must tell them what they need to know because they move en masse toward the elevator.

Something happened when I was in the office because Kayleigh rushes up to me with tears in her eyes.

"I told her because I thought she should know," Kason says, regret filling his young face which is also stained with tears.

"My momma?"

I look to Kayleigh. "Sweet girl, I'll protect your mom with my own life. I swear."

She nods, giving me a little sniffle before running across the room right into Anna's arms.

Kason stands before me, his eyes shining with fresh tears. "Please, Finn. Bring Momma home."

"I swear I will," I tell him, and I feel that truth in the deepest parts of me.

He nods at me before turning away to join his sister.

My throat is clogged with emotion as I walk across the room toward the elevator. Deacon claps me on the back as I climb on. The entire ride down, I pray I just didn't lie to that little boy. He'd never forgive me.

I'd never forgive myself.

Chapter 33

Kendall

My brain and my body aren't on the same page. I'm terrified, couldn't eat a thing if it were offered to me, but my stomach is still growling.

That noise is drowned out by the arguing going on in the warehouse. I'm back in the industrial building, and the man with the neck tattoo was here when we got back from the ATM. My captor, the one who has been with me the entire time, wasn't very happy to see him. He shoved me back in this room, reminded me of what was at stake, and then he left.

"And I told you it was taken care of!" neck-tattoo guy yells, growing increasingly frustrated.

The other guy murmurs too low for me to decipher what he's saying.

"They're gone. That's all you need to worry about. I'm not giving you the fucking details so you can hang me out to dry. Fucking look at you, all twitchy and shit. This is the last fucking time I do a job with someone I don't know."

More murmuring, but I can't focus on their fight.

They're gone echoes in my head, a broken record of words playing over and over.

He was the one who had my children.

They're gone.

They're gone.

They're gone.

I collapse to the side, curling into a ball. He was talking about my kids.

They're gone.

I'm numb, the sounds around me nothing but background noise as my heart breaks.

They're gone.

They're gone.

They're gone.

It can't be true because if he means what I think he means then I'll never survive it. I can't exist in a world where my children don't.

Laughter and the smiling faces of Kason, Kayleigh, and Knox flash in my head, drowning out the pops from the warehouse. I grin into my arm, feeling truly crazy as I try to remember holding each of them for the first time. I was alone in the hospital, only surrounded by hospital staff with the twins. Ty just couldn't be bothered to return my phone calls despite being in labor for hours and hours. He didn't pop back up until after I was already home with them.

It was two weeks before he met Knox, claiming some out-of-state job that prevented him from making contact like he was a fucking spy or something. The man seriously thought I was an idiot.

I frown, shoving all thoughts of that man away, trying to replace it with happy ones involving my kids. We have had a lot of happy times despite me scraping every extra penny I have into savings. They enjoyed trips to the park and didn't care if their clothes were from last season's sales rack. Kayleigh was the only picky one in that regard and so long as it was pink, purple, or had sparkles, she was as happy as a clam.

I think of Kason and the way he tried to boss them like he was the man of the house.

I think of Knox and his serious face when he's drawing with his favorite blue crayon.

My perfect little babies.

My angels.

This last thought makes me sob, all the good fading away into darkness.

They're too young for wings.

Maybe all of this could've been avoided if I'd only listened to Finn this morning. He offered to come along while I looked at the house. It was another give on his part, another thing I couldn't take from him because I've already taken so much, but losing my children is the worst *I told you so* in the history of them all.

My horrible choice in men brought me to this point, and that damage, all the pain Ty caused, made me push away a deserving man.

I'm fighting a battle in my head, trying to determine what's honestly worse—never having met Ty, meaning I wouldn't have my children, or this current situation where three innocent children die because of my choices.

I'm choking on sobs, my entire body convulsing when the door to the room opens. Let them kill me or rape me. I couldn't care less at this point. They've taken from me the only things that matter. I'm fucking numb to the rest of it.

Hands roam over me, and that fight instinct I thought I'd lost kicks in. I smack at the touch, crying out when I use my right hand to defend myself. The man who abducted me forced me to drive to the ATM earlier while he hid in the back seat to make sure I didn't just take off and leave. I was able to get a good look at my wrist, and it's clearly broken. Pain shoots up my arm and I try to curl into myself once again, the pain making my stomach swim with nausea.

"Baby, stop. You're safe."

My eyes flutter open, so sure this is another dream, and I feel my lips smile, my uninjured hand reaching up to cup Finn's scruffy jaw. His green eyes shine with tears, making me realize it really must be a dream. A man as tough as Finnegan Jenkins doesn't cry. He's not one to shed tears for any reason. He's too tough for that.

"Your wrist," he says, cupping the injury softly in his huge hands.

I look down at myself, noting the blues and purples have made their way up my fingers.

"Doesn't matter," I whisper, my voice broken and pained.

"Sweetheart," he says, pulling me to his chest and being careful not to hurt me further.

This is only half of what I need, and I hate that my dreams are betraying me right now.

"My babies," I sputter, my heart in pieces inside the very core of me.

"They were at the office, but it got late so Wren and Whitney took them back to their place."

I nod against him. At least he's not telling me that they're in purgatory.

"Let's get you up."

I comply, trying to get to my feet, but I'm weighed down with the guilt of what I've let happen. It wouldn't surprise me if this man was sent to drag me to hell.

I use my hands to push up to standing, only to fall back, screaming in pain.

"Fuck, Kendall. Let me help you."

My eyes snap to him, Finn's jaw clenching as he reaches for me.

"Finn?" I blink at him, my eyes hazy from the pain in my wrist, but somehow clearer than it was a few minutes ago. "You're here?"

"I'm here, baby. Did they hurt more than your wrist? You seem a little—"

"They hurt my kids," I confess. "And it's all my—"

"The kids are fine, Kendall."

I shake my head, knowing what I heard, and this man lying to me is the cruelest thing I can think of. I try to pull away, but he doesn't allow it.

"Baby," he says, pulling me against him and reaching into his pocket for his phone.

I sob loudly, uncaring for the other people I sense in the room at our backs.

"Put them on," he snaps when the call connects.

There's shuffling.

"Look," Finn snaps, hitching his shoulder to get me to lift my head from it. "Look, Kendall."

My tears fall even more when I look at the screen. There in a bed are my children. Knox even has his little blue dinosaur clutched to his chest.

"Glad you're okay, sweetheart," Wren says, turning the phone so I can see his face instead of it being a monster looking after my children.

"They're okay?" I ask as Finn hangs up the phone and pockets it.

"They're fine.," he assures me. "A little worried about you, but healthy. The guy who took them—"

"The man with the dragon tattoo," I clarify.

"That man picked them up from school and immediately dropped them off at the park. They were there unsupervised for a few hours, but a concerned citizen called it into the police. The police called us, and they were at the office all evening until shortly after you visited the ATM."

I nod, trying to absorb everything he's telling me, but my heart is stuck on the fact that my kids haven't been hurt. They're safe, tucked into bed at Finn's friend's condo.

"I need to go to them," I insist, trying to shove past him to move toward the door.

I gasp when I naturally use my right hand. The pain is unbearable.

"We need to get you to the hospital," Finn argues.

"My kids, Finn."

"Baby," he says, turning me in his arms and forcing my eyes up to his. "We have to make sure you're okay."

He presses his lips to mine before pulling back a few inches. His eyes roam over every part of me, and I don't think I've ever felt more valued than I do right now.

"You were crying," I say, reaching up with my uninjured hand to trace the scruff on his jaw.

"I'm really happy you're okay," he says.

"I didn't think you could cry."

He smiles a sad smile before brushing another soft kiss against my lips.

"I'll tell you why some other time, okay?"

I nod as he turns me around, his palm resting protectively on my lower back as he guides me from the room.

"Oh my God," I gasp as we walk across the warehouse.

"They must've gotten into a fight. The tattooed guy shot the other one then turned the gun on himself," Finn explains as he tries to usher me quickly out of the building, but my eyes are glued to the carnage in front of me.

Other than television, I've never seen such a scene in real life.

My mother's funeral was closed casket, and then realization hits me that I've never seen a dead person in real life before. The blood pooling around their bodies looks so much darker than what's portrayed in the movies. Their skin is an ashen gray, and I don't know that I'll ever fully get the sight of their corpses out of my mind.

"Hospital, Kendall. You're safe now."

I nod, letting him steer me away. It may be the end of those two, but I doubt this incident is the last time I hear from anyone connected to the Keres MC.

Three hundred thousand dollars will never be forgiven. Even bloodshed wouldn't satisfy Adrian Larrick. His pride has been wounded. He was bested by Ty Penman, and that won't go unpunished.

I cling to Finn on the ride to the hospital, his boss Deacon driving the sleek, black SUV.

I'm somehow wired and utterly exhausted, in a weird catatonic but functioning state when he shifts his weight in the back seat, telling me that we've arrived.

The numbness is setting back in, and because of that, I plan to take all he has to offer, at least until I can get my kids and me out of the state. I won't stick around and hope that Adrian grows a heart. Leaving and getting away is the only way to keep us safe.

My kids are the only things that can matter. My broken heart will always come secondary.

Chapter 34

Finnegan

"What color are you going to get?" I ask stupidly as I sit beside the gurney Kendall is lying on.

"What?" she asks, her head slowly turning toward me.

She was given pain medicine when we first arrived. Her wrist has been x-rayed, and it's definitely broken. Now we're waiting for the doctor to come put her cast on.

"Your cast," I clarify. "What color?"

I give her a weak smile, but she doesn't even attempt to give me one back.

"Doesn't matter," she whispers, once again looking away from me.

She's safe. The kids are safe, but I still feel like I'm in the middle of a nightmare. Ty Penman has been gone for years, but he's still managing to drain her, to take from her, and it kills me that I can't seem to find the right words to make everything okay.

Telling her she's safe now would be a lie.

This is Adrian Larrick's doing, although neither Wren nor the local police have been able to find a direct link between the Keres MC and the two dead men at the abandoned warehouse. They didn't have club tattoos nor were they wearing the custom-leather cut.

Wren has contacted the feds working the cases against the MC to see if those two have popped up on video footage, but I know they won't find anything. Larrick is meticulous with how he outsources jobs. Hell, the two men working for him may not even know that's who they were working for. Rumor has it from others arrested and suspected of carrying out jobs for Keres that all they get is an untraceable phone call, and once the job is done, they pick up money from a drop location.

I know Larrick isn't going to stop until he gets what he wants, and the man doesn't care who he has to plow through to get it. Pride will keep him moving the pieces until he produces the outcome he desires.

So, no, Kendall isn't safe. She's not in any immediate danger, because I'm sure Keres is regrouping, but it's far from over.

"Kayleigh would pick pink," I say, continuing the ridiculous conversation. I also want to remind her of those three special people waiting for her to return.

I doubt the woman is giving up, but I also don't want her mind racing. She gets a little crazy when she gets a thought in her head—the fake bomb at the office for example—and the last thing I need her doing is something outlandish to put her right back in Keres's line of fire.

"Or purple," she mutters, but there's no enthusiasm in her tone.

"You feeling okay?"

She shrugs, her shoulders only lifting an inch or so as if she can't manage more.

"Ready to see my kids."

I pull out my phone, unwilling to leave her side, but needing someone to light a fire under the doctor's ass. Before I can hit send on my text, the doctor walks in with the supplies needed for her cast.

She ends up with a plain white cast, showing no more enthusiasm when the doctor asked if she wanted a different color.

It takes another thirty minutes to get her paperwork signed and taken care of, and despite Deacon's offer to drive us, I decline.

I need some time alone with her, but I still can't find the words she needs to hear on the drive back to the condo.

I don't bother hitting the elevator button to my floor, choosing Wren's instead. Trying to convince her to get some rest would fall on deaf ears, so I don't waste the energy.

"You'll like Whitney," I tell her as I lift my hand to knock softly, remembering Kendall once complaining about people ringing the bell when the kids are sleeping.

Both Wren and Whitney are in front of us when the door is pulled open, and although Whitney has never met Kendall before, she doesn't hesitate to pull her in for a hug. My girl sinks against the stranger, wrapping her arms around her as tears stream down her face.

"You have the most amazing kids," Whitney offers, her face tucked into Kendall's hair. "Kayleigh is going to destroy hearts when she grows up."

Kendall chuckles at this, her head nodding as if she agrees.

"Knox may never grow out of his love for the color blue, and Kason is going to be a mad genius who tries to take over the world."

Kendall's laughter strengthens as she steps back, using the back of her hand to swipe at the tears on her face.

"Did they give you any trouble?"

"No," Whitney answers, stepping aside so we can fully enter the condo. "But they did try to convince us that you let them sleep with the TV on. Full disclosure, we allowed it, but turned it off about an hour ago because they were all conked out."

"We figured the distraction was good," Wren adds.

"Thank you both so much," Kendall says, her voice tinged with another wave of emotion. "I need to see them."

Whitney nods in understanding and guides Kendall to the guest bedroom.

I stick close to Wren who watches the two of them leave the room. The lights are turned down low in the condo, and I'm grateful not to hear the birds squawking and making noise. They must still be at the office.

Unable to handle the physical distance between us, I walk toward the bedroom. Wren sticks close, and I appreciate the moral support, but I just want to be alone with her and the kids. I'd never tell him to get lost, this is his condo after all, but he must sense it because he presses his hand to Whitney's back, and they walk away.

Kendall is standing at the edge of the king-sized bed, looking down at her kids. After brushing her palm over each head, she kicks off her shoes and curls up beside them.

Her shoulders shake with her silent sobs, and keeping my distance is no longer possible. I walk to her, bending down and pressing my lips to her temple, as I cover the hand she has on Knox's back with my own.

Knox doesn't move, but his eyes flutter open.

"Kendall," I whisper because her own eyes are squeezed tight.

She looks at Knox, giving him a light smile as she lifts her hand to caress his cheek.

"Momma," he says, her name a little sigh on his lips.

Then he sits up, jostling the entire bed in a way only a small child can. As if they're both attuned to Knox, Kason and Kayleigh open their eyes as well.

"Momma!" Kayleigh says enthusiastically as she slings herself at Kendall.

I have to press my hand to my woman's back to keep her from rolling over the bed from the force of it.

Kason looks up at me, giving me a nod that is well beyond his seven years, and I see exactly what Whitney was talking about. He's an old soul and understands more than he should have to at such a young age.

"White?" Kayleigh huffs as she gently holds Kendall's casted arm. "Should've gotten pink."

Kendall chuckles, pulling all three kids to her chest, and a pang fires through my chest at not being right in there with them. I don't know if that's selfishness or just longing to be a part of what they have.

"Finn said he'd make sure you were okay," Kason says as he pulls back from his mom, also wiping tears from his cheeks. "I believed him because he's a good man, and also because he helped Mystery Man Medano with that safe."

A smile spreads across my face. Kason has been the hardest one to win over, but it seems I'm finally making some progress.

Then he leans in close to his mom and whispers, "But watch out for all the other women. I heard the teachers talking about turning that sweat-wiping video into a GIF."

Both Kendall and I huff a laugh, and I wink at her when she looks over her shoulder at me.

Kason yawns, and although Kayleigh looks like she's ready to climb out of bed and start playing, Knox is already back asleep in Kendall's arms.

"Get some rest," she tells Kason as he lowers himself back down to the mattress. "You too, sweet girl."

Kayleigh listens to her mom, lying down, her eyes blinking slowly.

"You guys can sleep late tomorrow."

"No school?" Kason asks on another yawn.

"No school," Kendall promises, waiting on the bed until they're all back asleep.

I think she's going to curl up and sleep beside them but after watching them for a few minutes, she stands from the bed, covers them back up, and backs away.

I wait in the hall as she closes the bedroom door.

"We can bring them home in the morning," Whitney offers as we walk back into the living room.

"Thank you," Kendall says. "I'd stay, but I need a shower."

"Of course," Whitney says. "And you're welcome to come back if you want."

Wren tries to cover a yawn with the back of his hand, but Kendall notices.

"We'll get out of your way so you can go to sleep."

I clap Wren on the back in appreciation for all he's done for us and nod at Whitney before following Kendall out the front door.

When we get back to the condo, I have to guide her away from the hall bathroom. She doesn't say a word as I guide her into my en suite and start pulling her clothes off.

"Wait here," I tell her as I dart out of the room and head to the kitchen.

I'm back in front of her in a matter of seconds with a bag and rubber band to cover her cast.

She seems nearly catatonic when we climb into the shower, and although I can't control my dick at the sight of her naked body, I don't make any overtures for sex. I just need exactly this—washing her body, feeling her skin under the tips of my fingers. I'm happy just knowing she's whole and mostly unharmed.

Her bones will heal. It's the darkness in her eyes I'm worried most about.

She doesn't say a word in the shower or after we climb out and I dry her body. She doesn't argue when I pull one of my t-shirts over her head and guide her to my bed.

I curl around her back, holding her as close as possible without actually lying on top of her.

And the words I couldn't find earlier are still absent as she cries herself to sleep.

Chapter 35

Kendall

There's a moment, a flash of seconds when I first wake up, that the entire world feels right. The warmth of Finn's body at my back makes me want to hum in contentment, but my eyes land on my wrist, the white cast a stark reminder of just how imperfect my life is.

His arm holds me tighter, making me realize he's already awake, and I picture him telling me that I'm too much trouble to keep around, but that wouldn't really matter. I have my own plans, and since the safety of my children is all that matters, they don't include him. I can't take anything else into consideration, doing so would be selfish.

He tries to keep me locked against him when I shift to get out of bed, but when I continue to pull away, his hold loosens.

Leaving the room, I head straight to the hall bathroom, taking care of business then brushing the nasty out of my mouth.

I plan to hide in my bedroom, but I'm stuck looking at myself in the mirror. Placing my cast behind my back, I take a long hard look at myself. Someone seeing me wouldn't have a clue that I went through hell and back last night, but I can tell by the darkness under my eyes and the sadness that feels bone-deep. Yesterday changed me, and I don't think I'll ever get back the pieces those men robbed from me. Thinking my kids were dead, even for the shortest amount of time, took literal years off my life, and I'm determined to never feel that way again.

I give Finn a sad look when I find him standing in the hall waiting for me, but when I open my mouth to speak to him, he swallows my words with his mouth against mine.

The kiss isn't feverish, and if I let myself dream, I'd say it was passionate and appreciative.

His hands go around my waist, and he lifts my feet from the floor, carrying me back to his room.

He's gentle and attentive as he lowers me to his bed, his lips still locked on mine, tongue seeking, roving against mine slowly, sensually. All thoughts of my later plans drift away, and I just let myself be in this situation, knowing it will be the last.

I groan with pleasure when his huge hand starts at my knee and glides slowly up my thigh. I wrap that leg around his body, opening myself up to him, and I can't think of anything better than the heat of him at my core through his boxer briefs.

As if he feels the same way, he rolls his hips, pressing harder into me before backing off just an inch or so. My body, desperate for his, arches to regain that connection.

He doesn't smile against my mouth or make a joke about how needy I always am for him. There's no place for humor between the two of us right now.

That hand trailing up my leg pushes the t-shirt he put on me last night over my head, and once again he's careful not to let it get tangled over my cast. Once the fabric is free, he presses a palm to my arms, indicating that he wants me to keep both above my head. I obey, because the man has never steered me wrong in bed, and watch as his mouth lowers to my skin.

Hot breath and a warm mouth coat my chest, the tips of my breasts aching for him. It seems like an eternity before he finally gives me what my body is demanding, and honestly, it's perfect timing. My fingers twitch to touch him, to guide him, but the man's mouth is just as skilled as every other part of his body.

I'm a ball of tension within minutes, his mouth making it down my body, tongue licking at my navel before venturing lower.

I spread for him, needy and demanding when his lips find my clit, and we moan in unison at that first touch.

I've learned that he loves giving as much as I love receiving, and he knows all of me is on offer. He never hesitates to take. This morning is no different.

It seems like seconds before I'm teetering on the edge of that cliff, and with just one gentle swipe of his finger over my entrance, I fall apart, back arching, eyes going blurry. It's absolute bliss, and the man doesn't stop until I'm up on the edge again, looking down and preparing to take another leap.

But he doesn't push me over. He backs away, using one hand to shove his boxer briefs down his legs while he keeps his full weight off of me with his other arm.

He doesn't reach for a condom as he lines himself up, and I don't argue.

I've wanted him this way for a while but was unwilling to take that final step with him. I don't stop him because I don't want to walk away from him, wondering what it was like, what he feels like bare.

The first slide of his cock into me makes my mouth unhinge on a soundless moan. It's perfect, somehow better than I ever imagined it could be, and if life were perfect, I'd never leave this bed. I'd beg this man to fill me just like this every day for the rest of my days.

Life isn't perfect, and despite how he makes me feel, I know life will never be perfect for me. The very least I can do is protect my kids.

"Finn," I groan when he rolls his hips, his cock screwing into me.

He's deep and thick, overwhelming my nerve endings in the best possible way.

He doesn't say a word as he looks down at me, his cock driving in over and over on the slow rolls of his hips. He watches me, his fingers tangling in my hair, mouth slightly parted, breaths uneven from pleasure rather than exertion.

"Baby." He whispers the very first word he's spoken since our shower last night, and that's all it takes to make me fly.

He stills inside of me, body locked as I orgasm, and he does this often. He told me once that the grip of me around him is enough to set him off, and that's what happens. As I come down, his cock jerks inside of me, and this time is different from all the others because I feel the heated flood of him. It's intimate and perfect. He kisses me, his mouth slowly taking command of mine, and I offer it all to him, reluctant to let him go when he pulls back and falls to the bed on a gasp.

He doesn't waste a second, pulling me to his chest, cradling my hurt arm as I get settled. Warm fingers tease up and down my spine, reigniting the goosebumps that are always so familiar with him. The man lights my body on fire and makes my heart ache. I know I'll never find this again. He's one of a kind, made just for me, and it's going to kill me to walk away.

I press my lips to his chest, storing the feel of his skin against mine deep inside of me so I'll have it forever as he presses his lips to the top of my head.

"We need to talk."

I feel the rumble of his voice under my lips.

"And as much as I'd like to do that now, I have a meeting I can't miss."

I pull away from him, and he lets me, so this must be very important.

"We'll have plenty of time to talk when I get home," he says as he leans down and brushes his lips against mine before crawling out of the bed.

Shamelessly, I watch, also cataloging the sight of him as he dresses.

Unaware of what's going through my head, he notices, tossing a saucy wink my way as if promising me so much more is coming my way later.

I manage to keep the tears at bay, as he pulls on his boots. I even have a smile on my face when he leans down to kiss me, and I use the opportunity to wrap my arms around him and squeeze tight. He holds me against him for an extended moment, but then he's gone.

I have so much to get done, and very little time, so the second the front door closes, I jump out of the bed, clean up, and get dressed.

I'm in the middle of packing when the doorbell chimes through the condo, and I'm breathless when I answer it to find Whitney, Wren, and the kids standing there with big smiles.

"Hey," I say, immediately dropping to my knees so I can wrap the kids in a hug.

They must've really missed me because they all comply, even Kason who is already getting to the point where showing me affection in front of others is uncool.

"Thank you so much for looking after them," I tell Wren and Whitney when I stand.

"It's no problem," Wren says as he walks past me into the condo.

"Seriously," Whitney says. "Anytime."

She follows Wren inside, and I'm left staring at their backs, trying to figure out a way to get them to leave because I need to finish packing up the kids and get the hell out of St. Louis.

Unable to think of a reason quick enough, I close the door.

"How about some breakfast?" I ask the kids, walking toward the kitchen.

Knox is tugging Wren's hand toward the room he shares with Kason, and that terrifies me because two little suitcases are open and halfway filled on their bed.

"Breakfast!" I say again. "Knox, do you want some peanut butter toast?"

Knox pauses in the hallway, and relief washes over me.

"We already ate. Uncle Wren ordered Taco Bell."

My gaze shifts to Wren as I scrunch my nose and mouth. "Taco Bell?"

He shrugs, a youthful smile on his face. "Taco Bell is perfect for every meal."

Whitney laughs as if she's heard this more than a few times.

Knox continues down the hall, dragging Wren into his room.

"What are they doing in there?" I ask Kason a few minutes later when they still haven't come back out.

"Knox promised to show Uncle Wren how to use a blue crayon."

"Uncle Wren?" I ask Whitney once we're alone in the kitchen.

"Yeah," she says with a shrug. "Don't ask me. Knox started calling him that after Wren tried to explain that he was closer to Finn than just someone he works with. He said they were like brothers. Knox started it and now all three kids are calling him that."

It's fifteen minutes before Wren and Knox reappear, and although Wren meets my eyes twice, he doesn't say a word about the suitcases that were on the bed.

Maybe he was so attentive to Knox he didn't even notice them.

Chapter 35

Finnegan

I'd be a liar if I said my heart wasn't racing as I park my truck. I'm on enemy territory, and I don't mean personal enemy or even a Blackbridge enemy.

The Keres MC is an enemy to every law-abiding citizen worldwide. What they lack in compassion, they make up for in twisted apathy. Not only are these guys hardcore club members, but when it boils down to it, they're mostly about themselves. The loyalty to the club keeps them in money, drugs, and women, and all of that becomes insanely clear to me when I walk through the front door like I own the place.

Men are lounged around the common area—one getting his cock sucked by a naked redhead while another watches with his own dick in his hand. Cocaine dots a mirror on the coffee table as a baseball game plays on the massive television mounted to the far wall.

"You must have balls the size of Russia, walking in here like this," the one getting his dick sucked says without pulling the redhead off his meat.

"Maybe he's on a suicide mission," another asks on a growl, the warning clear in his voice.

"I'm here to speak with Larrick," I snap, making sure to keep my hands calm at my sides.

I'm outnumbered four to one, and despite my ability to handle myself in most situations, those are pretty shitty odds, considering the visible weapons lying around the room.

"He's not here," the guy stroking his dick says, his hand surprisingly stopping as he stands.

He stalks across the room, getting closer to me with his junk just swinging in the breeze as if my presence doesn't warrant enough concern for him to put the damn thing away.

"His bike is out front," I snap. "I'm not leaving until I see him."

"That so," the one getting closer snarls.

"Fuck, bitch. Suck don't bite."

The guy close to me turns back to look at his friend, grinning when the guy on the couch shoves his dick so far down the woman's throat that she gags.

"She just needs a little incentive," another guy says as he stands, unzipping his pants as he inches closer to her.

I'd be concerned about her safety and willingness if she didn't go from sitting on her haunches to getting on her knees and arching her ass in the guy's direction.

With no fanfare or even checking to see if she's ready, the man crouches low and thrusts his cock right inside of her.

I roll my eyes back to the guy close to me, reading *DIRTY* on the patch on his leather vest. He's watching me, evaluating my reaction to what I'm seeing, and I give him nothing.

"Larrick," I hiss.

"He's on vacation," the guy growls. "And unless you want to die, you need to leave."

"Vacation," I huff.

The man is here, and I fucking know it. His bike is outside, and the man hates regular vehicles more than he hates cops, and that's saying a lot.

Slowly, I cross my arms over my chest, indicating I'm not fucking leaving.

The guy narrows his eyes. "You a fucking cop?"

"We hate cops," the man on the couch mutters.

"Hate them," the guy thrusting agrees. "Think every one should die."

"Should you die today," the man in front of me growls, "cop or not, I think it's gonna happen."

"Fucking try me," I snap, eyes meeting his.

He can't be more than twenty-five, and that makes him dangerous. The young ones are impulsive, acting before they really take the time to think about the outcome.

"Dirty," a new man hisses from the far side of the room.

Dirty, like a broken puppy, backs away, his eyes snapping in the direction of the voice.

I turn my attention in that direction as well to see Adrian Larrick glaring at the both of us.

"Finnegan Jenkins," the MC president says. I shouldn't be surprised that he knows my name but hearing him speak it is startling. He was at my condo not long ago, so I knew I was on his radar as much as Kendall was after running into Brant Jesper at the grocery store. I'm not scared of him or his MC, but I am cautious, something the young buck in front of me isn't smart enough to be.

"Down boy," I tell Dirty before I turn toward Larrick. "We need to talk."

"Swallow it, slut," the man on the couch snaps before groaning out his orgasm.

My eyes go in that direction even though it's the last thing I want to see.

As if they planned it, the woman gulps him down before turning to the guy at her back and letting him paint her face with his jizz.

When I look back at Larrick, he's smiling, his eyes swimming with mirth.

"Here for an application? I'm sure a big bastard like you would be a solid asset for the club."

"Not a fucking chance. A little privacy?"

"Shake him down," Adrian demands, and I take a little pride when Dirty jerks when I snap at him with my teeth when he moves to do his boss's bidding.

I'm not armed. I knew better than to come in here and risk that, but that doesn't stop Dirty from running his hands all over my body. He jostles my dick, and I can tell from the look in his eyes that he's impressed with my size.

I smirk at him when he backs away after finding no weapons.

"Don't stop now, pet. I was close."

He growls at me, growing even angrier when the other guys chuckle.

"Follow me," Larrick snaps. He nods his head, indicating a door just off the common area, and I don't hesitate to follow him. I came here on a mission, and I'll be damned if I'm leaving without seeing it through.

"We're fine," Larrick calls, and it's only then I realize all three of the other men were following us into the room.

Dirty is growling when I close the door in his face, and it's probably best not to provoke these assholes, but I won't back down like a coward either.

Larrick strolls across the room, sitting gracefully in the chair at the head of the long scarred table. An overflowing ashtray sits in the center, but that's all that's on it other than a literal fucking gavel near Larrick's right hand.

I won't disrespect him by taking a seat at the table because I know only members are allowed. Plus, I don't want to be on that same level as him. He doesn't seem fazed when I walk closer, literally towering over him. The man is a stone wall, and I can begrudgingly admit that he's good looking. He's what some women would probably call gorgeous, but I know too much about his black fucking heart to consider him an equal.

Without a word, I pull a slip of paper from my pocket and toss it on the table in front of him. It slides across the wood, stopping two inches from his hand.

"What's that?" he asks without picking it up, and I suspect that's intentional.

Reaching for the thing would be akin to accepting what it says, and he's been in the game too long to ever do such a thing.

"It's an address."

He nods. "A good address?"

I return his nod. "My woman was abducted last night."

His face doesn't change. There isn't a hint of knowledge there, and I bet that's a skill he mastered many years ago. The man has been hauled in for police questioning a hundred times, I bet.

"Her kids were taken from school."

I get nothing from him.

"I don't appreciate my family being fucked with," I growl, letting my emotions get away from me. "That address is to the safe house the feds are using for Ty Penman."

And there, right at the corner of his left eye, is the only reaction I need. One little twitch gives me hope that I can resolve all this shit and get the heat off Kendall and her kids.

"You know what giving me that address means."

It's not a question, and he's well aware that he doesn't have to ask it. The man could easily take the address, shoot me in the head, and bury me in a shallow grave, but I get a feeling he's a little more honorable than that. At least I pray he is.

"I know."

"I thought Blackbridge stood for integrity? Thought all of you were law-abiding citizens and do-gooders?"

"I will burn the world down to protect my family, Larrick," I growl. "One less piece of shit walking the earth is of no fucking concern for me."

"His blood will be on your hands," Larrick counters.

"I'll sleep easy at night."

"Will you?" he challenges.

"The attacks on my family will stop," I demand, and I can tell by the way his eyes light up that he's a little impressed.

Larrick looks from the paper and back to me twice before he uses one finger to slide it closer to him. He doesn't pick it up and read it in front of me, and I'm sure that's just one more protective measure he's going to take.

"I don't have a clue what's going on with Kendall, but I'll wager that all of her bad luck has dried up."

I know it's the best I'm going to get, but it also feels like a promise. I suppose I'll have to take him at his word.

I would never compromise someone else, and that's the only reason I'm providing that information to him. Ty is terrified of the shitstorm coming from the Keres MC. The feds aren't even holding him. They leave him alone at that safe house, so I'm not putting an officer in danger.

I won't tell Larrick any of this. If he's as diligent as I've heard he is, he'll scope the place out before taking action.

"Was there anything else?" he asks, sitting back and steepling his fingers at his mouth. "Considering joining?"

"No," I hiss.

"Then get the fuck out of my clubhouse."

I don't waste a second striding away or apologizing when I swing open the door and it hits Dirty in the face.

I'm halfway back to the condo when I get a text from Wren.

Wren: Hurry the fuck up. Shit's going down.

I press my foot harder on the gas. I know they aren't in danger because Wren would've said if they were, but I have a feeling about what I'm going to find when I get home.

I saw the distance in Kendall's eyes before I left.

Chapter 37

Kendall

"We have to wait until Saturday because I have to work all week, but you've got a deal," Wren says with a grin.

Kason narrows his eyes. "I'm really good."

"You'll have to teach me," Wren counters.

They've been talking about some app game Kason has on his tablet for the last hour, and as each minute passed, I've grown more and more anxious.

My plan was to leave before Finn got back, but if Wren and Whitney don't leave soon, I'm going to have to figure something else out. Finn is too reasonable to let me load up the kids and leave. He'll beg me to stay, and when I still walk away, I'll be even more heartbroken. I think I'm more scared of him being perfectly fine with me leaving than anything else.

"Gotta head out," Wren says after typing something on his phone. "Needed at the office."

The kids hug the two of them like they're not going to see them for a long time, and it makes me wonder just how much damage was done to them yesterday.

I wave my goodbye from the kitchen, darting to the boys' bedroom the second the door shuts.

"What are you doing?" Kason asks, standing in the doorway.

"We're going on a trip."

"Will we be back by Saturday? We have school tomorrow." His eyes narrow on me when I look up at him after zipping up the last suitcase.

"It'll be fun," I tell him, avoiding the question. "Let me pack my things, and then we can go."

Kason watches me the entire time as I leave the room and pull out my own suitcase. Leaving and then asking Finn to ship me what I left behind would be incredibly selfish, so I spend more time stuffing my sentimental things into my suitcase. All the other stuff can be replaced. I work through a list in my head, knowing I'll have to go to the bank to withdraw my money, and it makes me even angrier about the guys from last night. That money was taken into evidence, and although I was assured I would get it back, that won't happen before I leave town.

Cutting ties with St. Louis means not ever looking this direction again. I have to consider that money gone.

"All done," I tell Kason as I pull my suitcase from the bed. "Time to go."

Looking a little stunned, Knox and Kayleigh are already standing near their suitcases at the front door. Kason isn't happy, and he makes that clear when he wraps his hand around the handle to his own suitcase, but he doesn't argue with me.

"Okay, my loves. Let's go on an adventure."

I shuffle them from the condo, praying no one comes up here, considering I left the door key on the kitchen counter.

I turn, pulling the door closed, and cuss under my breath when I realize I haven't pulled my suitcase far enough out.

"Can you take this? It's heavy," Kason complains.

"Just a second," I mutter, trying to maneuver my case.

"I think Momma forgot about you because she didn't pack anything of yours but an old t-shirt."

I freeze, as it dawns on me that she isn't talking to me. Finn is behind me; I just know it.

With guilt clogging my throat, I turn to face him. I won't apologize for taking his shirt. It seemed like a necessity at the time, and I know I'll be grateful to have it to cry into at night after the kids go to bed.

He doesn't say a word as he watches my face, and I find it impossible to look away from him either.

He doesn't look angry or upset. His face is just blank. It hurts to see him this way.

"Carry those things back inside, kids. Door Dash is bringing chicken nuggets."

The little betrayers cheer, pushing past me to reenter the condo.

I step out of their way, looking down at Kason when he walks back out and grabs the handle of my suitcase.

"I'm sorry," I tell Finn after the door closes at my back.

"For what?" he asks, his voice filled with more emotion than what's on his face. "For leaving? For taking what you did this morning, knowing this was your plan?"

I can't even deny it because the man is right.

"I'm sorry," I repeat. "For all of it. I have to go."

"You don't," he argues.

"I do."

"You're safe, Kendall. The kids are safe."

"I wish that were true."

"I swear on my life, you're safe."

"I know that's what you want, but we won't ever truly be safe. Getting out of St. Louis is the closest we'll get."

He steps into me, cupping my jaw in both hands. "I took care of it, baby. You're safe."

I blink up at him, tears ready to stream down my face, and I fight them, knowing if they fall, they may never stop. It's taken all I have already today not to cry in front of my kids, Whitney, and Wren.

His truth is right there in his eyes, and he's completely open for me, wanting me to see it.

"What did you do?" I whisper.

"I had to protect you."

"What. Did. You. Do?"

"I gave Larrick, Ty."

Four words, spoken with a simplicity that belies the weight of what he's saying.

I know exactly what he's telling me. I know the outcome.

I feel nothing.

There's no pain, no regret, no second thought.

I was faced with thinking my kids were dead last night. All of it was on Ty's head. The love I had for the man turned into hatred long ago.

"That's going to be a very difficult conversation with the kids," I whisper.

"It will be," he says. "And we can do it together."

"Together," I repeat, the word sliding across my lips with unfamiliarity. "How do you know it's over?"

Maybe he's just being hopeful, and I can't risk my kids' safety on hope.

"I had a chat with Larrick today."

"Just happened to run into him?"

"If by running into him, you mean went to the clubhouse and demanded to speak with him, then yeah."

I snap my eyes from his mouth where I was watching him speak to his eyes.

Green orbs look down at me, humor dancing in them.

"Are you crazy?"

"About you?" He grins. "Yeah, baby. I'm crazy about you."

I don't know how to feel or how to react right now. This man is telling me he took care of my problems, and if he's right, I don't have to leave, but I don't know what it means if I stay either.

I shake my head, needing some space and some time, needing some distance so I can figure out what to do next.

"I love you, Kendall." He presses a single finger to my lips to prevent me from speaking. "At first, it was just a slow burn, like this warmth in my chest, and I did my best to keep it under control. But one day, I just woke up on fire for you. I know you feel the same way. I could feel it this morning."

Tears burn down my cheeks. "Finn."

A sob escapes my throat, and he answers by pulling me to his chest, holding me close.

I never let myself hope for perfection, but somehow the stars lined up and gave me this man. I couldn't be happier.

I don't say the words back immediately. I don't want to cheapen the moment by making him think I'm just parroting them back, but I plan to tell him—or show him—exactly how I feel, very soon.

I shift back and up on the tips of my toes, pressing my lips to his. He returns the kiss, once again lifting me from the ground, my legs wrapping around his waist instinctively.

"Stop," he groans when I swivel my hips. "We can't go tell the kids you're moving into my room if I have an erection."

I chuckle against his lips, pressing my mouth there twice more before letting him put me down.

"We're telling the kids, huh?"

"I'm tired of you sneaking out of our room every morning."

He palms my face once more, pressing his lips to my temple before stepping back and shoving open the front door.

The kids are sitting on the couch, concern on each of their little faces when we enter.

"Did you kiss and make up?" Kayleigh asks, huffing as she crosses her arms over her chest.

"I don't want to miss my playdate with Uncle Wren on Saturday," Kason says.

"You won't," I assure him. "We have something to tell you."

Finn steps to my side, drawing me in close to him. Kayleigh grins, a little giggle slipping out like it did that night she caught us on the couch.

None of them seem concerned.

"Finn and I are together."

All three blink at us.

"We're dating," I say.

More blinking.

"Totally, completely, madly in love with each other," Finn adds, and I roll my lips between my teeth to keep from smiling like a fool.

"Tell us something we don't know," Knox says with a roll of his eyes.

"We're getting married," Finn says.

I gasp, looking up at him, ready to smack him and tell him that joking around about stuff like that isn't funny, but the look in his eyes tells me that he isn't joking.

I swallow, my eyes still locked on his.

"Really?" I ask, unconcerned that this isn't the most romantic way to ask a woman to marry him.

"Really," he whispers, his head lowering to press a soft kiss to my stunned lips.

"Can I be the flower girl?" Kayleigh asks on a squeal.

"Of course," Finn says.

"Can I get a puppy?" Knox asks.

"Anything you want, little guy."

I continue to glare at him, my head shaking a little.

"Can I stay up late watching *YouTube* tonight?"

"Don't see the harm in that," Finn answers immediately.

All three kids cheer.

"What can I get for you, baby?" he whispers as they dance around us joyfully for getting their way.

"I want two more kids," I tell him, somewhat jokingly because the room is utter chaos right now.

"Anything you want," he says.

I gasp my surprise, but he swallows it with a kiss.

Chapter 38

Finnegan

"Well, hell," I say, looking at the notification Wren just sent to my phone.

"What is it?" Kendall asks from the bathroom.

She's standing at the sink, washing her face, her naked skin flushed from the morning's activities.

I'm still in bed, my legs a little shaky from the phenomenal sex.

With a sigh, unsure how this was going to go, I climb out of the bed and cross the room to her. I turn the phone around so she can read the text instead of having to say it out loud.

"I see," she whispers, her eyes finding mine. She doesn't seem sad, just resolute.

We knew it was going to come to this, so I'm not surprised with Wren's text saying that Ty's body was found floating in the Mississippi River in Quincy, Illinois. It's been six days since I went to the Keres MC clubhouse, so Larrick really didn't waste any time solving his problem.

I can say I didn't fully trust that she had come to terms with how things would end, but she doesn't seem very affected by the news.

"You okay?" I ask, because I swore to myself after telling her that I love her that I would stop guessing at what she's feeling. I don't want to ever get it wrong and asking is the best way to cut through all that shit.

"I'm fine. We have to tell the kids."

We talked about this as well. I thought she should just never mention the guy again, but she assured me that the twins still have memories of him. If they asked later on down the road about him only to find out he died, they'd hate us for not telling them.

"Okay," I agree. "Together."

"Together," she whispers, her eyes meeting mine in the mirror.

She finishes in the bathroom and gets dressed for the day, and like I always do, I keep my eyes on her, drinking her in as she wraps herself in clothes. It's nearly as sexy as when she takes them off for me at night.

She gives me a saucy wink, rolling her eyes when I start to prowl toward her.

"After the kids go to school," she says, smacking my hands away before I can get them on her perfect body.

"You have that meeting with Anna," I remind her.

"And you have work," she adds.

"So why are you promising things you can't follow through with?" I know I sound like a whiney kid, but I just can't get enough of her.

We spend our evenings with the kids, and I love all of it, but I also love the quiet—or not so quiet, we discovered when the kids are gone—times I get with her just as much.

I wasn't joking about marriage, and it turns out, she wasn't joking about wanting more kids. We've been studiously working on both since that day.

"I have my meeting with Anna at the office. Your door has a lock." She winks at me before walking out of the room.

I dress quickly, wanting to help her as much as I possibly can because that's just how we do it around here.

She already has all three kids in the boys' bedroom by the time I make it out there.

"I don't understand," Knox says, his brows drawn together.

"Your dad was hurt," Kendall says.

Knox's eyes dart to mine.

"Like you have a tummy ache or something?"

Kendall looks over her shoulder at me, but I can only look at the little boy who just acknowledged that he considers me his dad. Talk about getting hit in the gut with emotions first thing in the morning.

"Our 'real' dad," Kason says, a little of his attitude slipping through.

"Who?" Knox asks.

"The piece of shit who abandoned his responsibilities a long time ago," Kayleigh supplies helpfully.

I cough a laugh as Kendall scowls at her daughter.

"Ohhh," Knox says. "Can I have yogurt with my breakfast?"

"It gives you stinky gas," Kayleigh says, pinching her nose.

Kason laughs, lifts his leg, and lets one rip.

Kayleigh and Knox scatter from the bed.

Kendall makes a gagging noise as she waves her hand in front of her pretty face.

Ty Penman is never mentioned again.

***

"How's the wedding planning going?" Kit asks as I take the seat beside him on the sofa.

"Good, I guess. Kendall wants something small, so there isn't really much to do."

"There's always something to do," Jude says. "*Modern Bride* has complete lists."

We all look at him. "What?"

"You read *Modern Bride*?" I ask.

"I flip through *Modern Bride* when Parker takes forever to get ready."

"Parker has those kinds of magazines at her place?" Brooks asks.

Jude shrugs. "They're leftover from when Hayden was planning her wedding."

"*The Every Modern Bride Guide* came out this month," Wren says from near the coffee pot.

Brooks chuckles. Jude looks confused.

"Who's going to tell him?" Kit asks.

"Parker is planning your wedding, dude," I say, uncaring if I'm the bearer of bad news.

"Yeah?" he asks with a grin, as if this is fabulous news.

"That's really sweet," Kit says, that familiar dreamy smile on his face.

Brooks huffs, his surly ass attitude out in full force today.

Brooks is the anti-relationship man, and Kit, I think, has always wanted that, and has just never found the right girl.

"Who is that?" I ask, watching two very pretty women walk into the room.

"Beth?" Kit asks. "Jules? What are you two doing here?"

Brooks springs up from the sofa before Kit can manage to stand.

"The blushing bride," Brooks says, pressing his lips to Beth's cheek. "You are one fine sight, Jules."

We all watch as Brooks kisses the other woman's cheek.

Beth peels off from the two of them, plopping down beside her brother.

"What are you two doing here?" Kit asks again, his eyes locked on Jules, a scowl marring his face.

Beth chuckles as he watches her friend. They're leaning close, whispering to each other. Brooks is still holding both of Jules's hands between the two of them, and they seem very familiar with each other.

"Jules just found out that she's pregnant," Beth whispers, but it's loud enough for me to hear on the other side of Kit.

I feel the man stiffen.

"What?" he hisses, his head swinging between his sister and looking across the room.

"She's not very far along, and she was hesitant to tell the father, but I talked her into telling him. She said she wanted to do it alone, but I did what any best friend would do. I tagged along, and here we are."

"She came here to tell the dad?" Kit asks, his voice filled with something I can't quite decipher.

Oh, shit. I recall a conversation between Kit and Brooks about his time with Jules at the wedding. Kit didn't come right out and say he hooked up with Jules, but it was seriously implied.

"Apparently, they hooked up at my wedding. Isn't it sweet?"

"Th-they—did you just say she got pregnant at your wedding?" A smile spreads across Kit's face, and I'm right there with him.

From conversations I've overheard through the years, the man has been in love with his sister's best friend for years. I can see his face light with happiness with what his sister just said.

He hooked up with Jules at the wedding.

She's carrying his child. I grin, realizing my friend is going to be a father. If I'm lucky, we'll have kids right around the same time.

We all watch as Brooks takes a step back. He drops Jules's hands, but then one presses to her lower belly.

No. Fuck. Oh shit.

The smile slides from Kit's face as he watches all of this.

No one is smiling when Brooks turns around to face us. His eyes go to his best friend, but Kit's gaze is glued to Jules's. The mother-to-be looks sad.

"I'm going to be a dad," Brooks announces with no fanfare.

Beth cheers, clapping her hands. "Going to be such a good-looking kid!"

Brooks swallows, stepping forward, but stops in his tracks when Kit stands and gives them both a disgusted look before walking away.

No one chases after him. Brooks doesn't laugh and say it's all a joke. He isn't smiling the way he did weeks ago when he teased Kit about flirting with Jules in an effort to get out of going to the wedding.

Shit just hit the fan in a serious way.

THE END

OTHER BOOKS FROM MARIE JAMES

Blackbridge Security
Hostile Territory
Shot in the Dark
Contingency Plan
Truth Be Told
Calculated Risk
Heroic Measures
Sleight of Hand
Controlled Burn
Cease Fire

Standalones
Crowd Pleaser
Macon
We Said Forever
More Than a Memory

Cole Brothers SERIES
Love Me Like That
Teach Me Like That

Cerberus MC
Kincaid: Cerberus MC Book 1
Kid: Cerberus MC Book 2
Shadow: Cerberus MC Book 3
Dominic: Cerberus MC Book 4
Snatch: Cerberus MC Book 5
Lawson: Cerberus MC Book 6
Hound: Cerberus MC Book 7
Griffin: Cerberus MC Book 8
Samson: Cerberus MC Book 9
Tug: Cerberus MC Book 10
Scooter: Cerberus MC Book 11
Cannon: Cerberus MC Book 12
Rocker: Cerberus MC Book 13
Colton: Cerberus MC Book 14
Drew: Cerberus MC Book 15
Jinx: Cerberus MC Book 16
Thumper: Cerberus MC Book 17
Apollo: Cerberus MC Book 18
Legend: Cerberus MC Book 19
Grinch: Cerberus MC Book 20
Harley: Cerberus MC Book 21
A Very Cerberus Christmas
Cerberus MC Box Set 1
Cerberus MC Box Set 2
Cerberus MC Box Set 3

Ravens Ruin MC
Prequel: Desperate Beginnings
Book 1: Sins of the Father
Book 2: Luck of the Devil
Book 3: Dancing with the Devil

MM Romance
Grinder
Taunting Tony

Westover Prep Series
(bully/enemies to lovers romance)
One-Eighty
Catch Twenty-Two

Made in United States
Orlando, FL
26 June 2025